THE HARD WAY

DUNCAN BROCKWELL

Copyright © 2021 Duncan Brockwell
The right of Duncan Brockwell to be identified as the Author of the Work has been asserted by him in accordance to the Copyright, Designs and Patents Act 1988.
First published in 2021 by Bloodhound Books.
Apart from any use permitted under UK copyright law, this publication may only be reproduced, stored, or transmitted, in any form, or by any means, with prior permission in writing of the publisher or, in the case of reprographic production, in accordance with the terms of licences issued by the Copyright Licensing Agency.
All characters in this publication are fictitious and any resemblance to real persons, living or dead, is purely coincidental.
www.bloodhoundbooks.com

Print ISBN 978-1-913942-44-1

ALSO BY DUNCAN BROCKWELL

Mr Invisible

The Met Murder Mysteries by DC Brockwell

No Way Out

Bird of Prey

Bad Blood

MONDAY, JUNE 11TH

1

Colin Fisher rose from his seat. "Great show, everyone, as always." His co-star, the delightful Brandy Reid rose from her chair opposite him. It was midnight, and the *Fright Night* show was being broadcast at their sister building in Croydon. "I don't know about you, Bran, but I need a shower. Kurt, I'm going to my dressing room, okay? You'll be here for a while, right?"

Kurt Austin, the producer, used his microphone to confirm he was staying for a while. "Absolutely! Editing doesn't happen by itself."

Meeting the blonde bombshell he'd chosen as a co-star at the door, Colin opened it for her. She was delightful, a real charmer with a great personality, great sense of humour. If he weren't gay, and married to Henry Curtis, the station's owner, Brandy would be right up there as his choice of wife. "After you, my lovely."

"That really was a cracking show, wasn't it?" Brandy, in a short denim skirt and low-cut white top, walked with him along the corridor to the dressing rooms. She wasn't a big enough name to have her own, so she used the generic dressing room on the right, while Colin used his own on the left. "I guess this is good night."

Sensing that something was bothering her, Colin asked, "You know you can tell me anything, don't you? I'm here to listen, as your manager, your friend. If something's wrong, you would tell me?" She could hide behind her smiles and laughter all she liked, he'd worked with her long enough to know when something was wrong.

Even her face gave her away. "I'm fine, Col, really. My boyfriend's being a jerk, but other than that, I'm perfect." She opened her dressing room door. "Well, night."

Something was definitely up. Brandy always kissed him goodnight; she'd not once gone without at least a hug. "Night, Bran. We'll talk more about this tomorrow." By the time he finished his sentence, she'd shut the door. "Rude!"

Entering his own room, he closed the door behind him, undressed, putting his clothes on an armchair, before walking through to his luxury bathroom. Henry had spared no expense renovating the factory outlet into a radio station.

Colin loved his life now, which was a far cry from his former life. Meeting Henry had changed him for the better. Henry was the sole reason why Colin and his older brother, Richard, were on speaking terms, not that he could blame Richard for disowning him. Colin had done some vile things to his family over the years.

Naked, he stepped under the shower, bending to turn the taps, as the jets probed his back. Having a shower at the end of his late shift was the icing on the cake. It was so different to his old life, living on the streets, doing anything he could to get hold of some heroin.

All his life, he'd lived under his brother's vast shadow. Richard was the brightest, the best, the first and only to go to university. Hell, he was the first to marry, the first to buy a house, have kids, the works. Colin had always looked up to Richard in so many ways, but he knew from a young age he was different.

Knowing he was gay was the hardest part of growing up. Colin had straight, very straight friends at school, who were forever talking about girls, about their bodies, the usual. Colin couldn't comment back with any conviction, because the girls at school didn't make him feel anything. It was unfortunate that one or two of the boys did.

Growing up pretending to be something he wasn't took its toll on his mental health. When Colin was old enough to leave home, to leave the pressure his parents exerted on him to follow Richard's example, he moved in with a couple of friends.

He still considered those days his best, until he found cocaine. His housemates introduced him to coke, which he fell in love with. It made him feel invincible. Coke helped him explore his sexuality. Colin went to his first gay bar high on the white powder, and had his first sexual experience on that same night.

Building it up in his head, he finally had the courage to tell his housemates that he was homosexual. They laughed and told him they knew, and that they'd always known. Relieved beyond words, he used his new-found confidence and confessed all to his parents. He made his mum cry. His dad ordered him out of the family home.

The black sheep of the family, Colin went in on himself. He started using cocaine more, which affected his performance at his office job. Out on the streets, meeting unsavoury people, he was introduced to his biggest love, and greatest enemy, heroin. He could only afford it for six months, before he couldn't contribute his share to the house anymore. His friends threw him out.

Colin rubbed shampoo into his hair. Turning to face the door, his eyes closed, he thought he heard a scream. Stopping, he listened. He thought he heard a pop. Listening again, he turned back, shrugged, and continued washing his hair.

Out on the streets, he squatted for a couple of years with some unsavoury types. Who was he kidding? He was unsavoury himself, stealing to buy his heroin. Shoplifting, beating people up for their wallets and handbags. He hated himself for so long, he used that hatred to commit these vile acts.

If it wasn't for his gorgeous sister, Charlotte, he didn't think he would ever make it off the streets alive; they'd have swallowed him up. He finally reached rock-bottom when he beat his dad up, and stole his wallet.

Charlotte took him to rehab, where her husband, Samuel, paid for the best treatment available. It didn't take one trip, but two to rehab to sort Colin out. He relapsed in between, back on the streets, until Charlotte came to the rescue again. Richard wouldn't speak to him after beating up their dad, not that he could blame his brother.

After rehab, Charlotte and Samuel put Colin up in their guest cottage, which was really an annex on their house. For the first time in his life, he had a lovely place to live, and he wasn't taking drugs anymore. On his first night out – with good friends – he went to a gay bar in the city, where he met his future husband, Henry Curtis.

Attraction was immediate. As soon as he saw the dashing radio station owner at the bar, Colin knew he had to have him. They conversed for hours that fateful night, laughing over drinks into the early hours of the morning. Henry invited him back to his house, which was more like a country manor, surrounded by an eight-foot wall topped with razor wire.

For the first time in his life, Colin found himself in a loving relationship. He was with Henry a good couple of years, working in offices on the phones generally, before his partner offered him a spot on the radio once a week. Henry found Colin funny, all the time, so he thought the humour would translate well over the airwaves.

In time, Colin's role within the radio station changed. He went from part-time to full-time, learning the ropes until he was the main voice of Accord FM. At the centre of his role within the radio station was inclusion. Henry wanted the listeners to be involved in every aspect of the broadcast. It was a radio station chosen by the people, for the people, with no playlists. All day, listeners sent in requests, and it was the presenters' job to spin those tunes.

There was another pop. Colin turned off the taps, wiped his face with his hands, and stepped out of the shower. Grabbing a towel, he wrapped it around his waist. A third pop, louder this time, made him jump.

Curious, he stepped out of the bathroom into the dressing room, where his clothes were waiting on his chair. Colin was about to reach for his trousers, when the door burst open and a thickset man in jeans and a leather jacket stood in the doorway, carrying a pistol with a long muzzle. Looking at it, Colin realised it was a silencer.

"Found him!" Leather Jacket said, stepping inside.

Swallowing hard, Colin tried to speak, but he was too afraid. His bladder made its presence known when Leather Jacket raised the pistol to chest height. "What do you want? If it's money, I'll get it for you. I'm married to Henry Curtis; he'll pay you whatever you want. Please, don't hurt me."

A second intruder entered the room carrying a pistol. Colin noted he was wearing jeans and a black T-shirt. "Don't take it personally. It's just a job."

Wanting to run, Colin couldn't move, even when Black T-shirt raised his pistol and pulled the trigger. The force of the bullet hitting Colin in the chest lifted him off the floor. Landing with a dull thud on his back, the carpet burned him.

He thought maybe he was winded, unable to take a breath in, until he realised his lungs were shredded. Blood was pooling on his chest, dripping down his side. When he couldn't breathe, panic set in.

Black T-shirt stood looking down at him. He placed a foot on Colin's chest, aimed the pistol at his face. "This'll be over quickly, I promise."

Colin gasped for air, looking up at the smirk on his attacker's face.

The last thing Colin saw was the muzzle flash.

2

"God, I'm bored." Detective Sergeant Rachel Miller drummed her fingers on the steering wheel. "You see stakeouts on TV, and they make out they're so exciting. No one tells you at the training centre how dull they are."

"The clue's in the name." Detective Inspector Amanda Hayes sat in the passenger seat, watching the front door of the block of flats through binoculars. "It's called surveillance for a reason." A guy in a bomber jacket approached the building. "Wait! This could be him." She sensed Miller's excitement. "Oh, no, false alarm."

"At least let me look through the bins for a bit."

Hayes sighed. She handed her glasses over and sat back in her seat. It was just gone eleven and by rights she should be in bed, cosying up with a good book. Miller blew a bubble with her gum, as it popped and stuck to her lips. "You're so annoying when you're bored, did anyone ever tell you that?"

Miller smirked. "Nope. Just you. When are we going to see some action?"

"I keep telling you, soon. If our informant is right, our suspect should be visiting his girlfriend any time now." Her partner was right: it was so boring being sat in a car waiting for something to happen. "She said tonight, be patient."

She had been partnered with Miller for little over five years, having trained her from a detective constable, not that Miller had needed much training having been a uniformed police officer for eight years. Hayes was more than satisfied with Miller's performance on the job, even if she did annoy her at times, like tonight.

Hayes and Miller had worked day and night to identify and apprehend the killer of a woman whose body had been found by the side of a motorway. For almost two weeks they'd interviewed potential witnesses, questioned CIs, scoured hours of CCTV footage – her favourite. All the man-hours they'd submitted culminated in them being in the car, backed up by an armed response unit hidden further up the road.

The radio crackled on the dashboard. "Please be advised possible sighting of suspect on his way to you."

"Finally!" Miller turned in her seat and looked behind her. "Is that him?"

Searching with her binoculars, Hayes watched the tall, heavyset black man walking towards the block of flats. He had the right build and height. "It's possible. He's wearing a cap, so it's hard to tell."

Recently released ex-convict Eric Helsey stood six feet four, according to his sheet. A prolific drug dealer, who'd carved out a name for himself as the local kingpin by terrorising his enemies and threatening their lives, Hayes and Miller both believed he was responsible for shooting the thirty-year-old woman in the back and disposing of her body by the roadside.

Their victim was the girlfriend of the leader of Helsey's biggest competitor. Helsey murdered her as a warning to all his rivals: *mess with me and it's not just your life at stake; it's your loved ones' lives, too*. Hayes was sure his message had sunk in, for none of the locals dared talk to her or Miller. "You know what? I'm calling it. That's him."

Miller picked up the receiver. "That's affirmative. We have a visual on our suspect. And it looks like he's going inside the block of flats... Yes, that's it. The operation is a go, I repeat the operation is a go."

"Copy that," the radio crackled. "We are a go."

Taking the receiver from Miller, Hayes held the button down. "Hold fire. Let's give him time to get comfortable. Hang back for three minutes."

"Copy that. Holding back for three minutes."

"We'll meet you at the entrance. Miller will keep an eye on the rear exit, and I'll keep tabs on the front. We know there's no other way out."

She replaced the radio and looked at her partner. "Time for the action you wanted. Let's go!" She stepped out of the car and checked her pocket for her cosh. The extendable metal baton was her go-to weapon and it had saved her life on a number of occasions. "Are you ready?"

"Hey there, ladies," a confident voice from behind her said.

Luke "Not the Sky Variety" Walker, clad in black combat uniform, bulletproof vest, and black cap with "Police" emblazoned on it, smiled at her, then turned his attention to Miller.

He had a Glock 17 holstered on his hip, while he clutched a Heckler and Koch MP5 carbine close to his chest. Hayes thought he was a poser, with his bulging biceps, perfectly straight, impossibly white teeth, trendy haircut, and cheeks so sharp he could stab someone with them. "Hi! Miller, let's get going. I've been asked to escort you both across the road."

Her partner didn't move; she stood there smiling at the cocky gun-carrier.

"Miller! Let's go! We're moving." Her comment worked. Her

partner met her at the front of their car, while Walker remained behind them. "I make that three minutes."

With cosh in hand, Hayes ran across the road towards the block of flats. Their suspect disappeared inside over two and a half minutes earlier, so she estimated he must be in the lift, or on his girlfriend's floor by now.

Arriving outside the front doors, Hayes leaned against the wall. The rest of Walker's team arrived carrying the artillery, another five carbines and Glocks. Prior to commencing the stakeout, both teams met and discussed the operation. They were there to take Eric Helsey down, either by force, or with his co-operation; it was Helsey's choice.

"Good luck in there." Hayes watched the team enter the building.

The commanding officer, Sarge, tipped his cap.

The last one to enter was Walker. "We don't need luck," he said, his words smug.

"Yeah, whatever!"

Miller stood next to her. "Why are you like this? He's lovely."

Her armed colleagues marched through the ground floor. They climbed the stairs. Two officers, including Walker, took the lift. "Who, Walker? He's a poser! Have you ever seen anyone love themselves as much?" When she turned her attention to her partner, Miller looked mad. "What? The guy's a joke. I've met so many blokes like that, Miller. They're only ever after one thing."

"You're just jealous!"

Miller went to walk round the rear of the building, but Hayes grabbed her arm. "Jealous? Of what? You think I fancy Walker?"

Shaking her off, Miller faced her. "You know he likes me, and you don't like it. Anyway, I need to be out back; we'll talk about this later."

"That's a load of crap, and you know it!" Miller started walking away but Hayes continued. "Why would I care if he likes you? He's so not my type. What about Billy? I thought you wanted to see how things went with him?"

"Billy?" Miller made a funny noise with her mouth. "I don't think so."

Hayes couldn't keep up. The last time she spoke to Miller about her personal life, her partner told her she was seeing Billy. How could it have all changed in such a short space of time? She gave up. "Whatever! And what are you still doing here anyway?"

"I was going, and you pulled me back, remember?"

Her partner huffed and strutted off in the direction of the rear car park. There were only two ways in or out of the block of flats, through her or through Miller. Hayes hoped the boys upstairs would emerge with Eric Helsey in cuffs.

3

Waiting behind a car, watching the fire exit door, Miller couldn't believe Hayes. Who the hell did she think she was! Her partner had no right to tell her who she liked, or didn't like. She wanted to march over there and give Hayes a mouthful. The truth: she and Billy had gone their separate ways. She liked him for a time, but they weren't compatible, not really.

Luke Walker, however, she could imagine being with. He was handsome, fit, talented... A smile crept over her as she thought about the first time she met him. During a raid at a potential suspect's home, Walker introduced himself. Their eyes had locked for longer than was necessary. She'd held the same smile then, before Hayes disturbed their connection.

The fire exit door flung open and Helsey came charging out.

"Helsey's on the move! I'm in pursuit," she shouted into her radio. "Heading east towards Vauxhall Park."

Miller ran after Helsey. When she grew closer to the fire exit, he spotted her tailing him and increased his speed, his feet beating the concrete so fast, she thought she might have trouble keeping up.

There was one thing her charge didn't know: how quick she

was. Pounding the car park after him, she kept the pace up, until she was running along the pavement, cars speeding past on the main road beside her.

"Miller, wait!"

With Hayes tailing her, Miller stayed on Helsey's tail. He ran into the street, causing three vehicles to screech to a halt, before running across one lane and stopping in the middle. She followed him, apologising to the drivers, who beeped at her. "Helsey! Stop! You're under–"

A car screamed past her, beeping its horn, as Helsey legged it across the second busy lane, just missing a lorry's wrath. "Shit!" In between the two lanes, she caught sight of Helsey running into the park. "Oh no, you don't," she said, gauging the space between cars and making a run for it.

She laughed out of fear when she reached the other side safely.

In front of her, the suspect disappeared into the darkness of the park. Some lamp posts worked, others didn't. Her lungs were burning, but she continued running. "He's heading south through the park." Using the radio slowed her down.

Twenty metres ahead of her, she heard voices complaining.

When she reached them, she saw a young couple picking themselves up. "Out of the way!" She had to jump over the girl, who complained behind her, as she carried on chasing Helsey. "Sorry!"

He wasn't slowing. Miller was approaching a children's playground when Helsey stopped behind a couple of girls in their twenties.

When she was almost on them, her charge pushed one of the women at her.

Managing to avoid the youngster, Miller made sure she wasn't injured, apologised, and headed off in the same direction as Helsey.

After ten seconds, she saw his feet back pounding the path.

Her body was fighting her.

Finding a burst of energy, digging in, she gained ground on him.

It looked like he was winding down.

Reaching inside her jacket, she felt her cosh and extended it. "Don't make me do this, Helsey," she shouted. "I don't want to hurt you."

She was right on him, her feet and his almost touching, when she threw the metal bar at his legs. The cosh caught between both, sending him flying through the air.

Helsey hit the grass and rolled.

Miller launched herself on top of him.

Rolling, first on top, then under him, she landed on her back with his eighteen stone sat on her belly, grinning down at her. While he was congratulating himself, laughing, she reached inside her trouser pocket, pulling out her pepper spray.

"You don't get your man this time, pig," he said, slapping her face playfully. "Don't feel bad though, baby. Plenty have tried."

When Helsey went to stand, she held the spray up, and pressed the button, missing him. A bit caught him. She'd forgotten how victims react; he staggered about, clawing at his eyes, while calling her every name he could think of.

On her feet, she aimed the spray at his face and fired again.

His screams increased in fervour; he swore at her.

When she went to confront him, he lashed out at her and punched her cheek.

She should have been more careful, she told herself, knowing how dangerous wounded animals could be. Half-blind, Helsey took off again.

Miller groaned, hearing Hayes behind her.

Putting her pepper spray in her jacket pocket, Miller ran after him.

She'd lost all momentum. Even injured, Helsey was faster than her. "Don't make me come after you," she cried. "Stop! Before I hurt you again."

Her pleas were ignored. As she sprinted, his feet pounded ahead.

Finding her stride again, she was taken by surprise when Helsey stopped and faced her, reaching into his leather jacket, and pulling out a flick knife.

"Come on, bitch!" The blade shot out, pointing at her. He rubbed his eyes with his free hand. "Let's see what you've got. Come on!"

Thinking she could use the pepper spray once more, she retrieved it, pressed the button but nothing happened. "Oh shit!" She saw him smile, then edge closer. Why didn't she pick up her cosh earlier?

He laughed. "Come on, then."

When he came close enough, she lunged and punched him on the bridge of his nose. Standing back, she heard him groan and hold it, blood pouring through his fingers.

Helsey launched himself at her, throwing his whole weight behind the knife.

Miller was thrown to the floor, his big frame on top of her for the second time. "No you don't," she hissed, grabbing his wrist, the tip of the blade pointing down at her.

While she was desperate to try to prevent him stabbing her in the face, the knife edging closer, Miller heard movement around her.

Miller felt relief at Hayes' presence.

"Get your hands off her!"

With the blade centimetres from her face, she lay on the grass trying to keep the knife from sinking into her flesh, a crazed look in Helsey's eyes, when Hayes hit him on the back of the head with her cosh.

He flew off Miller, taking the knife with him, and she stared up at her breathless partner. Miller tried to catch her own breath. "Thank... you!"

"Not bad for an old girl, hey! That's two you owe me." Hayes rolled Helsey on his front, grabbing both arms and cuffing him. Helsey groaned, barely conscious.

"Miller, are you all right?" Walker asked, his carbine trained on Helsey.

Walker and two of his team helped her to her feet. If Hayes hadn't arrived when she had, she might be dead, or seriously injured.

Miller enjoyed the attention from Walker, who held her chin and checked her swollen cheek. "It's nothing; he sucker punched me." It was bravado, but she wanted him to think she was tough, or rather the toughest. "I'm fine; stop fussing."

When Walker was handed a first aid kit, Miller had no choice but to accept the fuss, as he fixed her up. Miller didn't realise she was bleeding from a cut on her forehead. There was no denying she felt like she had been in the ring.

DAY 1
TUESDAY, JUNE 12TH

4

Hayes stooped down and kissed Molly, the tabby cat, before heading out of her front door. After the previous night's excitement she felt her age. Fifty-four. When did that happen?

The journey from her house to work took roughly forty-five minutes in rush-hour traffic. Hayes listened to the radio on her way there, tapping on the steering wheel as she went, hoping she would manage to get the paperwork finished today.

After driving Helsey to their station on Cobalt Square, she and Miller spent the best part of two hours grilling him on his involvement in the murder of the woman left by the side of the motorway. As expected, he feigned ignorance, not that it mattered; they had enough trace evidence supporting their suspicions to take to the Crown Prosecution Service. A confession would be the cherry on top of the delicious cake.

She arrived in the open-plan office to find Miller busy on her computer. "Oh! I thought you'd be in later? You can't have had much sleep." She took off her suit jacket and placed it on the back of her chair.

"I'm fine. I was jazzed all night, so I didn't bother trying to catch any zees." Miller stood and handed her some paperwork over the partition. "Here's my version of events for you to sign off."

"Thanks." Hayes took the report and placed it on her desk. "Do we know how our guest is doing? Did he have a wonderful night in the cell?"

"I don't know, shall we go check?" Her partner smirked.

"I was thinking that. Let's go have a little chat with Mr Helsey."

~

After keeping him waiting for forty-five minutes on purpose, Hayes let Miller into interview room two first. Eric Helsey sat cuffed behind the battered, graffiti-covered table, his face the picture of annoyance. "Here he is."

"So I see." Miller perched on a chair opposite, eyeballing him.

Hayes took the chair next to her partner, a smile forming. "You know we've got you, don't you? We have enough trace to put you away for murder, plus eyewitness testimony placing you at the motorway at the time. That and CCTV footage of your car on the road is enough to place you there."

"Killing your biggest rival's girlfriend, I mean it sends a message all right, but it wasn't the brightest thing to do, was it, Eric? What were you thinking? Did you think we'd ditch the investigation after a few days? Or did you think you would intimidate us?"

"Yeah, it was stupid." Hayes looked at her partner. "It wasn't as stupid as trying to murder a police officer, though, was it?"

"He couldn't even do that properly." Miller gripped the table, staring into Helsey's eyes. "You see, I'm still here. It's going to take more than you to get rid of me, you piece of–"

Joining her partner, Hayes jovially put herself between them. She laughed, pulled Miller back and made her sit.

"What the fuck do you two jokers want?" Helsey leaned forward, his hands cuffed behind his back. "Am I under arrest, or what? And where's my fucking lawyer? You can't question me without him, you bent pieces of shit."

"He's on his way." Hayes loved the bravado. "And who's questioning you? We haven't asked you anything yet, have we? Ah, well, my partner here might have asked a rhetorical question, I guess, but it doesn't count unless the audio recorder's on."

"But you'd better believe we'll be charging you, with everything we can think of. Now let's see, that's murder, attempted murder – on me – assault, GBH, ABH, and resisting arrest, for starters." Miller grinned at Helsey. "Yeah, where's your lawyer? I want to get started."

A knock on the door made Hayes walk over and open it. Greeted by Helsey's sleazy barrister, Garrett Barlow, she didn't like to even look at him. Unfortunately, he represented a few undesirables in her district, so she had to converse with him more often than she would like. "Let's get this over with, shall we?"

Hayes spent a couple of hours interviewing Helsey, in the presence of his sleazy lawyer, who it turned out was great at his job. She played a game of "tug of war" with Barlow, until their suspect stipulated that he wanted to make a deal. "What kind of deal do you think you can make with us? We're investigating a murder, and now we have our guy, you, cuffed and in custody. You might as well be tied up with a nice little bow."

"All that might be true, but I know people." He regarded her, then Miller. "I know people who've done some bad shit."

It was her turn to glance at her partner.

"And let me guess, you'll be willing to give them up for a

lighter sentence, is that it? You'll roll over on everyone to save yourself, isn't that right!" Miller folded her arms and glared at Hayes. "What do you think? Should we listen to him?"

"I don't think we have a choice, do you?" She followed Miller's lead and crossed her arms as well. "All right, we'll hear what you've got to say, but it'll have to be pretty good to secure a deal, I hope you know that."

"It's good enough for you both." Helsey nodded almost imperceptibly. "But if you think I'm telling you without a signed document, you're even stupider than you look."

Without conferring with Miller, Hayes stood and glared down at him. "We don't need it that bad. Eric Helsey, you're being charged with all the aforementioned. We'll bring back the appropriate documentation."

Helsey's lawyer put up a fight, but it wasn't until their suspect spoke again that Hayes' interest piqued.

"That skip body you found a few weeks ago."

She froze at the door, Miller eyeing her, and they both turned back to him. "What about it? Colleagues of ours closed that case already."

"No, they didn't. The guy who killed her is still around, but you go ahead and walk out." He sat back and crossed his arms. "What do I know?"

Hayes didn't know how to proceed. "I'll have to consult my colleagues."

In the corridor, she turned to Miller. "What do you think? Is he full of shit, or what?" A part of her wanted to forget she'd heard him.

"I think we should speak to Inspector Gillan and Sergeant Jackman. It was their case; they called it. They won't be happy with this."

Finding DI Alfie Gillan in front of his computer, she beckoned DS Travis Jackman over. Hayes explained the situation to them both, noting their exchanged glances, the fear in their eyes. If Helsey was telling the truth, they had an innocent man in prison, awaiting trial. "I'm so sorry about this. At first, we were ready to walk away and dismiss him as a liar, but there was something in his expression."

As they were about to leave for the interview room, Gillan's phone bleeped.

Hayes stood back. Judging by his responses, they had another case.

"We've got a triple murder."

"We don't mind starting it, if you want to take over the Helsey investigation?" She would do anything to get away from Helsey, especially if their suspect was telling the truth about the skip body. "Where is it?"

Gillan sent her the file by email. "A small radio station called Accord FM. Apparently the owner, a Henry Curtis, renovated a factory and turned it into a broadcasting station. From what I can gather, it's popular. Their guiding principle is inclusion, so it's favoured by the LGBTQ community."

Hayes took her phone out, scan-read the file, and put it back in her jacket pocket. "We're on it, sir. On our way now."

5
———

Miller kept her focus on the cars ahead, hands holding the steering wheel at ten-to-two.

"Are you all right? You look pale," Hayes asked her.

Hayes' concern annoyed her. Pulling up outside the renovated factory outlet, Miller parked, put the handbrake on and switched off the engine. The real reason she couldn't sleep the previous night: Walker. She couldn't stop thinking about him. So stupid, she thought. "I'm fine, I'm just tired."

There was a tent in front of the building, which Miller had grown accustomed to seeing at crime scenes. "Let's get this over with, shall we?"

Inside the tent, Miller said hello to Sheila, the pathologist, while changing into the overalls, gloves, face mask and shoe covers. After putting on safety glasses, she was ready. Miller listened to Hayes and Sheila natter, wishing they would hurry up.

Sheila left the tent first. Miller let Hayes go next.

"We'll take this one room at a time." Sheila opened the front doors.

Before Miller stepped inside, she glanced up at the sign:

Accord. There was no mention of it being a radio station, no mention of the letters F or M.

Miller walked into a hallway with four rooms connected to it, two either side. Sheila opened the door to the first room on the left, nosed for a couple of seconds then backed out.

There were two recording studios on the premises, complete with glass partitions separating the host from the guests, or whoever else sat the opposing side. Never having seen the inside of a radio station before, Miller found it fascinating that presenters would actually know what all the buttons were for. There were so many of them.

Back outside, in the hallway, there were two more rooms, one on the left and one on the right. Both had brown wooden doors with little signs on that Miller couldn't read from that distance. They looked like name signs.

The front door behind her opened and noise filled the hallway. Miller turned to find a good-looking guy in his fifties fighting with uniforms to get inside.

"Please, I have to see my husband!" The man dressed in a brown suit wrestled with her colleagues until Hayes stepped forward and spoke.

"Sir, you can't be in here. This is a crime scene."

It was heartbreaking listening to him grovel to be let in. The man identified himself as the business owner, Colin Fisher's husband, Henry Curtis. Miller stood back. She left it up to Hayes to handle the heartbroken husband.

Feeling bad for him, she walked with Sheila to the rear of the building, where the signs on the doors indicated they were dressing rooms, and where the murders took place. "We'll be through here when you're ready," she shouted to Hayes, who struggled to keep the husband away.

The furthest room was what appeared to be the cutting and editing room. A man sat on a swivel chair, slumped over a desk that held a bank of monitors and equipment used to edit audio footage. They were covered with the man's blood.

Miller stepped up to the man and peered down at the back of his head, where a huge hole showed her where the suspects stood when they shot him. The man had headphones on, so must not have heard the suspect enter. "It appears to be a single gunshot to the back of the head." She looked to Sheila for confirmation.

After filming the scene with a small camera, the pathologist asked her to help move the victim. When they lifted his head, a portion of his face was a bloody, pulpy mess, where the bullet had exited. "I concur. I can't see any other entry wounds, can you?"

Miller saw that a monitor in front of the man was broken. "It went straight through him, into that." She took out a pen and poked about in the remains of the monitor, looking for the projectile. "This must be the producer. Inspector Gillan said his name's Kurt something."

Hayes stood beside Miller. "What have we got?"

"Single gunshot to the back of the head by the looks of it. I'm not sure how this guy didn't see the intruder coming in. It's not a huge room, and the door's in his peripheral vision. Personally, I'd see that door open."

"Maybe he was too engrossed in what he was doing."

Miller nodded. "Maybe."

Hayes looked down at the slumped body. "I've checked, and the building doesn't have any cameras outside. How can this place be so high-tech, yet not have any cameras either inside or outside. We'd best pray the neighbours do."

6

From what Miller speculated, Hayes agreed. It would appear that the suspect had entered without the victim noticing. How, was anyone's guess. Perhaps Sheila was right: the victim was glued to the monitor. He had headphones on. "We know his name's Kurt something."

Miller took the victim's wallet out of his trousers. "Austin. Kurt Austin. He's local. Born in 1964. He has an NHS exemption card, and four, no five credit cards. Oh, and a business card for here. He calls himself a producer."

Hayes took the card from her partner. "Right, we need to find out as much as we can about him anyway. Any of these victims could be the intended target, Colin Fisher, Brandy Reid, or this poor guy." Hayes checked the corners of the room for cameras.

"Shall we move on to the next one?" Sheila, the pathologist, walked out of the room.

"With three victims, how are we going to find the suspect?" Miller asked.

Hayes was thinking the same. In all her time on the force, she'd never investigated a triple murder before. With three victims, she wondered who the intended victim was herself. If she were a betting person, she would put her money on it being the star, Colin Fisher, but she might be wrong.

Not that she knew anything about Brandy Reid. The co-presenter might have had a past that caught up with her; it could be an ex-boyfriend, or jilted lover for all she knew. It was folly to suspect Fisher. She hadn't even seen the body yet, and already she believed he was the target. "We're going to need help whittling down the suspect pool. We can't handle this case alone."

Allowing Miller to go ahead, she followed her partner to the second crime scene. The first thing she noticed: the blood, lots of it, over the carpet, bed covers, everywhere. Lying naked, her dead eyes staring up at the ceiling, Brandy Reid showed off her wares.

There were stab marks on her chest and stomach, together with a bullet wound in her chest and forehead. The brown carpet beneath her was red. Hayes made a note of where the shooter could have stood, although, judging by the mess below, it looked like Miss Reid had been sexually molested before they shot her.

"One in the chest and one in the head. It couldn't be any clearer if you ask me. This was a professional hit, but the knife wounds don't fit the MO of an assassin." Miller crouched and studied said blade wounds. "What kind of hitman does this?"

"It puts her in the front-running, though, doesn't it?" They needed to get lucky on this one, or it would become a drawn-out investigation. Hayes didn't want that. "We'll see what trace the SOCOs come up with, but I've changed my mind. I think Miss Reid might be the target. Look at those stab marks, how deep they are. Whoever did this knew her intimately."

The pathologist nodded grimly. "Poor woman. No one deserves that." She shook her head, turned to the door. "Shall we?"

"After you." Hayes followed Sheila out of Brandy's dressing room, across the hall to Colin Fisher's. When Hayes entered, she couldn't help but notice Colin's dead body sprawled on the blood-soaked carpet in front of the door to his en suite shower room.

Hayes studied the body. "A single shot to the chest and another to the forehead. I'm definitely thinking an execution."

SOCOs walked in and started filming the crime scene. The room was suddenly a hive of activity, with white-clad professionals marking the room, bagging evidence, dusting for prints and recording everything. "Let's do a walk-through," Hayes suggested.

Miller, Sheila and Hayes strolled out of the dressing room to the front of the building, to the hallway between the two recording studios. The radio presenter's husband stood inside the doors, still trying to get past security. "It's all right. We'll take it from here, sergeant."

"Make sure he doesn't get past." After whispering to her taller partner, Hayes met Henry Curtis at the front doors. "Is there somewhere we can go and talk privately, Mr Curtis?" Her question was greeted with a nod. She followed him to a small conference room at the front of the building.

There was room for twelve people to sit around the oblong table. Hayes took Henry's arm and walked him to the chair at the head of the table. "Please, have a seat, Mr Curtis. You're in shock."

"When can I see him?" Henry's eyes were red, puffy.

Hayes sat next to him. She reached out for his hand. "We'll need you to identify him formally at a later time, Mr Curtis. I'm afraid we can't allow you through the crime scene; you may contaminate it, which will make it harder to apprehend the person responsible."

Henry bowed his head and sobbed.

"I'm so sorry for your loss." Realising they weren't going to get anything useful out of him, she stood and nodded to the female uniform in the doorway, who gently took the owner out of the building. "We'll chat to Fisher's husband soon," she said to Miller.

All through the exchange, Miller remained quiet. Hayes squeezed her partner's shoulder and attracted the pathologist's attention. In the hallway, she started the walk-through. "Is this where we think they came from?"

"I noticed a fire exit at the rear, but I can't see the suspect gaining access through there. It's more than likely the victims left the front doors unlocked, isn't it? The emergency exit's a push bar to open sort, notoriously difficult to unlock from the outside."

"So we have our point of entry sorted." When she glanced behind her, a SOCO was busy dusting the handle and glass for fingerprints. "Let's walk in their shoes for a minute. They're probably going to check the recording studios for activity first, right? Like we did when we arrived. Which means we need all door handles, light switches and surfaces checked for prints. Let's assume they're professionals, and judging by their MO, they're assassins, they're going to be wearing gloves."

"They'll take glove prints as well. We've caught a number of suspects using their gloves. And they'll dust for footprints. So we have every area covered."

Hayes agreed with Sheila. She started their walk-through. "So, let's assume they've checked all the recording studios, if they have come in through the front doors, they're going to come to the editing room last. If they came in through the fire exit, the editing suite will be the first room they come to."

Miller walked in that direction. "They walk over here, find the producer listening with headphones on. And when he doesn't look over, they stand behind him, boom, one to the back of the head, and he slumps over his desk."

"Right, then the suspect backs out, and strolls to either his left or right." Hayes had to decide which victim they killed next, Fisher or Reid? "I don't know which one they visited first. Brandy had stab and bullet wounds."

"And she was molested, which adds time," Sheila pointed out.

"The two guys were taken care of quickly, cleanly, no fuss, but the suspect spent time with Brandy Reid. I don't know about you two, but I'd put my money on her being our target. What do you think?"

Miller nodded. "It makes sense. Are you thinking jilted boyfriend, or crazed fan? I noticed she was about to snort a line of coke. It's on her dresser. She might have had an altercation with her dealer. Who knows!"

"And that's what we're going to find out." Hayes didn't want to focus on only one victim in case they were off the mark. "We're going to divide the work up evenly. I don't think we can count on Inspector Gillan or Travis to help us on this, though. Something tells me they're going to have their hands full with Helsey and backtracking on the skip body case."

7

Charlotte Edwards busied herself in her kitchen. Her husband, Samuel, loved her baking, especially her signature chocolate cake. With flour down her apron, she slid the risen sponge off the oven tray and carried it over to the counter with her heatproof gloves, leaving it to cool on a metal rack.

Spying the clock above her, she made a note that it was time for her workout. With her two daughters at school, she loved her morning ritual.

Bar baking, she had a routine which consisted of getting the girls ready for school, then she would give the house a once over with the hoover before doing her circuit in their home gymnasium. After a shower she would read the newspaper, followed by a spot of lunch, sometimes out with friends, or she would provide for them. After lunch she would read for an hour or so before picking up her girls. It didn't get much better than that.

Upstairs, she stripped off and changed into her black jog bottoms and white strappy vest. First: her bike ride to warm up. A good fifteen-minute workout, starting slow, working up to a mad frenzy at the end. If she didn't finish the cycle ride dripping she had not worked hard enough.

Catching her breath, Charlotte sat on her rowing machine, and when ready, began the familiar motion, back and forth with her arms. Her knees bent and straightened with the motion. The front of the machine whirred and blew air over her.

After fifteen minutes of frantic rowing, sweat dripping down her back and chest, she stood, her knees weak, and picked up her resistance bands, which in her opinion were the epitome of inventiveness because she could workout anywhere in the world with them. She didn't require a gym subscription to build her core.

As per her weekly schedule, that morning she focused on her upper body and core, using three bands together, as was her level of experience. She didn't need a full-length mirror in front of her to show the gains. Charlotte could see and feel them herself. Over the course of a year, she had lost two stones and burned off fat to produce a tidy, taut physique.

There was nothing she relished more than meeting her friends for lunches. They were all so complimentary about her looks, and she noticed random men couldn't walk past her without turning their heads. Of course, she did enjoy wearing short skirts and small tops that showed off her new abs.

Her husband, Samuel, the most gorgeous black man she ever laid eyes on, had a lot to do with her new trimmer figure. It was only fair to make herself the best she could be. He looked after himself by going to the gym four times a week. Together they made a handsome couple, everyone said so.

Their union had produced two gorgeous daughters. Charlotte loved them both so much, everything from their milk chocolate skin, to their inquisitive, naughty natures. Yeah, life was pretty perfect in many ways.

Samuel earned an obscene amount as a stockbroker in the

city. The money was so much, she feared the bubble would burst one day. Until then, she would enjoy the high life, enjoy the six-bedroom house in a highly desired postcode just outside the capital, and four cars parked on their gravelly driveway. She would relish the three holidays a year and exclusive romantic getaways he surprised her with periodically.

After her resistance bands workout, she stripped out of her damp training gear and stepped under the shower head, soaking up the lukewarm jets. Twenty minutes later, she dried herself, and as she dressed into her lunch attire, cursed at the time. "Bugger!"

She flew out of the front door, into her red convertible Mini Cooper, and after opening the home's gates, raced along the A road towards her lunch date. Using her hands-free mobile, Charlotte dialled her best friend's number. "I'm running, maybe five minutes late, honey. Go grab a table and I'll see you at the club soon."

Charlotte struck it lucky with finding Samuel. Unlike her elder brother, Richard, she was not blessed with an intelligence level that made MENSA members jealous. No, she made it through school with grades that allowed her to enter hairdressing college. From there she graduated and started work at a local salon.

After ten years of hard graft, she decided to go solo and style hair from clients' homes. She loved her old job, but she preferred her new, carefree, lady-of-leisure lifestyle. Yeah, these days she didn't have the stress of work; she felt so much more in control of her own destiny. Amazing the joys money brought.

Life would be so much easier if she had been born an only child. Ever since she could remember, she had played referee to her brothers. Richard, the eldest and most intelligent of the three of them, wanted everything done his way. Their parents doted on him, which upset Colin, her younger brother. Growing up, Colin was blamed for everything that went wrong. It grated on her nerves, and helped push her sensitive younger brother away.

She wished her family life wasn't so complicated. More than anything, though, she wished Colin had not found drugs. They changed him from the quiet, sensitive lad he was at school, to the narcissistic liar, and violent thug he became.

Colin and Richard almost came to blows after Colin beat their dad up. The only reason her elder brother didn't go through with it was because he didn't know what kind of state his brother was in. Being a heroin addict, Colin could have had any combination of needle-related diseases.

They were the bad days, though, back when Richard and Colin weren't on speaking terms. It was different now. Two stints of rehab, and meeting Henry had done wonders for Colin's lifestyle. Free of drugs, her younger brother was a delight to be around.

It took Charlotte years to convince Richard to speak to Colin. Finally, they spoke their first words to each other on Colin and Henry's wedding day two years earlier. Charlotte cried when she witnessed them hug. They weren't best of friends after, but at least they were on talking terms.

Pulling in at the customer car park of the Roehampton Club, she found a space near the main building and parked up. Wearing a strappy vest and short skirt that showed off her long legs, Charlotte fiddled with her hair, using the reflection in the driver's window, before heading towards the country club.

She found her friend and joined her. Picking up the menu, she decided on a club sandwich and bottle of water. The calories didn't matter too much; she would be playing tennis with her girlfriends later. Every Thursday the girls were picked up from school by Samuel's parents, who spoilt them with sugary drinks and cakes, much to her annoyance.

Greeting her friend with a kiss to both cheeks, she ordered her food and settled in for a natter and gossip. Gail was one of her most complimentary friends, always there with a "you look great in that", which boosted Charlotte's confidence.

She tried to find nice things to say in return, but Gail was overweight and dressed down.

"You always look so made-up, Lottie, you put me to shame."

She pretended to be all coy, waving Gail's comment away. "Oh stop! It's just a vest." Of course, she knew how great she looked; she felt great. "So, what's the goss? Tell me everything you know."

It was a safe bet that one of their many friends had something going on. Gail would know what that something was. Her friend was about to talk when Charlotte's mobile rang. "Hold that thought." She smiled and answered the phone. "Henry? Is that you? Calm down. What're you saying? I can't understand you."

When he told her that Colin was dead, she covered her mouth with her hand and gasped.

8

Richard Fisher turned away from his computer and took a couple of deep breaths. His team were waiting for him downstairs in the workshop, all eager and excited. He opened his desk drawer and popped out two paracetamol from the packet, put them in his mouth and swallowed them with water from his glass on the desktop.

Getting up, he strolled over to his internal window, and parted the blinds to find his team leaning on the blue Ford Fiesta, chatting. Test number fifteen coming up, he thought, heading towards the door.

When he emerged from the office and stood at the top of the wrought-iron stairs, they cheered and clapped him. He had to steady himself as he descended the twenty steps, adrenaline pumping. "How's she looking?" The question aimed at them all.

His second-in-command, Vanu, a highly intelligent Indian engineer with two doctorates to his name confirmed with excitement, "We're ready for test fifteen, Richard."

He regarded his team for a moment, taking stock of this momentous occasion. They were the best team of employees he could have put together. Two women and two men, each leaders in their respective fields. He hired Vanu Parekh for this project three years earlier, and paid him handsomely for his expertise.

At the blue Ford Fiesta, he walked around her, stroking the chassis as he circled her. When he peered through the passenger window, he thought how ordinary she seemed, yet everyone here knew she was anything but. This little car would change the world like nothing else had, more so than the last great invention: the internet.

"Are the cameras set up and ready to go?" He stared through the window and up at the ceiling, where Germany-born Paula Lang had mounted the tiny audio and visual recorder. When she replied in the affirmative, he nodded. "I guess it's time to go."

Paula opened the driver door for him. Richard had hired her for her technical wizardry. She was the fastest techie he'd ever met, an asset to his crew. "I think we should mark this occasion. She'll work today, I can feel it."

Having marked fourteen previous tests, Richard went along with the group photo opportunity in front of his record-breaking Fiesta. He put his arms around his top two teammates and smiled at the camera. "Is that it? Are we done yet?"

Going around each team member, he shook their hands and thanked them for their tireless efforts over the years. They had put themselves out there for him, working through weekends and into evenings sometimes.

Stood by the open door, he stared at the camera Paula held. "As you know, my name's Richard Fisher. This is test fifteen, and today's the day. Come join us as we make history in this 'ordinary' little Ford Fiesta."

When he sat in the driver's seat, Vanu was already in the passenger's seat, strapped in, raring to go. After closing the door, Richard did all his checks, including a dashboard monitor. "Everything looks ready. The ceiling camera's running. Can everyone hear me?" The rest of his team confirmed they could, through Vanu's mobile phone.

Richard gave the green light to open the workshop garage door. Paula obliged by pressing the button on the remote control. And when he started the engine, he accelerated out onto the courtyard. From there, he turned right onto the main road.

He had to admit to feeling better about himself now he was on talking terms with Colin, thanks to Charlotte's intervention before his brother's wedding. He'd almost cried at witnessing his brother marry Henry, because his parents never had the chance to see their youngest happy.

For years, he blamed Colin and his drug habit for the family's misfortunes, never forgiving him for breaking them apart. Charlotte told him on a couple of occasions, it was their parents' fault for not accepting Colin's sexuality, and favouring Richard over her and Colin that pushed their younger brother into the arms of recreational drugs, but he didn't believe her. Their younger brother was a selfish bastard.

It took Richard years to finally forgive Colin and shake his hand. He missed his stupid little brother, not that he admitted it back then. Despite Colin's behaviour, he still loved him. This love was partly the reason he'd confided in Colin and Henry about what they were trying to achieve at the workshop, and once they knew, Henry had offered to invest.

At a time when funding was tight, the extra investment helped. With Henry and Colin as ghost investors, he didn't need to worry about them; they were happy to help, and didn't involve themselves. All Henry asked for was to be kept in the loop and informed when they achieved their goal. Richard looked forward to phoning Henry later, fingers crossed their test worked.

On the A23, he checked the dashboard. "Won't be long now. I'll take her out to the M25 and give her a good run."

Once on the M25, he ramped up the speed to a little over seventy, sticking to the fast lane, only pulling into the first inside lane to let faster cars pass. "It won't be long now. Are you all still with me?"

The rest of the team replied in the positive, although their voices were almost drowned out by the sound of travelling at high speed along a motorway. "The gauge says empty. Any time now." He took the car up to seventy-eight.

Bombing along, Richard heard a clunk. He glanced over at Vanu. "Was that it? Was that the changeover?"

"What does it say?" His passenger leaned in. "That was it! We bloody well did it, everyone. Test fifteen was a success." His voice held the excitement of a five-year-old boy on Christmas Day, waiting to open his presents.

The team back at the workshop cheered. Richard was beyond words. The gauge went from empty to full, and the car ran still. Adrenaline peaking, he searched for an exit, not wanting to drive along the M25 anymore. His hands and feet shook with excitement. "You know what this means, don't you! This is so fucking huge, I can't get my head around it."

"You've had three years to digest it, Richard." His usual frown gone, it was replaced with elation. "I can't believe we've done it. It works; it bloody works. It only took three years and fifteen tests."

After turning off the M25, and managing to traverse the complex road system, Richard sped along the A24 towards the workshop. At a convenient place, he pulled over at the side of the road and got out, his legs wobbly.

He did a circuit of the Fiesta, stroking the paintwork as he walked around her. The bonnet warm to the touch, he figured he'd given her a run. "You did it, baby. I always knew you would." Standing back, he admired her ordinary appearance, and knew that beneath the hood, she was the most extraordinary car in the world. No other engine resembled hers. His phone rang.

"Go ahead, Richard; I'll wait in the car."

Taking his mobile out of his jeans pocket, he identified the caller: Lottie.

"He's dead, Richard! Someone murdered our Colin."

It took Richard a couple of moments to register the information. He smiled first, not believing it, waiting for the punchline. When his sister continued to cry, his smile faded. "What? That can't be. I only saw him on Tuesday. He was fine."

Charlotte explained that Colin had been shot at work, or so Henry had informed her. Colin's co-star and producer were also shot and killed. Richard's first question to her was "why?" Silly, really, how could his little sister know? He had to lean against the car to prevent himself from falling.

"Hey, are you all right?" Vanu got out of the passenger seat and rushed over to him. "What's happened? Richard? Talk to me."

"He's gone!" Richard still couldn't believe it. He dropped his phone and sank to the ground, numb. "Colin. Someone killed my little brother." Even saying it aloud didn't make it feel any more real.

Vanu helped him up. "I'm driving us back to the workshop. Here, let me help you. Let's get you all strapped in." He closed the passenger door and ran around to the driver's side. "We're on our way back now, peeps."

Richard sat staring out of the window for the duration of the journey back. Someone had murdered his little brother. His Colin was dead!

9

Miller climbed out of her coveralls and left them in the tent. After brushing off her suit jacket, she binned the face mask and foot covers.

Hayes met her at the door to the tent and she followed her partner out to their waiting car. Journalists swamped the police cordon, the uniforms trying their best to keep them at bay. "They're a lively bunch today."

"Two local celebrities have been murdered. Of course they're going to be eager. Must be a slow news day."

"Except on the Brexit front." Hayes pulled a distasteful face.

"Right!" She opened the passenger door. "They're getting louder."

"Hayes! Can you answer some questions? Is it true Colin Fisher was murdered? Was it a gangland hit?" A male reporter at the back of the fray stuck his microphone in the air. "He was into the Demirci family for thousands."

"Inspector Hayes, can you tell us how many victims there are, and how they were murdered?" A female reporter stuck her microphone between two uniforms in front of her. "Is it true they were executed?"

Miller didn't say a word, instead she left Hayes to speak to the press.

"Is it true Kurt Austin was shot, Hayes? Is his boyfriend a suspect?"

Getting in the car, Miller closed the door and waited for her supervisor to join her. When Hayes sat, she stared at the throng of journalists. "They've got theories already. How the hell are we going to play this? We've got three lots of suspects to chase down."

Hayes sighed, starting the engine. "Tell me about it. We're going to go through each suspect's background with a fine toothcomb." She reversed, turned and steered towards the cordon, the journalists clearing a path for them. "First, we're going to interview the next of kin of each of the victims, starting with Fisher's and Reid's."

"Do you still think Reid's the intended target?"

"I'm not sure. The extra stab wounds suggest she's special. The male victims got a bullet a piece in the head and chest, but Brandy also has stab wounds. My money's still on her."

At first, Miller would have bet on Brandy being the target. "But what about Fisher being into gangsters for thousands?" She stared at a brunette journalist through her window, as Hayes drove them off the plot's car park and past the cordon.

"I think we're looking for someone with a military background."

She nodded in agreement. "Makes sense with how precise the entry wounds were, especially Fisher's central forehead shot. I think the suspect stood over him and fired that kill shot. It was too perfect."

"I was thinking that myself. Keep your eye out for cameras along this road, would you? I saw one on our way in, so I'll contact the council and see if we can get a car type, or registration."

"The neighbouring factory had one above their doors." Miller received a surprised reaction from her supervisor. "What? First rule of studying the crime scene: look out for cameras. I'm surprised you didn't see it yourself."

"Well done. While I'm pratting about with the council, you contact the factory and ask for their footage. Then, we're going to set up interviews for tomorrow morning with the families of the victims." Hayes wiped her forehead with the sleeve of her suit jacket.

"I'll make a start on Brandy Reid's next of kin."

"And I'll contact Fisher's husband. They'll all need to identify their loved ones before we interview them, so we'll ask to meet them at their homes. No need to make it too formal just yet, not until we've dug into their histories."

"You think it could be a hired hit?" Miller pondered the hired assassin scenario. It wouldn't be against the realms of possibility for someone to hire a hitman to murder a radio presenter.

"Anything's possible. Like you said earlier, it wouldn't be the first time."

10

Charlotte Edwards pulled up outside Henry and Colin's five-bedroomed palatial detached house. Surrounded by an eight-foot perimeter wall topped with razor wire, Henry's home was an impenetrable fortress controlled by a remote in Henry's charge. "We're home, Henry. You need to open the gates, honey."

Her brother-in-law reached into his pocket and pressed the "open" button on his key ring, as the wrought-iron gates opened. Every time she drove there, she wondered how Henry could own such a magnificent home. The interior décor matched the awe-inspiring exterior, every touch and nuance chosen by Henry.

Stopping outside their huge pillared front doors, Charlotte switched off the engine and sat waiting for Henry to move. Numb. She picked him up from the radio station, where she found him trying to get through the police cordon. "Let's get you inside, shall we?"

Getting out of her car, she went round to Henry's side and opened his door. He sat motionless, staring into the void, his eyes dead. She reached across him and unclipped his seat belt.

"Come on, Henry, help me out here. I'm not strong enough to carry you."

Not comatose, he put his arm around her shoulder and pulled himself out. Charlotte walked with him up the three concrete steps to the huge front doors. He handed her the key and she opened up, helping him inside. After closing the door, she walked him through to the huge lounge and eased him onto his expensive sofa. "Can I get you anything to drink?"

Fussing over Henry made her forget about her poor little brother, slain. In the kitchen, she prepared two mugs of tea, while waiting for the kettle to boil. Her Colin was dead! Too numb to believe it, she made the beverages and carried them through.

After placing Henry's mug on the coffee table, her mobile went off in her handbag. "That'll be Richard." Her brother-in-law lay on the sofa, sobbing. Charlotte went through his trouser pocket and took out the gate remote key ring. "I'll bring it right back."

She answered Richard's call and pressed the "open" button. A couple of minutes later, she opened the door to her elder brother, who greeted her with his customary kiss on the cheek.

"How is he?" Richard seemed genuine.

"As you'd expect, devastated. He's lying on the sofa." She walked with him through the hallway to the lounge. "I've just made tea. Do you want one?"

While Richard sat with Henry, she went through to the kitchen and made another mug of tea, this time to her fussy brother's specifications. She was used to his meticulous ways. Charlotte couldn't fathom how her sister-in-law had put up with his habits for so long before separating from him. "Here!" In the sitting room, she handed him the mug.

Silence. When she sat on the sofa next to Henry, he crawled

towards her, and lay his head on her lap, sobbing. Charlotte stroked his hair. Her poor Colin. She tried swallowing the lump in her throat.

Richard leaned forward. "Do you know what happened? Do you know how he died? Has anyone spoken to you?"

Charlotte shook her head. "I drove to the radio station and found Henry trying to get through the police cordon. I didn't get a chance to speak to anyone before I drove him back here. I'm sorry! This is all too surreal for me. Who'd want to hurt Colin?"

Richard stood. "I don't know, but I'm going to find out."

When her brother took out his mobile, Henry's landline phone rang. It sat next to the sofa, within Charlotte's reach. "Shall I answer it, Henry?" When he failed to reply, she lifted the receiver. "The Curtis residence. How can I help?"

"Yeah, hi, I was hoping to speak to Henry Curtis."

She looked down at him. "I'm afraid we've received some devastating news. He's unavailable right now."

"Oh, excuse me. I'm Detective Sergeant Rachel Miller, I'm investigating Colin Fisher's murder. I was hoping to arrange a convenient time to come and speak to him?"

Charlotte waved at Richard, who stood faffing with his phone. She covered the mouthpiece on the receiver. "It's the police. They want to set up an interview." Her brother strutted over and took the receiver from her, identifying himself as Colin's brother.

Still unreal, dreamlike, she listened to Richard converse with the detective with the lovely voice. "And? What's going on?" She waited for him to place the receiver on its docking bay. "Did she tell you what happened?"

"Detective Miller and Hayes are coming over tomorrow at eleven. I'm going to identify Colin's body at nine, and then drive over here straight after."

"Identify his body?" Shit was becoming all too real, although it felt like a dream, a bad dream that she wished she could pinch herself to awake from. She only saw Colin a couple of days earlier, and he was in great spirits, all excited about his upcoming holiday with Henry. They were borrowing a friend's luxury yacht and crew for a couple of weeks. Charlotte wanted to wake up now.

"Someone has to, sis. Henry's not up to it, and I don't want you to remember Colin lying on a slab in a morgue. So I said I would."

She had to hand it to Richard, he always came through for the family, every time. Richard was a reliable rock. Whenever she found herself in trouble, she would seek out Richard's advice. The family would have imploded without him. Charlotte nodded her understanding, while stroking Henry's hair.

"I'll do it." Henry's tiny voice, barely audible, broke their focus. "He was my husband. I'll go and identify him. I need to say goodbye."

Richard objected. "I don't want you remembering Colin lying on a slab, either. Please reconsider, Henry. You mean a lot to us."

"I've made up my mind. It's something I have to do."

Charlotte stopped stroking his hair and he sat up. "This is a shock, Henry. Lie back down, please?" He sat there, staring into space. Instead of forcing him, she got up and took the mugs back to the kitchen.

After putting the plug in, she filled the basin with hot soapy water and started washing up the plates left on the counter from the previous night. It seemed as though Henry and Colin had entertained at some point. Obviously not the previous night, because Colin was working at the radio station until late. There were a dozen plates to wash.

She would do anything to take her mind off Colin, including

washing-up, which she detested. She opted to handwash the plates, just to have something to do in the background. Now she'd spoken to a detective, it felt more real. Her mobile phone rang.

Marching into the hall, she retrieved it from her handbag and answered the call from her husband, Samuel. Taking it in the kitchen, she closed the door and unloaded on him, telling him everything in one outburst. Charlotte was angry with him for not picking up when she'd needed him earlier. "You weren't there, again. I needed you, Sam."

He apologised, kept on, until she'd had enough and forgave him. Only a few hours earlier, she'd been happy with him, but today wasn't the first time he'd not been there for her. After the last time, she thought he would be faster at picking up his damned phone and calling her, especially after the urgent nature of her voicemail.

He agreed to drive over to Henry's. Terminating the call, she finished the washing-up and dried her hands on a tea towel, before meandering into the hallway. Charlotte listened to Richard trying to talk to Henry.

"I thought you'd like to know it works. We took her on her fifteenth test-run just now, and she passed with flying colours. Who'd have thought it would only take three years, and fifteen tests? She's sat in the workshop now."

Silence. Henry failed to respond.

"Did you hear me, Henry? We made history today."

Charlotte entered the lounge and her brother sat back in his armchair. He was not a subtle man; she felt like she'd interrupted something. "Everything all right in here?" Richard looked away. "What works now, Richard? I heard you say something works."

"Oh nothing, a work thing. It won't interest you."

"But it will interest Henry? Why?"

"No reason, Lottie. Forget about it. Forget I said anything."

Charlotte sat on the sofa and coaxed Henry to lie with his head on her lap again. She didn't mind Richard having secrets, but he didn't have to be so obvious about it. Now she wanted to know what he was talking about.

11

Hayes put her desk phone receiver on its dock and turned her attention to her computer. "I spoke to Fisher's older brother, Richard. We'll be meeting Curtis, Richard Fisher and Charlotte Edwards, the middle sister, at Henry Curtis' home. Looks like we'll get the whole extended family in one hit."

Miller poked her head over the partition. "And we have an interview lined up tomorrow afternoon with Brandy's daughter, Ellie, and Brandy's mum." Getting up from her swivel chair, Miller strolled up to the board and wrote Ellie's name beneath her mum's.

Hayes went over to the whiteboard that she had drawn three equally spaced vertical lines down. At the top of each column she wrote the names of each of the victims: Colin Fisher, Brandy Reid and Kurt Austin.

She wrote the names of Fisher's relatives beneath his name: Richard Fisher, Charlotte Edwards and Henry Curtis. And then she wrote the name of Kurt Austin's partner underneath his name: Fernando Linares. "Here's our next of kin for all three victims. This is going to get complicated."

Three lists of interviewees, three lives to trawl through,

which would lead to three shortlists of suspects. Hayes sighed, going back to her computer. She picked up her phone and dialled the number for the local council. It took her a while to connect to the right department.

After a lengthy exchange with the council worker, she finally managed to acquire the footage she needed, except she had to wait for the email to ping through, and she wouldn't hold her breath for it arriving today. She leaned back and stretched. "How're you getting on with Brandy's background check?"

"She's led a colourful life, I can tell you that much. Brandy Reid's been in trouble most of her life, by the length of her sheet. At fourteen she was expelled from her first school for beating another girl up so badly she spent several weeks in hospital. The second expulsion was for having sex with her female history teacher."

"Quite the charmer, then." Hayes continued listening.

"It gets better. She eventually graduates with eight GCSEs in all the decent subjects, and not bad grades, mostly Bs, with a couple of Cs, so she's not unintelligent. But it's post-school that her record gets really interesting."

"Go on! I'm listening." Hayes sat back and took it all in.

"In and out for minor offences, the last one being solicitation. In all, she's been inside five times, for a total of four years and eight months. Brandy's been clean and out for six years. That's where her sheet ends."

"We'll have to find out more about her through interviewing friends."

"What about you? Have you found out much about Colin Fisher?"

"He has a record, but nowhere near as lengthy as our Brandy's. Colin Fisher was arrested for solicitation back in 2009, and for ABH in 2012. One count of lewd behaviour in a public toilet. He's only been sent down the once, though, an assault charge, and spent fifteen months inside."

Having read out his criminal record, Hayes clicked on Google and typed in Colin's name. Thousands of entries appeared on her monitor. There were already news reports of Fisher's murder on various online news outlets. Clicking on one, she caught Miller's attention. "They're still shouting the gangland hit theory. One local reporter claims Fisher was into Melodi Demirci for thousands in gambling debts."

"Demirci, why have heard that name before?" Miller went to her PC.

Pulling up another Google window, Hayes typed in the gangster's name. "Melodi Demirci took over the family's casino after her father was found dead in the car park. He had eight bullet wounds in the chest, a little over two years ago. It says here, in an interview with her, that she almost had to close the casino, but thanks to her business savvy, it's now a profitable enterprise."

"Yeah, I bet she's a real pillar of the community. Here it says she was pulled in for questioning last year over the death of a croupier who fell off a nearby roof. And I bet if we dig, we'll find more on her. If Fisher was into her for thousands, she doesn't sound like the type to let debts go, does she?"

"No, she doesn't." Hayes went over to the board and wrote "*Demirci*?" in red pen below the list of Fisher's family. "We have our first suspect, if we can put the two together. I'll call the casino later and see if I can book an interview in with the lovely entrepreneur."

"I'm onto Kurt Austin now. It seems he's clean. No arrests, charges, or detentions, as far as I can see. The PNC has him living with a Fernando Linares, who does have a record. He's done time for aggravated burglary. Oh, and he's ex-Forces in

Spain. He's lived here for seven years, still registered as living with Kurt."

Up at the whiteboard, Hayes scrubbed out Fernando's name in black and rewrote it in red felt pen. "Ex-Forces, he has to be added to our suspect pool. Right, I think we have enough to be getting on with."

12

Miller pulled her navy jog bottoms up and put on her white vest. Once she tied her shoelaces, she came out of the cubicle and walked through to the gymnasium, where her colleagues worked out.

Joining the police gym down the road from the station was the best idea. She started with a gentle jog on the mill, which turned into a frantic sprint at the end to get her lungs burning.

Next up: the rowing machine. She climbed on and started the motion, back and forth, the wheel at the front whirring away, blowing air in her face, cooling her down. She found it hypnotic, the same motion for fifteen minutes.

A couple of people she'd spoken to before came in and nodded at her. She acknowledged them in return, before wiping her face with her towel. Leg press next. She sat on the seat and adjusted the weight pin. Holding the handrails either side of the seat, she pushed down hard on the foot panels.

After her first set of ten, the tenth almost killing her, she relaxed. Catching her breath, the doors opened and there he was: Luke *"Not the Sky Variety"* Walker entered with Zuccari, one of his armed unit colleagues. He was too pumped, even before his workout. She could only imagine what his biceps would feel like after.

Deciding to play it cool, she put her earphones in and listened to her compilation on Spotify, a mix of heavy metal, hard rock, and country. Miller adored country music more than any other genre. Her dream was to visit Nashville one day.

On the chest press, she started her reps, occasionally catching glimpse of him. Luke and his mates stuck to the free weights area, picking up huge dumbbells that she thought obscene. He almost caught her staring at him, but she turned her head in time.

As he walked towards her, Miller jumped off the chest press and meandered over to the cross trainer, where two female colleagues were halfway through their workouts. She hopped on, set the programme, and commenced when Luke leaned on her machine. Miller pretended she had not seen him. "Oh! Hey, Luke." She continued using the cross trainer.

"Hi! I didn't think you used this gym. I haven't seen you here before."

She smiled while doing the action, sweat forming on her brow, and dripping down her back. "We must keep missing each other. I'm here three or four times a week."

"Huh! Strange. You'd have thought we'd have bumped into each other by now."

She wiped her forehead, then placed her hand on the bar. "Well, I only joined a couple of months ago."

He hit his forehead gently. "Of course. That'll be it."

Miller smiled while cross training. Her eyes went from his face down to his pecs, which were on display. When he'd entered, he wore a vest, but he'd taken that off and now stood next to her in his glorious perfection. Hayes was right: he was a poser. With a body like that, though, it would be a crime not to. Shame about the lack of smarts.

The long awkward silence between them made her want him to leave.

She kept on the cross trainer, occasionally looking at him.

He didn't seem to get it. "Are you after this?"

Walker woke up. "Huh? Oh, no, you're all right. I only do free weights. I get my cardio from early-morning runs."

"Me too." She smiled, then blew hair out of her eyes. "I only come here as an extra workout. My ex and I had a gym at home, so I never used to have to use a public gym."

"Were you married? I notice you're not wearing a ring."

"I'm recently divorced, actually." She stopped the apparatus and stood on the foot panels, her vest clinging to her skin. "What about you?"

"Me? Nah, married to the force. Funny, but for some reason women don't seem to like dating armed cops. I can't say I understand it."

His colleague called for him. Miller felt a little disappointed when he made his apology and went back to lifting huge dumbbells. Walker liked her; it was in the way he wouldn't take his eyes off her when he had to go back to his colleague. Even from his area, he kept checking her out, so she hovered on the apparatus near him, showing off her gains.

Miller smiled at a couple of female colleagues as she went around the gym.

After a further forty minutes, she decided she'd had enough and headed for the changing rooms, where she stripped and showered, before sauntering to the cubicles, grabbing her belongings and changing into her civvies: running shoes, light blue jeans and white T-shirt.

After blow drying her dark hair, Miller picked up her gym bag and made her way out to her car. She placed her bag in the boot.

"Hey, Miller!"

The voice made her jump. "Jesus Christ, Luke. Has no one ever told you off for sneaking up on people?"

Walker held his arms up in surrender. "I'm sorry! I didn't think you'd jump. Please, forgive me?" Again, his concern appeared sincere.

She waited for her heart rate to slow. "It's all right." She laughed and closed the boot. "So, what did you want to say just now?"

He looked scared and shuffled his feet. "Well, it's all gone to shit now, hasn't it? I might as well go back and start over. Shit! I hate this crap."

"What crap? What're you talking about?"

"I was all confident just now. I was going to ask if you want to join me for a beer, or something. I was going to be all smooth, like, but now I've gone and botched it."

Miller smiled. "You're asking me out?"

"It looks like it, yeah. I know a decent bar nearby if you fancy it?"

Walking round to the driver's side, she waited until she opened her door before replying. "No, I don't fancy a bar tonight. Sorry!" She noted his disappointed expression. "I'm trying to avoid bars at the moment, but you're welcome to join me for a beer at my place. I've got cold ones in the fridge. Best I can do, I'm afraid."

His gorgeous face lit up. "You're on. My car's back there, I'll follow you?"

"I was going to offer you a lift, but–"

"I'm on call tonight, so I need my motor with me. Give me a sec, I'll be right with you." He strutted off.

His strut made her grin. Such a lad, she thought. The dash clock said it was 21:25. The night was but young. And Miller was looking forward to an energetic evening with the lovely Luke Walker.

13

"So, what's it like working with the legendary Amanda Hayes?" Walker held Miller in his lap tighter. "I bet you've learned loads from her."

Miller sat up, her TV on in the background. "She's a workaholic. That's why she's so legendary. The woman lives and breathes the force. Don't get me wrong, I put more than my fair share of hours in, but Hayes, man she obsesses. She's already on her second divorce, no children. I can sum her private life up in two words: she reads. Like, a lot. It drove her second husband mad, apparently. She either works, or she reads."

Finishing her can of Carling, Miller placed it on the coffee table in front of her. "Anyway, enough shop talk. Are you ready for another?" By another, she meant squash for Walker, who'd already drunk his limit of one can of lager. She'd polished off three cans already, not that she was counting.

"Nah, you're all right. Don't want to go into the station in the morning with a squashover, now, do I? What'll the boys think?"

She chuckled to herself, unfolded his arm from around her waist and stood from the couch. They had some banal action-drama programme on in the background. Whenever he stroked her arm, he sent shivers down her. She loved it. "I'll be right back."

Grabbing her hand, Walker pulled her towards him and forced her to sit on his lap again, which Miller pretended to fight against, until he leaned forward and kissed her. With his strong hands on her waist, she let go and enjoyed him.

Opening her eyes, her palm on his stubbly cheek, she stared into his blue eyes. "Hi!" Was the only thing she thought of to say.

"Hi!" He seemed equally nervous.

Instead of getting up, she leaned forward this time, her lips meeting his. As she kissed him, deeper and longer each time, she thought how she'd never felt like this before.

Miller felt safe with Walker, protected, which was a strange sensation, as even her husband had never made her feel safe. Miller was strong, in both body and mind. She didn't need protecting by any man. So, why did she feel so feminine sat on Walker's lap?

His hands began to wander. This was the part she dreaded. "Wait!" She pulled away from him, remained sat on his lap and stared into his lust-filled eyes. "I have something I need to tell you, before we go any further."

He pulled a surprised face. "You're not a man, are you? You're not going to whip something bigger than mine out from between your legs?"

Miller liked him, liked his sense of humour, his body, everything. Walker was the first guy she'd liked since her marriage had broken down. Her fling with Billy, a stockbroker, didn't count. Now was crunch time.

After she moved into this awful, tiny flat, and after the divorce, she tried dating on three occasions. All had ended badly. Miller was by no means a girly-girl, in any sense of the term. "Of course not. I might even be too much woman for you to handle."

"Ouch! Then what's up?" He tried lifting her T-shirt.

"Stop it! I'm being serious. I have something I need to tell you."

Walker pretended to zip his mouth, wiped it from smirking to serious. "Go on. I'm listening. I'm sorry! You have my undivided attention."

Now she had him quiet, she didn't want to go through with it. "God! This is so embarrassing. I'm sorry to even tell you this."

"Whatever it is, Rach, don't worry. I'm not going to laugh, I promise."

She believed him. "I've only been with my husband. We met at school. We married when I was twenty. He had his career, I had mine. So, I haven't had much experience with, you know, other men? Oh, and a guy called Billy. That's it."

Walker wiped his brow with the back of his hand. "Is that it? Phew! I thought you were going to say something serious. None of this bothers me. We can take this as fast or slow as you like. You're in charge, okay?"

When he started unbuttoning her jeans, she wanted to run, but stayed, as he gently tugged them down. He stood and pulled her T-shirt over her head, leaving her in just her bra and knickers. It was erotic, sensual, having him feast his eyes on her.

"You are beautiful."

Calling her Rachel compounded her desire for him. Even her ex-husband called her Miller. The only people who ever called her Rachel were her parents, and only because they named her. From primary school up, she was always Miller.

"And you're not the only one with a confession." He sat her down on the sofa and started to undress himself. Walker took off his vest and fumbled with his trainers, then his jeans, sliding them off and dropping them on the carpet.

Miller waited with anticipation. "So? What's your confession?" Everything was perfect so far. His back was so muscular, she ran her hand over his glutes and delts. Everything about him was perfect.

"A few years ago I got stuck up Annapurna with my climbing crew for three days and nights." He took his left sock off. "We all suffered from severe hypothermia." When he took his right sock off, there they were: artificial toes. "I think I got off lightly; a quarter of all climbers die on that mountain."

She leaned over and took a closer look. "Oh man, they're so realistic."

Walker took off his toes and handed them to her, leaving the residual limb on the carpet. "The NHS wouldn't pay for them, so my parents and I stumped up the cash. Two friends of mine lost fingers."

Handing them back, Miller waited for him to put his toes back on, stood, and held out her hand. "Shall we go somewhere more comfortable?"

Walker took no time in kissing her, holding her buttocks in his hands. Mostly naked already, Miller sat on the edge of the bed. She felt every kiss, every lick, loving his unfamiliar touch.

DAY 2
WEDNESDAY, JUNE 13TH

14

Specialist Firearms Command (SCO19) officer Luke Walker had hated his name since primary school age, since being introduced to his very nearly namesake Luke Skywalker of *Star Wars* fame. His parents were avid fans of the space saga, so when his dad had the chance to name him, what other name could he choose when his surname was Walker?

Lying in Miller's bed, stroking her back, Walker stared at the digital display from her alarm clock on the ceiling. 03:16. He needed sleep, but he was too excited. He'd tried to find the courage to speak to her for ages. Their paths had crossed briefly on duty when his unit were asked to raid one of Helsey's crew's homes. But he only managed to introduce himself.

The previous night at the gym was fortuitous. He would have found a reason eventually to talk to her, and he thought he made a good impression the night he and his unit went to apprehend Helsey, although Miller ended up in a tussle with their target. He thought she had to be the bravest woman he'd ever met. And she was in good company, partnered with Amanda Hayes, a legend everyone knew had balls of steel.

His mobile phone buzzed next to him. Reaching across to

the bedside cabinet, he picked it up: work. Without hesitation, he sat up and answered it with the words, "Be right there", flung his legs over the edge of the bed and proceeded to put his toes on.

Miller stirred next to him. "I've got to go. No rest for the wicked and all that." Locating his boxers, he stooped down and put them on. He stood and stared down at her lovely face. She smiled up at him, mostly covered in a sheet. "Can I call you later?" He straddled the bed and kissed her.

With the clock ticking, he tried to tear himself away, but she kissed him deeper each time he threatened to leave. "I've really got to go." Miller pouted as he walked away. At the door, he ran back to her for one last kiss.

The drive to the station took no time so early in the morning. He pulled up in a space close to the reception doors as a couple of his unit arrived. Zuccari, a British-born Italian, met him at his car.

"How'd it go with Miller?" Zuccari held a knowing smirk.

"That's my business, mate." Walker closed the door and walked towards reception. "Do we know why we've been called in?"

"Come on, man, don't try ducking the question, how'd it go?" Zuccari made gestures with his hand that made him smile. "Hey, Vodka, Luke's trying to dodge the question. He asked Miller out last night. I saw you talking to her at her car, mate. Spill."

Vodicka, nicknamed Vodka, or Voddy for obvious reasons, marched up to him. "Spill the beans, Walker. She as good as I imagine she is?" She opened the door and marched through reception, using her card to access the security gate. "Well? Don't be a pussy, come on!"

"Fuck you guys." He swiped his card and the gate opened. "I'm not telling you shit. What's the matter, Voddy, you not getting enough pussy of your own? And Zuccari, you're not that hard up, are you? You sad git!"

Laughing with his colleagues and friends, he marched into the locker room and started getting changed into his combat gear. Their sarge strode in, hurrying them up. Walker noted his tone, and judging by the early morning wake-up call, this was big. "Does anyone know what's going on?"

The rest of his unit shook their heads as they geared up. Wearing his bulletproof vest, shirt, black khaki trousers, tough black boots and cap, he was ready for action. In the lock-up, he and his colleagues signed out their weapons, their Glock 17 pistols and HK MP5 carbines, and marched to the garage at the rear of the station.

Their sergeant stood in front of their vehicles. "Listen up, people."

Walker figured it must be urgent for the briefing to take place in the garage, instead of upstairs in one of the briefing rooms. He listened to the sarge explain that they were being tasked with raiding a warehouse. It was part of a wider operation. "So, take no chances with these scumbags, understood? Stay alert, but if one of these bastards opens fire, you do what you need to."

The sergeant and two more of his team got in the BMW 530d, their Armed Response Vehicle (ARV), which would be their unit's lead car, while Walker sat in the driver's seat of their BMW X5 Xdrive 30d. In the top left and right corners of both front windscreens were yellow circular stickers, identifying their vehicle as armed.

As part of his ongoing CPD, Walker had taken additional driving lessons, which taught him emergency manoeuvres, as well as specialist weapons training. There were few weapons he wasn't qualified to use during deployment. "Here we go!" He pulled out of the garage after the sergeant's BMW, their lights flashing.

Vodicka leaned in between him and Zuccari. "Man, I love this fucking job."

"Voddy, you know the rules: strap yourself in." He chided her playfully, never wanting to take her on physically. Vodicka may be a woman, but she was tough as they came, and could probably take Miller out in a ring. Czech women were notoriously tough, in his experience, and he'd dated two through Vodicka.

After she strapped herself in, Walker drove the car behind the sergeant all the way there, pulling up behind him on a side road, the warehouse just down the street.

Getting out, he checked his weapons.

Walker took his half of the unit to meet the sergeant and the others in front of their BMW. "How do you want to play this, Sarge?"

Their sergeant explained their assault formation. Three groups of two; one left, one right, one central to the rear. They waited for a full ten minutes in position. The sarge had to receive the green light from his superior, some commissioner.

Walker and Vodicka took the left, while Zuccari took charge of the right and the sarge took the rear centre. In his earpiece, Walker heard the sarge's command and signalled to Zuccari that they were going to breach.

15

Charlotte Edwards lay next to her husband, unable to sleep. It appeared Samuel wasn't asleep either, judging by his fidgeting. The girls would be asleep at four in the morning, which was where Charlotte would like to be. She sighed. "Stop fidgeting!" Her voice barely a whisper, it failed to register a reaction from the lump next to her.

She couldn't get Henry or Richard out of her mind. The way her brother had abruptly ended his conversation with Henry made her suspicious. Richard made it sound like he was discussing his work with their younger brother's husband. But why?

What could Henry, a radio station owner, have to do with Richard's business? Her brother was an engineer, a brilliant one at that; he was well-respected in the engineering community, according to him anyway. So, why would he discuss business with Henry?

When she'd tried to illicit a response, Richard clammed up. What didn't he want her to know? These questions ran around her mind all night, and into the early hours.

"You awake?" Samuel's whisper disturbed her thoughts.

"Yeah, you?" Silly question. Of course he was awake.

"You thinking about Colin?" He turned onto his back and held his arm out for her. "I am. I can't believe he's gone."

Lying next to him, her chin on his chest, leg entwined with his, she stroked his stomach, feeling the ridges of his abs. "Yeah, I can't believe it either. Poor Colin."

A silence settled between them.

"It's not just Colin you're thinking about, though, is it?" Samuel glanced at her. "Come on, what's up? Your cogs are turning; I can practically hear them. Unload on me."

She wondered for a few seconds whether or not to tell him. "It's Richard. I walked in on him trying to talk to Henry earlier, and he balked when I walked in. He sat back in his armchair and cut the conversation off, just like that."

"So? So what?" Samuel stared at her. "I don't mean to sound harsh, honey, but he probably doesn't want you hearing about his work. What's wrong with that?"

Charlotte put her cheek on his chest again. "No, I get that, I do. But it was the way he did it. Like he was scared of me listening in, or something. I don't know, you had to be there, I guess."

Her husband stroked her back. "What do you want me to say here? Your brother's a secretive prick? And he is, as well as stuck-up. But I wouldn't lose sleep over it, Lottie. We've got bigger things to worry about right now."

They did. Knowing Henry, he would need help with planning the funeral, whenever that would be. Her brother's body wouldn't be released for a while, as was standard with a murder enquiry. "I know. We need to look after Henry. He's the one I'm most concerned about."

When Samuel didn't answer her, Charlotte lifted her head and looked at him. Samuel had frown marks. "Sam? What is it?" He didn't answer for a few seconds.

"Nothing. Don't worry about it." He took his arm away from her and sat up.

"It's not nothing, though, is it? I can see it in your face. What is it?"

"Oh, it's probably nothing."

"But?"

"But Richard turned up one day, when I went to visit Colin and Henry at the radio station." Samuel stared up, like he was trying to recall an image. "I remember now because he looked shifty, and when he saw me, he wouldn't look me in the eye. When I asked Henry what Richard was doing here, he just shrugged and said Richard wanted a word with Colin about something. But his face gave him away. Henry was shifty, too, come to think of it. He ushered me out shortly after Richard arrived."

"And you're telling me this now, why?" She sat up and glared at him.

Samuel got up and put on a pair of boxers. "I didn't think anything of it back then. Why would I? Your brothers are odd at the best of times. It didn't strike me as all that strange then, but now you mention Richard acting all suspicious."

"And Henry didn't give you anything else to go on? Nothing at all?"

"No, nothing, I swear." He mounted the bed and sat facing her. "I just remember the desperation in his eyes. Richard never looks desperate to me; he has too much self-respect for that, but he did that evening."

"Wait! When was this? When did you go to the radio station?"

"A few months ago, maybe. Nine, yeah, eight or nine months ago."

Charlotte was pretty speechless. The way Samuel described

her older brother didn't sit right with her. Richard wouldn't behave like that.

The mystery thickened. Richard didn't look shady yesterday; he seemed more frightened than anything. "I wonder what he was doing there?"

Samuel sat thinking. "You don't think they're in business together somehow?"

"Who? Richard and Colin?" Charlotte smiled. "I think that's the stupidest thing I've ever heard you say. How? Why? Richard wouldn't go into business with Colin, ever."

"But what about Henry? He's savvy. He's smart."

"You're right, he is, but I can't see it, can you? He's got a radio station. How would Richard's and Henry's business interests cross?" Her husband's question did make her think. She would study the two of them later.

16

"Get down, get down, now!" Walker surged through the warehouse with his carbine pointed at the night workers, who raised their hands and turned to face him, shaken. The noise of taking the metal shutters off their rollers was enough to startle them. "Did you hear me? I said, get on your fronts, now! Knees first, hands behind your backs and lie on your bellies. Do it, now!"

All six young lads in their late teens and early twenties complied, first getting on their knees, then lying face down on the concrete floor. His colleagues joined him in scaring the drug dealers. They cuffed the youngsters.

"Let's spread out. These are just the cannon fodder, the generals are still around, somewhere." The Sarge pointed to his left for Walker.

The warehouse was huge. From the outside, it seemed small, but like the Tardis, opened up internally. The building went back a fair way. Walker, carbine in hand, finger on the trigger and adrenaline peaking, made his way slowly towards some floor-to-ceiling shelving units. The generals could be hiding anywhere.

Having Vodicka with him made Walker feel secure. She was his rock. If he had to choose anyone to go into combat with, he would choose her. Not only was she a skilled marksman – or woman – she also had a black belt in Ju Jitsu, and a brown belt in kickboxing. He signalled for her to take the left while he took the right.

With his nerves heightened, he checked the aisles, crouching to check beneath the lowest shelves. "Clear!" He received the all-clear from Vodicka and the Sarge. "Zuccari, talk to me!"

He turned and ran back to the main factory floor at the sound of raised voices. He stopped when a gunshot echoed through the warehouse.

When he reached the table in the middle of the warehouse, he saw his friend stood over a body.

"It was a clean shoot." Zuccari held his hands up, his carbine on the floor, as was policy after a shot was fired. "He had a pistol in his hand, look."

The rest of his unit sounded off after checking the large room. Walker couldn't believe these youngsters were the only ones here, except the dead general. Sarge took Zuccari away, while Walker and the rest of his squad made the area safe.

Once the dealers were squared away, he made a note of the inventory. The table in the middle of the room held enough cocaine to put these men away for a long time. They were dealing in kilos, not grams. Two had possessed firearms as well, so this haul was worth their effort.

"Hey, Walker, what's going to happen to Zuccari now?"

"You know what's going to happen, Voddy." Every SCO19 officer knew what happened as soon as a firearm was discharged, regardless of fatalities. "He'll be relieved of duty, pending an investigation by the IOPC. If he's found to have acted lawfully, he'll be allowed back to work, if he passes his psych evaluation. Come on, you don't need me to tell you this. You know it."

"I just think it's really shitty that we get questioned as soon as we fire a gun."

"I agree, but it is what it is. We signed up to the scrutiny as soon as we took on the job. We're not in the States, don't forget. And Zuccari did shoot this guy in the head."

When they went on patrol, Walker drove, Zuccari navigated, while Vodicka worked as communications operator.

His comms operator turned and walked back towards the car park. A SOCO crew arrived and started their role documenting everything. A coroner was en route to process the dead general. Walker started after Vodicka.

17

Richard Fisher opened the door to his workshop, slipped inside and closed it. He peered through the glass, checking no one was behind him. Locking himself inside, he turned the main lights on and they flickered to life, his little blue Fiesta sat in the centre of the room.

He walked up the metal stairs to his office, where he switched on the light, before sitting behind his desk. His PC whirring away in the background, he clicked the mouse and the monitor sprang to life. He'd waited a long time for this email.

Four years earlier he'd applied for a patent on his revolutionary idea. Only an idea back then, it was now a reality, sitting downstairs in the middle of the workshop.

The Intellectual Property Office's logo appeared at the top of the email. When he scrolled down, he saw the words "delighted" and "successful" and grinned. It was his, all his. Hell, it only took fifteen tests and three years to build it.

In his desk drawer, he had a cigar reserved for this occasion. He opened the drawer, took it out and put it in his mouth, searching his pockets for a lighter.

The first inhale was always the harshest. For the rest he

simply held the smoke in and blew it out. Now that he had his patent confirmation, he could set up a press conference whenever he liked. Having a working model was the icing on the cake.

On the monitor, he noted it was eight o'clock, and he had to pick up Henry and go with him to identify Colin's body. Then the detectives were visiting for an "interview". Such a silly term for it, he thought, switching off his monitor.

After finishing his cigar, he switched everything off and headed back downstairs. As he reached the front door, he spotted Vanu on his way in. "Hey! What's up?" His second-in-command's mind was elsewhere. He stared down the road.

"That van's been there for days." Vanu gestured a white transit sat by the kerb, no driver or passenger present.

"So what? It's a parked van." Richard shrugged. "I'm off to Henry's."

"No, wait! Listen to me. It's been hanging around a lot lately. Everywhere I go I see it."

He'd never seen Vanu paranoid, even though the poor guy took medication to help reduce his neuroses. "You're just imagining it. Look, there's no one inside." He even pointed at the van. "Relax! Go on, the others will be here soon."

18

Hayes pulled up outside the wrought-iron gates of Henry Curtis and Colin Fisher's home. She wound the window down and extended her arm, pushing the intercom button. "Mr Curtis, it's Detective Inspector Amanda Hayes and Detective Sergeant Rachel Miller." The buzzer sounded, and the gates whirred open.

Driving through, Hayes kept an eye on the closing gates in her mirror. She pulled up outside the huge country house, getting out and locking the car with a touch of the key fob. Crunching along the gravelly drive towards the front door, she climbed the three stone steps. She whistled.

"Curtis' parents are wealthy. I–" Miller didn't get to finish her comment.

The door opened and a woman answered. She introduced herself as Charlotte Edwards, was Fisher. Miller glanced over at Hayes.

When Charlotte opened the door for them, Hayes stepped inside the hallway first, followed closely by Miller. Charlotte showed them through to the huge lounge, where a man in his late forties, maybe early fifties, stood waiting for them.

"Detectives, please join us. I'm Richard Fisher, and you've already met my sister, Charlotte. Please, have a seat."

"Can I get you anything to drink? Tea or coffee? Squash?" Charlotte hovered.

Hayes sat next to her partner and shook her head. "No, thank you, we're fine. Will Mr Curtis be joining us?" She could tell by their demeanours he wouldn't be.

"I'm afraid we've just returned from identifying my brother's body. As you can imagine, it was traumatic. Henry's taken himself off to bed for a while."

"We'll try to answer any questions you have, detective." Charlotte smiled down at her with a nervousness Hayes had come to expect during interviews.

Hayes smiled. "I'm sure you'll try, Mrs Edwards, but we'll still need to question Mr Curtis. He and your brother were married and lived together, am I right?"

Charlotte nodded.

"So, he'll have a unique perspective on your brother's day-to-day activities. I'm sure you understand that while you know your brother, his husband will know him far better. Could you call him down, please."

Charlotte looked at her brother for approval. "I'll bring him to the station tomorrow. How about that? I really don't want to disturb him while he's sleeping."

"Or I will." Mr Fisher shot her a pleading look.

When she studied Miller, her partner shrugged. "Very well. If you promise to bring him by tomorrow, I guess that's fine. We probably wouldn't get much out of him today anyway. So, firstly, I'd like to start by offering our deepest sympathies on your loss. Losing your brother in such a way is traumatic. And thank you for taking the time to speak with us."

Brother and sister sat side by side, Charlotte nervously playing with her fingers.

Mr Fisher still straight, spoke first. "Before we begin, though, detective, tell me, do you have any idea at all who did this? Do you have any of those, I don't know what you'd call them–"

"Leads?" Charlotte finished her brother's sentence.

Mr Fisher nodded.

"We have a couple of theories, yes." Hayes gave Miller the go-ahead.

"We believe the suspect we're looking for might have a military background, Mr Fisher. Someone who has been, or still is, in the armed forces. I don't suppose your brother knew many ex-soldiers, did he? We've checked his sheet, so we know he wasn't in the army himself, but we were wondering if he socialised with anyone fitting that description. Would you know, Mrs Edwards?"

"Or if you've heard him talk about having had an altercation with anyone fitting that description? It could be through work, for example?" Hayes waited for a reply.

Both interviewees shook their heads. "No, nothing like that. I mean, Lottie would know more about Colin's movements than me–"

"Oh? Why is that?" Hayes checked his response facially, looking for tells.

"It's no secret that I disowned him for years, detective. His drug use, stealing, the violence. He beat up our dad and stole his wallet. As you can imagine, it caused a terrible rift in our family. My poor sister had to mediate between us; she never gave up on him."

"Yeah, we've read his sheet." Hayes watched Richard closely.

"He could've done anything he wanted, my little brother. He could've gone on and done important things, you know? He was intelligent, and he decided to throw it all away to spite me. And now look where he is."

Hayes exchanged glances with Miller. "This must be very

painful for you, dredging all this up, but we have to ask some sensitive questions, Mr Fisher. Some will be hard to hear."

Mrs Edwards' face crumpled. "You want to know where we were on Monday night, don't you? You're trying to eliminate us from your enquiry by asking us for an alibi."

"We ask it of everyone we interview." It felt mean asking them such questions, but the animosity with which Fisher spoke about his younger brother called for it. "So, how about it, Mr Fisher? Can you tell us where you were late Monday night, early Tuesday morning?" Hayes wasn't sure of his willingness.

"What're you waiting for, Richard? Tell them!"

Richard Fisher stared at Hayes for a moment. "I was at my workshop until around one in the morning. And before you ask if anyone else was there, Vanu, my second-in-command, was there until around nine. After that, I was there alone."

Miller wrote it down in her notepad. "With cases like this, we ask if you can verify your whereabouts another way. So, does your workshop have cameras in or around it that will corroborate your alibi?"

"There are cameras on the way into the business park, sure. And my computer will show what time I switched it off at least, won't it?"

Miller asked for the address of his workshop. "I'll get onto that."

While her partner was busy, Hayes asked Mrs Edwards where she had been. Having exhausted the alibis, she decided to dig further. "It's such a shame we can't ask Mr Curtis some questions. I don't suppose your brother spoke of any conflict at work? Did he have any fights with colleagues, anything like that?"

"Colin was loved by all his co-stars, everyone. The gay community loved him for everything he did to include them on the station. If you're asking did he have enemies? Maybe, he'd been a violent drug addict years ago, so sure, he must have. There must be people out there he beat up for their wallets, or what have you, but I don't know who they are."

"Okay, Mrs Edwards." Hayes tried to calm her down. "Let's look at this from a different angle. There's a rumour circulating that Colin had debts outstanding with Melodi Demirci. Do you know if there's any truth to them?" She asked both brother and sister.

Fisher sat back in his seat. "My brother was an addict, detective. It could be true, I don't know. He had an addiction to pretty much everything at one time or another."

"So, it could be a possibility?"

"With my brother, anything's possible. All I know is that we made amends just before he married Henry, and since then, Colin hasn't put a foot wrong. Henry's the best thing that ever happened to him."

Miller took over, aiming her questions at the sister. "But you were still on talking terms with your brother, right, Mrs Edwards? Is there anyone from his past who sticks out? Previous boyfriends? Anyone at all you can think of?"

"No! Nothing like that. He was on good terms with everyone he worked with. He never mentioned any altercations to me."

Hayes thought she seemed genuine enough. Becoming more frustrated by the second, Hayes grew restless. They were getting nowhere with Fisher's siblings. She had a few more questions to fling at them, but she wasn't hopeful. It still looked more likely that Brandy Reid was the main target.

19

Miller smiled at her text message from Walker, who'd asked her how her shift was going. The five hearts made her chuckle inside like a seventeen-year-old. She tried not to show it to Hayes, who sat next to her driving the Peugeot.

"Something funny?" Hayes glanced over at her.

"Hmm?" Miller looked up from her phone. "Oh, no, nothing important. A text from my mum." She started typing her reply.

"Give me a break. You're sat there with a great big smile. It's not your mum texting. Let me guess: you bumped into Luke Walker last night, am I right?"

The mere mention of his name made her look at her partner. "What? No!" Her tone belied her words. "What would make you say that? This is my mum."

"Where'd you meet him?" Hayes wouldn't drop it. "Come on, we're partners, remember? That means sharing information. Come on, where'd you meet him?"

When she wouldn't play along, Hayes decided to play by herself.

"Let me see! Walker works out, a lot, judging by those bulging biceps. You like working out, too. I'm going to hazard a guess and say you bumped into him at the gym last night. How's that? Am I right?"

She hated Hayes' smug grin. "How could you even know that?"

Hayes chuckled to herself. "Trade secret. A friend saw you two talking in there. So, how'd your first date go? Did you kiss him?"

Hayes slowed the car to a stop at some traffic lights.

"What? I'm not answering that."

She finished the text with a flurry of kisses. She liked Walker, a lot. The night they shared together was nothing short of heaven. If his texts were anything to go by, they would have round two tonight. The thought excited her. All she had to do was get through the afternoon. "And you're wrong about him, by the way."

Miller put her mobile away, determined to focus on the job at hand. "So, what did you make of Fisher?"

Hayes stared straight ahead. "I think meeting Fisher's brother and sister was a waste of time. We should've made them wake Curtis. He's the key. He'll know what's going on in his husband's life more than they do."

As they entered a run-down part of town, Hayes brought the car to a stop outside a row of terraced houses. The estate was covered in graffiti and everywhere Miller looked, kids stood on street corners, rough-looking kids, all between the ages of around ten and eighteen. They would rob their car given half the chance, she thought, unbuckling her belt.

A group of kids of varying ethnicities crowded their car as Miller opened her door. She took out her warrant card and showed it to the teenagers. "Metropolitan Police, lads. Back off!" And as she stood, taller than them, they backed up. "Thank you! Now, can one of you tell me which house Brandy Reid's mum lives at?"

"She lives over there." A kid of no more than ten said, pointing.

"Thanks." Hayes joined her.

"Hey, I know you. You're that pig who arrested Martin's dad."

Miller grabbed the twelve-year-old boy's shirt. "Don't ever use that term in front of us again. We're police officers, or detectives." Her partner made her relinquish him. "Be respectful, boys."

With confidence, Miller strode through the pack of teenagers, towards the Reid residence. "You've got to project strength to these little shits, or they'll walk all over you."

"You know as well as I do you can't touch them. They could put a complaint in against you now." Hayes sounded more concerned than angry.

They reached Brandy Reid's mum's front door, with its red paint peeling off. "Them? Nah, they hate the police. They'd sooner spit on us than call us, and that's why we need to nip that whole 'pig' attitude in the bud before they become adults."

Hayes turned and watched their car. "Yeah? Don't expect our car to be there by the time we leave. They'll be off looking for a crowbar as we speak."

She knocked on the door and moments later a woman answered, opening it a crack. "Miss Reid? We spoke earlier on the phone. I'm Detective Sergeant Rachel Miller. This is my partner, Detective Inspector Amanda Hayes. May we come in?"

"Yeah, sure." The woman stood aside, allowing them access.

The first thing to hit Miller was the girl's lack of emotion. Ellie Reid took them through the thin hallway, into the lounge. She offered them the settee, while she plonked herself on the armchair. All the furniture had seen better days. There was a potent smell lingering under Miller's nose, and when she saw the cats, she knew what it was. "Oh I just love cats." She tried not to pull a face. "How many do you have?"

"Eight now, or is it nine? I forget. They're all around here somewhere."

Frumpy and lazy were the two words that jumped out at Miller when she studied Ellie. Dressed in an Adidas tracksuit that she'd obviously bought several years ago. With straggly dark hair and pounds of excess fat, she thought Brandy's daughter must have been a disappointment to the radio co-presenter. "You said your nana would be here."

"She couldn't make it. She's got bingo."

Miller wondered how could Brandy Reid live like this? It was beyond disgusting. The stench would seep into her skin. She wrinkled her nose, the smell cloying.

"I just want to say how sorry I am for your loss." Hayes wrinkled her nose.

"Don't be. Mum was a total bitch."

As was expected. "Oh? Can I ask why?"

"All she cared about was that arsehole boyfriend of hers, and getting high. She didn't care about me. Nana raised me here. I only ever saw mum when she came begging Nana for money."

"Your mum had a drug habit? That surprises me. Colin Fisher was dead set against drugs. How did she come to get her spot presenting with him?"

"I don't know. She hid it well? She would take whatever she could get her hands on, but her drug of choice was coke. I'm surprised her septum didn't fall off like that *EastEnders* actress."

Hayes wasn't buying Ellie's story. It sounded like the daughter hated her mum so much, she was making it up. "I'm sorry to hear this. Can I ask where your mum lives, Ellie? We have this address for her."

"No, she's shacked up with Dylan somewhere." Ellie reached in front of her and picked up her packet of cigarettes. She offered them both one.

Miller waved her refusal. "Could you find her address?"

The girl lit her cigarette, then asked how?

"Does your nana have an address book?"

Ellie laughed. "You don't know my nana at all, do you? She's an alcoholic. I doubt she can even write, she's so pissed all the time. I only ever see her sober for five minutes in the morning when she wakes up on that couch, before she pukes in the toilet and washes it down with half a bottle of vodka. Then she's ready to get on her scooter and head to Wetherspoons. Thinking of it, you might have more luck speaking to Nana's friends there. They know Brandy better than I do."

"Do you know your mum's boyfriend's surname, Ellie?" Hayes regarded Miller, indicating that they should leave soon.

"I don't know! I've only seen him parked outside in his clapped out Rover. Mum never introduced us."

"I see. You really don't know her well at all, do you?" She looked over at Hayes, suggesting they leave.

Standing up, Miller regarded the slovenly girl. "We might take you up on your suggestion and visit your nana's friends in Wetherspoons. We'll see ourselves out, Ellie. And for what it's worth, I'm sorry you didn't know her better."

Ellie Reid shrugged. She didn't care. "It is what it is."

Miller let Hayes leave first.

"Did she suffer?"

"It was over quick." Miller lied, not wanting to burden the poor girl, who'd grown up in the worst possible conditions, apparently without any kind of maternal love. "Take care of yourself."

Miller was keen to get out into the fresh air.

Hayes waited for her outside. "Looks like we've got company."

Miller closed the door and took in a long lungful of air. She took the time to gauge their situation. Sat on the bonnet of their Peugeot were two guys, one black, one white. They attracted the attention and adulation of the kids around their car. "Which one do you want to take?" she whispered. "I'll take the white guy, if you're okay taking the black fella."

"Let's just act calm, get in our car and go, right?"

"Sure, but if there's trouble, which one do you want?"

"I'm comfortable taking on the black guy, yeah."

"You see? That wasn't so difficult." Miller walked towards their car, never taking her eyes off the tall, white guy sat on their bonnet. The teenagers made room for them as they approached, which she took as a sign of respect. "Thank you, boys."

To her surprise, a couple of them smiled. When she reached her door, she regarded the white guy. "Off the bonnet, please, sir. This is a police vehicle."

Both guys jumped off the bonnet and stepped towards her and Hayes. "You just seen Reid's mum in there?"

Miller glanced at her partner, then back at them. "Nope, but it's really none of your business who we speak to, is it?"

"Come on, Miller, let's go!" Hayes went to walk towards them.

The white guy put his hand up, stopping Hayes. "Hold on. You're investigating her murder, though, right?"

"Don't put your hand on me," Hayes warned.

"That's assaulting a police officer, right there." Miller waited for her supervisor to make the first move, which she would; she could feel the tension in the air, everyone could. The teenagers moved back, giving her and Hayes room. To the right of her was the passenger side door. "What do you guys want? Trying to intimidate us?"

"We want to know where that worthless piece of shit, Dylan Oldham's hiding, and we know you must have asked that fat bitch daughter of hers by now. If you tell us where he is, we'll walk away–"

"And if not? If we refuse to tell you, what then?" Hayes was defiant.

Miller could feel the anger emanating from her partner. "Yeah, we know where Oldham's at, but we're not going to put him in harm's way by telling you, are we?"

The white guy grabbed Hayes.

Hayes gripped White Guy's hand, twisted it until he groaned, bent his arm and turned him round, almost breaking the guy's arm in the process. She tripped him, and he went belly first on the ground, with Hayes kneeling on his back while she cuffed him. "What're you waiting for, Miller? Stop playing with him; we haven't got all afternoon."

Black guy stared at his partner cuffed, then back at her. Miller gave him a "Well?" stare, and he put up his fists, like he was about to fight her. Going along with it, she raised hers, hearing the excitement from behind her.

Bored, Miller dropped her guard, lunged forward, grabbed his T-shirt, and brought her knee through. It connected with his genitals with a satisfying thud. He collapsed on the floor. "You see, boys? It never pays to pick on girls."

Their mouths hung open. Miller grinned, as she crouched and forced Black Guy onto his belly while she cuffed him. She read them their rights to cheers from the teenagers. She noticed some teenage girls had come to see what the fuss was about.

"Now it's your turn, boys. You're going to tell us everything you know about Dylan Oldham, starting with why you want him, and who you work for."

Miller yanked Black Guy to his feet and opened the back passenger door, while Hayes walked her collar to the opposing side. With the two suspects in the rear, she sat in the front passenger seat and waited for her supervisor.

20

"It was good of Inspector Gillan to offer to interview them for us."

Hayes opened the front door of The Half Moon Wetherspoons pub on Mile End Road and held it open for Miller to walk through. "Yeah, they know we're under the cosh. Besides, I think they're repaying us for giving them a second chance with Helsey." She followed her partner into the open plan pub.

"I bet they're shitting their pants, though, right? How's it going to look if they have the wrong guy in lock-up?" Miller huddled in towards her. "I know I would be."

"It's not just Gillan and Travis, though, is it? The CPS must've thought they had enough evidence. They're lucky it hasn't gone to trial yet. Can you imagine the shitstorm if they'd convicted the wrong guy?" She tried attracting the barman's attention by holding up her warrant card.

Even at half four in the afternoon the bar was busy. Hayes leaned on the polished surface and scanned the room. There were two large groups of regulars. A group of fifteen heavy drinkers to her left and about a dozen to her right. The other tables were occupied by a mixture of older and younger punters. "My bet's on her."

Miller spotted the old woman. "Mine too. Excuse me!"

After Miller's less-than-subtle attempt at grabbing the server behind the bar, the young lad excused himself from the couple he was serving. "Yes, I'm right in the middle–"

"Detective Sergeant Rachel Miller." She held up her identification. "I just need to ask, is that Katherine Reid over there?"

"Kat, yeah, sure." He apologised to the couple. "Is that it? Can I go now?"

"By Kat, you mean Katherine, right?"

"I wouldn't call her that – she'll throw you out if you do. She likes to be called Kat." He walked back to his paying customers. "And good luck, by the way, she hates cops."

Hayes joined her partner and walked towards the group of fifteen drinkers, who looked like they'd started when doors opened. As soon as they headed in the group's direction wearing their suits, the comments began. "Afternoon everyone, we would like a word with Kat, please."

One of the men said, "You can have two words from me: fuck and off. Or is that three?"

Hayes laughed with the group, like she hadn't heard it before. She encouraged Miller to join her in laughing. "Yeah, that's really good. And you are?"

The craggy old guy seemed confused. "I am what? You asked me."

Both tables of well-oiled drinking machines erupted in laughter, with a couple of heavy-handed old guys thumping the table, spilling drinks. "We're not going to get much out of anyone here," Hayes whispered. "Look at them; they're wasted."

"Let me try it a different way." Miller took out her identification. "I don't mean to break up this party, but you're all under arrest, unless one of you tells us which one of you is Katherine Reid." She made a point of emphasising Katherine.

"Ooh, Katherine! Toffee-nosed twat," one old boy shouted.

An old woman, the one she'd pointed out to Miller, mumbled to herself.

Behind the tables, the woman mounted a mobility scooter.

Hayes ran to get in front of her. "Oh no, you're not going anywhere, Mrs Reid. You're going to answer some questions about your daughter."

Katherine "Kat" Reid, drunk, pushed her, hard.

Hayes stumbled back as the old woman zoomed towards the glass doors.

"What's the matter? Can't you handle her?" Miller grinned, before sprinting after the drunkard on her scooter.

Hayes brushed herself off, straightened her blouse and suit jacket, and went after Reid and Miller. Her partner had no trouble stopping the batty old woman, and fought with her for the keys. "Here, Miller." She caught the keys.

"Listen, Mrs Reid, Kat, we can either ask you questions here, or book you for assault and do this back at the station. It's up to you." Miller clicked her fingers in front of Reid's face. "Hello? Mrs Reid? She's not going to give us a thing, look at her!"

One of the drunkards from Reid's table stumbled towards them, dribbling. He looked to be in his late fifties, early sixties, maybe. He almost fell into a table of empties on the way to her. "Leave Kat alone. She's a good sort."

Hayes glanced over at Reid sat on her scooter, whose face told her to take a sidestep away. "She's going to puke." The old guy kept on towards her. Bracing herself, the old boy clenched his fist, as he lunged at her, and fell flat on his face.

"Damn it!" Miller turned away as Reid vomited on the worn carpet.

"I'd call that assault, sir, wouldn't you?" Hayes took out her cuffs and slapped them around the old fella's thin wrists. She looked up at Miller. "Looks like we're doing this the hard way, back at the drunk tank. Why doesn't anyone ever take the easy way?"

The pub burst out in clapping and cheering, Hayes walking the drunk man out while Miller directed Reid on her scooter. They received stares from shoppers and locals on their way back to the car. Hayes helped Miller with their passengers, making sure they didn't hit their heads on their way inside.

Hayes placed the scooter in the boot. "It's lucky this thing folds up." She walked round to the driver's door and sat down, starting the engine.

Reid pitched forward and vomited in the footwell, the smell immediately cloying at the back of her nose.

"That's just great!" Hayes held her breath as much as she could, and left the windows open as wide as they would go.

Forty minutes later, she pulled up near reception in the station car park. When she exited, Hayes took several deep breaths of fresh air, hoping the smell didn't cling to her suit. She attracted the attention of two uniformed constables and asked them to help their passengers into holding cells. "I've got to go wash; I stink. And someone needs to wash this upholstery."

Miller stood back, her hands up. "Hey! Don't look at me. It's not in my job description. I'm a detective, not a cleaner."

"Yeah, and I'm not doing it by myself, so we'll both do our fair share. How's that? Go and get some hot, soapy water, would you?" When Miller went inside, Hayes took a look inside the car at the footwell behind the driver's seat. "Great!"

Tutting at Miller, who stood watching her clear up Reid's sick, Hayes carried the bucket back inside and threw the dirty water down the toilet. With Reid's mobility scooter stored for the woman's release, the pool car was prepped, ready for the next driver. "Right, let's go and speak to Inspector Gillan, see what he has for us." She washed and dried her hands. "What're you washing your hands for? You didn't do anything, except carry the bucket out."

"I told you, I'm not a cleaner." Miller left the room, waiting for her outside.

Hayes finished drying her hands and met her partner in the corridor. In the lift, she wanted to say something to Miller, but didn't. She rolled her eyes when her partner started texting, with a grin. "Loverboy again?"

Miller said nothing but followed her while texting.

Hayes found her desk and sat with a slump. The smell of Katherine Reid's vomit still lingered, either on her suit, or had it seeped into her skin? Either way, she wanted to take a long, hot shower to wash it away.

"Great, you're back!" DS Travis Jackman joined her at her desk. "I know one of your guys, Inspector. You were lucky this afternoon. The white guy you arrested, he works for Melodi Demirci, one of her high-end enforcers."

Hayes sat back in her chair. "Him? I had him on the floor inside two seconds."

"Yeah, some enforcer if Hayes can have him like that."

Hayes ignored Miller's comment. "So, did you talk to him?"

"He wouldn't talk. His lawyers made him keep things close to his chest, but I thought you'd like to know who he worked for. Melodi's not above taking hits out on people. Just thought this might help, because I know you're looking at a possible hitman taking out Fisher, Reid and Austin."

She contemplated it for a moment. "But why would Melodi Demirci want to assassinate Brandy Reid? This guy's after Brandy's boyfriend, a Dylan Oldham."

"And we had Demirci as a possible suspect for Fisher, not Brandy." Miller frowned. "But Melodi has to be top of our suspect list now, doesn't she?"

"With a connection to two of the three victims, yeah." Something didn't sit quite right with her, though. "Except why would she send her enforcers to murder Brandy, or Fisher? Either way, supposing Fisher was her intended target, and this guy kills all three. Why would Demirci order the hit on Fisher? If he owes her money, she's not going to get it back by putting a bullet in his head, is she?"

"The same goes for Brandy Reid. If Brandy owed Demirci money, she wouldn't get it back by killing her."

Travis sat on the edge of Hayes' desk and folded his arms. "What if shooting Brandy, or Fisher was a message?" He sat up straight. "Let's look at it: you said yourself that he was after the whereabouts of Brandy Reid's boyfriend, this Dylan Oldham, right? What if killing Brandy was a direct message to him to pay up?"

Hayes saw what he meant. "And that works for Fisher. As far as we can make out, Fisher's not the wealthy one in the relationship, Henry is. Maybe offing Fisher was a message to Henry to pay up?"

"I'll look up this guy's record." Miller went back to her desk. "Hey, Oldham's ex-military. Spent ten years in the army, and took three tours, one in Iraq and two in Afghanistan. He was discharged in 2012, and since then he's been on the Demirci payroll, as a security guard. He fits the bill."

"I think we need to speak with the lovely Melodi Demirci,

don't you?" Hayes rolled her chair back before standing. As she fetched her suit jacket, Inspector Gillan joined them.

"Leave it for now. Try getting more information from your collar before you go all guns blazing for Demirci. She won't appreciate being fingered for this, and she's lawyered up. You'll need more evidence."

21

Melodi Demirci turned on the television to Sky News. The flat-screen TV on the wall of her office above the casino came to life, a brunette news broadcaster talking animatedly outside the radio station, formerly an old factory unit in a business park nearby.

The lovely-looking presenter pointed at the building behind her. Melodi noticed two women in suits the other side of the police cordon walking towards a white Peugeot. Taking a closer look, she noticed the tanned, shorter woman was the famous Detective Inspector Hayes, the one who'd rescued illegal immigrants from an abandoned factory fire.

She'd read quite a lot about Hayes. About how she and her partner had been instrumental in catching the Suitcase Killer, who had left the capital in fear after he abducted and butchered half a dozen sex workers over the course of eighteen months. The killer dumped the bodies in suitcases in the River Thames.

No, one thing she didn't want was Hayes sticking her oar in. Her business with Henry Curtis needed to stay quiet. Melodi picked up her desk phone. "Yeah, it's me. I think it's time. You know what to do. Look, I don't care how you do it, just make sure it doesn't come back on me, understood? I don't know, use your imagination."

Slamming the phone down, she spun in her chair. "I have to do everything around here!" She was sad about Colin Fisher and Brandy Reid; they were great presenters, had good chemistry.

When Henry Curtis had come to her asking for investment in his broadcasting station, she'd been reluctant at first. The thought of a radio station aimed at the LGBTQ community didn't seem like a viable business proposition to her. But when she saw the forecast for Return on Investment (RoI), pound signs flashed in her eyes. Demirci had no idea how under-represented the LGBTQ community were in local, regional or national radio.

For the past three years she'd had a good working relationship with Henry Curtis. Being a silent investor was an easy win for her. Handing over the money to him was the extent of her involvement, and she was receiving her forty per cent of the profits, which had grown exponentially over the years. The problem she had now: Henry was getting greedy, trying to buy her out of the company she helped establish. If anything, she would buy his shares, not the other way round.

Being the figurehead of a family dynasty had its perks and pitfalls. She held people's livelihoods, and ultimately their lives, in her hands. The casino was a huge burden on her, but with cunning and ruthless business acumen, another cash cow. Her father had almost run her birthright, and inheritance, into the ground. It didn't surprise her to find him riddled with bullets in the casino's car park.

As much as she wasn't surprised to find her father filled with lead, it still hurt. The police even suspected her of hiring hitmen; they took her in for questioning and everything, not that they had any proof. She was more careful than that. He deserved everything he got, the alcoholic prick that he was. In the end, they collared a business associate, a dealer he'd double-crossed.

Now Melodi was in charge of the casino, and guided her family's fortunes. The first thing she did when she took over was to fire the pit boss and cage manager; it was clear they were skimming. She made sure they received her message not to steal from her. Neither would use their left hands again.

Next on her list of priorities was to hire trustworthy dealers and inspectors, which meant screening existing staff. Those who failed were beaten by her security team in the cellar, and told never to return. The lucky few retained their jobs, and she hired only those she trusted, or those she thought she could scare into behaving. Inside six months, she had a working casino taking more money on a daily basis than her father had.

Yeah, she knew what she was doing. Melodi acquired quite the reputation for business, so much so that small business owners approached her for loans. She took this as a compliment. One bicycle shop owner asked her for a loan, to which she obliged. But when he couldn't front the repayments, she had her security visit the shop, steal the bikes, and when the insurance money came through, made him pay her. He folded.

Melodi turned the TV off when a knock came at her office door. She shouted for the visitor to enter and one of her security team came in. "I'm coming. Wait outside."

She walked over to her corner bar and poured herself a whisky, not a high street brand. She only drank decent whiskies. Feeling the liquid warming her insides, she took a deep breath and headed towards the door. "What's so urgent? I said no interruptions."

"There's some guy downstairs, says you'll spot him."

Melodi knew immediately who the guy was. The useless piece of shit lied to her that he was some hotshot stockbroker.

She'd had him checked out, and was pleasantly pleased to find out he was a member of SCO19, a unit of the armed police.

If there was one type of person she despised it was dirty cops. Unfortunately, there were a lot of them in the capital, and they all seemed to want a piece of her action. They came by her place frequently, threatening this and that if she didn't comply with their needs. This guy was acting more like an undercover though, a real scumbag.

Downstairs the night was young. At half ten, the doors only opened half an hour earlier, and this dirty pig was already into the house for ten grand. Instead of going straight to the cop's table, she visited the bar and poured two glasses of whisky, one for him and one for herself. It would loosen him up.

"There she is, my girl, Melodi," the cop said, his moustache twitching. He put his arm around her waist while sat on a high stool, his hand stopping on her arse. "The night started off well, and just keeps getting better. How about it, beautiful? Are you going to spot me fifty? You know I'll pay you back."

She smiled. "If my man says he's good for it, I guess he is." She smiled. "But before we get to that, I need to see you upstairs in my office."

Taking his hand, she guided him up to her office, where she opened the door for him and followed him inside. He slammed the door and pinned her against the wood, kissing her neck, his hands all over her. She gasped.

With prowess, Melodi forced him onto the sofa in the middle of the room, where she pulled his jeans down around his ankles and sat on his lap, kissing him, deeper each time. His hands were under her dress, pleasing her. "This is the last time."

"Where have I heard that before?"

Melodi rode him to the finish line, perspiration beading on her brow. She cuddled him, as she tried to regain her composure. Not being married had its perks. It meant she could take whoever she wanted up to her office. She had to be careful of her overbearing, psychotic cousins, who hated her sleeping with British guys; they wanted her to find a wealthy Turkish man. "What's the matter with you tonight anyway? You shouldn't be this drunk so early. How do you expect to beat the house like this?"

"I had a bad day on the stocks, nothing major."

"Oh!" She didn't care about him. Melodi used him for sex every now and then. He was a good-looking guy, fit, muscular. "What happened?"

"Ah, nothing for you to worry about. I'm still good for the fifty."

If this pig clocked up a huge debt tonight, she would treat Zuccari the way she treated all customers indebted to her, harshly. If he couldn't pay up, she would set her cousins on him, telling them he'd taken advantage of her. "Is fifty going to be enough? Or would you like to double it?"

22

Henry Curtis lay on his couch in his fabulous dressing gown, with the lights off and the huge television on in the background. He'd had it tuned to Sky News all day, in the hope of finding out more about his Colin's murder. Formally identifying his husband's body earlier was the hardest thing he'd ever had to do.

And now he was conflicted. He'd done nothing but argue with Colin since his husband had confessed to his gambling debts with that Turkish bitch, Melodi. There he was, about to extricate her from their lives by buying her out of Accord FM, and Colin went and got himself in the shit. Of course Henry bailed him out, yet again, but he told Colin it was the last time. Henry knew it wouldn't be.

A news presenter came on talking about the murders. Henry looked over at the screen. Two female detectives were pictured walking to their white Peugeot. He would have still been there at that time. The shorter, tanned detective he met, and the taller white detective, but they had face masks on. He recognised the tanned detective as Amanda Hayes; she'd been on television a lot. If anyone could find Colin's murderer, she would.

Henry cursed when he heard the buzzer go. Ignoring it, he lay back and covered his eyes with his arm, wanting to sleep yet unable. Even a tumbler of whisky had not helped. All he wanted was to fall into the abyss, never to be seen again. Life wasn't worth living without his Colin.

The news turned to a drugs seizure in the capital, during which a dealer was shot dead. According to the news presenter, a member of SCO19 had been suspended, pending a review of the siege. The Metropolitan Police retrieved five million in cash, and blocks of cocaine with a street value of two and a half million, not to mention recovering illegal weapons and arresting those involved.

The front gate buzzed again. Henry sat up, took a mouthful of whisky, and set the tumbler back on the table, hoping whoever was at the gates would disappear. At the third buzz, he stood and listened. "Bugger off!"

After the fourth buzz, his temper frayed. Henry strode out of the lounge, into the hallway, where the control panel for the doorbell camera was located. He jabbed the microphone button. "What!"

"Metropolitan Police, sir."

Henry stared at the screen: two guys sat in a car outside his gate. The driver held up what looked like a police warrant card, not that he could read it. He introduced himself and his colleague. Henry didn't listen to their names. "Where are the female cops? Hayes, where's Amanda Hayes? She's investigating Colin's case."

"Detective Inspector Hayes sent us to keep an eye on you, sir. It seems your husband might not be the intended target, you are. We're here to see that no harm comes to you, Mr Curtis. Would you let us in, please?"

He had to think about it first. Something felt off. "Can you hold your ID closer to the camera, please? I can't read it." His visitor got out of his car and held the identification up close enough for him to read.

"Is that good enough?"

"Very well. Come in if you must."

The driver returned to his Peugeot.

Hanging up, Henry pushed the green "Enter" button and the gates whirred to life. The detectives' car drove into the compound and he closed the gates after them. "You'd better not need feeding," Henry mumbled.

He waited at the door until they parked up and rang the bell. "Come in, detectives. You don't need feeding, do you?" When he received confirmation in the negative, he showed them through to the lounge, where he lay back down on the sofa.

The two detectives sat on armchairs. After a few minutes of silence, he felt eyes on him. Sitting up, both stared at him. "Can I get you something? Tea, or coffee?" They shook their heads, not ones for talking, he guessed. "Something stronger?"

Henry stood, picked up his tumbler and sauntered over to the corner bar. He went behind it and poured himself another triple measure of the "good stuff". The detectives' eyes followed him wherever he went. "Are you sure you don't want a whisky? It's no bother."

Coming out from behind the bar, he leaned against it.

"Sit down, Mr Curtis!" the driver said, stern, his voice non-negotiable.

Henry was taken aback by the man's tone. "Hey! You can't talk to me like that."

The driver stood, reached behind him, and pulled out a pistol. Pointing it at Henry's chest, the "detective" gestured at the sofa. "Over there! Sit on the sofa, be a good boy."

His glass shook, his legs turned to jelly. "It's you, isn't it? You murdered my Colin. You murdered Brandy and Kurt."

"Give this guy a prize. You're sharp, Mr Curtis. Now sit on

that sofa, or shall I force you to sit by blowing out your kneecaps? I don't think you want that, do you."

Henry felt sick. He was face-to-face with his husband's killers. The room started spinning; everything went black. The last thing he saw before he fainted was the passenger getting up from his armchair. Henry fell to the carpet.

Big, strong arms pulled him up, before carrying him over to the sofa. Having the driver's gun pointed at his chest made him want to cry. "Please, I don't want to die. I've got money; if it's cash you want, I can get you whatever you need, please. Put that gun away."

Pleading didn't seem to help. All he received for his troubles were angry scowls. "Whatever it is I'm doing, I'll stop it. Please, tell me."

"No dignity," Driver said to his colleague. "You *are* going to die tonight, Mr Curtis. It's your choice how you go."

"I'll find a piece of paper and pen," Passenger said.

"In a drawer behind the bar, there's a pad of paper in there." Henry thought being helpful might stand him in good favour. "Please, you don't have to do this."

Driver sauntered over to the coffee table and sat on the edge, the pistol still pointed at Henry's chest. "I'm afraid we don't have a choice, Mr Curtis. I promise, it won't hurt, if you play ball. If you do as we say, it'll be quick and painless. Mess us around, and, well–"

"I'll go find the bathroom and get set up." Passenger left the room.

Henry stared at the pad of paper Passenger had left on the table. Driver stood and handed him the pen. Henry looked up. "What's this for?"

"It's quite simple. All I need from you is to write the word 'sorry' on that pad of paper. Then sign it from yourself. If you do that, I'll make this as quick as I can."

"You want me to write my own suicide note?" He dropped the pen on the glass table in front of him. "I'm not doing it. You can't make me, either. And besides, no one will believe it. Me? Kill myself? Why would I do that? I have a fabulous life."

Driver's expression wasn't angry; it was confident. "Oh, you'll write that note, Mr Curtis. I know you will." He reached into his suit jacket and retrieved his mobile.

Taking the phone from his attacker, Henry stared at the photo Driver intended him to see. "You bastard! You wouldn't." His hand shook at the picture of his sister's ten-year-old boy.

"You see? It's not just your life you're playing with. If you don't follow our instructions to the letter, we're going to pay your little nephew a visit at his boarding school. You don't want anything bad to happen to him, do you?"

Henry welled up at the thought of these two thugs hurting his sister's son. A tear rolled down his cheek. He wiped it away, took a deep breath and picked up the pen. "Just the word 'Sorry'?" Driver nodded. He attempted to write it.

Putting the pen down again, he couldn't do it. He angered Driver, who stood next to him and placed the nozzle of his pistol in the back of his head, hard, to the point of almost cutting him. Henry put his hands up. "I'm sorry! I'll do it."

"In the next thirty seconds, or we're driving to your nephew's school next. He won't be a happy kid by the time we're done with him."

Henry could still feel the gun in the back of his head when he scrawled the word "Sorry" on the paper. He signed his name and looked up at his murderer.

"Are you ready up there?" Driver shouted to his partner.

Receiving the affirmation, Henry did as instructed and walked up the stairs followed by Driver, who nudged him a couple of times in his back with the gun. "I'm going." He saw lights on in his bathroom and burst into tears.

The Passenger stood. "It's all good. A lovely temperature for you."

"Take your clothes off and get in the tub, Mr Curtis."

Fighting back the tears, Henry untied his dressing gown belt, let it fall to the floor and stood naked in front of his guests. He lifted his right leg and put it in the warm water, then the left, before submerging his legs and waist. Shivering, petrified, he sobbed when Driver went into his pocket and took out a razor blade.

Passenger took the blade from Driver and squatted by Henry's side. "This will only hurt for a couple of minutes, Mr Curtis."

Henry tried to fight Passenger for control of his wrist, but Driver held out his phone with the picture of his nephew. Henry relented, giving Passenger his left wrist. "Please, you don't have to do this."

The blade sliced into his flesh, horizontally, but deep. So deep, a torrent of crimson erupted from his severed vein, turning the water red. Henry shrieked.

"Now the other one, please."

What did it matter? He was a dead man. Henry gave his right wrist to Passenger, and his guest opened his vein. In less than a minute, he started to feel drowsy, the bath water turning a darker red. Instead of being tense, he let his arms fall in the water either side of him, too heavy to lift.

"Yeah, it's me. It's done."

Henry closed his eyes, his heart rate decreasing. He heard the intruders talking, but their voices grew fainter by the second, further away. Everything around him turned dark. His breathing slowed. Each breath shallower, with a bigger gap between the last.

DAY 3
THURSDAY, JUNE 14TH

23

"Oh shit! I'm late. I'm going for a run before work. Fancy it?" Miller thought Luke would refuse. Instead, he rose out of bed faster than she did.

Ready in record time, Miller put her trainers on and opened the front door for him. Out on the pavement, she started off with a gentle jog, Luke by her side.

When they reached the fields behind her flat, she ran faster, seeing how fit he was. To her surprise, he barely raised a sweat. Cross-country wasn't everyone's forte, but it seemed to suit Luke, which pleased her.

Pounding the grass, she increased her speed when she saw the road they were heading for. Miller wanted to beat him there. Without telling him they were racing, he kept up, increasing speed with her. One final spurt was all she needed.

Just when she thought she'd won, Luke went soaring past her, jumping up and down when he arrived at the gate they needed to traverse. Trying to catch her breath, she bent over, hands on knees. "You barely... broke a sweat."

"County cross-country champion two years in a row." Luke

wiped his forehead with his sweatband, not that he needed to, to Miller's annoyance. "Did I forget to tell you? Sorry!" His chest rose and fell, but nothing like hers.

Miller should've been annoyed. For whatever reason, she wasn't. If anything, it made her appreciate him more. Luke looked after himself more than she did. Deciding she needed to stop the booze, Miller regarded her watch. "Time to call it quits. Got a big day ahead of me. You're welcome to stay at mine, but I need to dash."

Luke had a couple of days off to look forward to. Miller made him promise to cook at hers that night. The previous night, she had taken a spare key out of a drawer and given it to him. He'd promised to cook a healthy, wholesome meal from scratch, but wouldn't tell her what he had planned.

After spending an age kissing him goodbye, Miller got in her car and drove to the station, where she parked in a staff bay. Hayes' motor was already there. She cursed to herself, liking to be the first to arrive. Not letting it ruin her morning, she locked her car and made her way up to the office, where her partner was busy on her computer. "Morning!"

Her partner looked up at her with raised eyebrows. "Morning!"

Standing next to her supervisor, Miller grabbed her own chair and sat down. "How's it going? Have you found anything?" She leaned in to find Hayes screening the CCTV film from near the factory outlet.

Hayes stopped the footage and flipped over to another set. "I've found their car," Hayes pointed at the black and white footage, at the number plate, "but as you can see, they've taken it off. It's a Rover of some description, but it'll be nigh on impossible to make out the exact model and colour from this."

"It adds to our theory about it being a hit, though, doesn't it?

They went as far as unscrewing the number plates. Are we looking for a burnt-out Rover now?"

"I've already flagged it. Oh, and Kurt Austin's boyfriend, Fernando, is a ghost apparently. He's not at home, and according to his manager, he hasn't been seen since Kurt's murder. I've managed to locate Dylan Oldham. I've asked for assistance bringing him in, so I thought we'd start by meeting Henry Curtis, and move on to trying Kurt and Fernando's place. Does that sound like a plan?"

"What about the boys we picked up yesterday? Are they still in holding?" Miller believed they had something to do with it, although it seemed they were only after Dylan Oldham. One of them fitted their profile of being ex-military.

"Inspector Gillan and Travis are interviewing them. They've said they'll help out where they can. And I've let Brandy's mum go; she was stinking up the place."

"I'd hate to be the next person in her cell." Getting up, Miller wheeled her chair to her desk and sat down. When her mobile vibrated, she studied the screen: Luke. Grinning, she sent a reply saying she would see him tonight, and not to keep texting.

"You ready?" Hayes put on her suit jacket.

Miller pressed "Send" before guiltily putting her phone in her suit jacket pocket. She could tell Hayes scorned her, not that she said anything. With her jacket on, she joined her partner and they walked to the lifts together.

On the way down Miller stood in silence, thinking about her night with Luke. She had to prevent herself from smiling, which was difficult. Hayes was about to say something. "I'm sorry!"

"What for?"

"Oh, yesterday when I snapped at you. I didn't mean to. I was a bit crabby, so I apologise. It won't happen again."

Hayes nodded, hands behind her back. "Nice. No offence

taken, by the way. I've got thicker skin than that. Nothing you can say will hurt me."

It was a load off. She wouldn't tell anyone, but she regretted snapping. "After you!" She let Hayes off first. Her partner handed her the keys to their requisitioned Peugeot in the car park. Miller didn't mind driving.

On their way to Henry Curtis' gated mansion, she thought about Luke again. The previous night he'd called on her about half eight, carrying a takeaway Chinese. Miller did not have the heart to tell him Chinese was her least favourite, being too greasy. She still ate her plateful.

"He came over to yours last night, did he?"

Miller stared at Hayes. "Huh?"

"You're grinning away to yourself. Luke came to yours, or did you go over to his?" Hayes grinned, waiting.

"Fine! If you have to know, we're seeing each other. And he came to mine with a Chinese. Any other questions?" Miller smiled, making sure her partner knew her irritation was only by half. "You never quit, do you?"

"I'm famous for it," Hayes replied. "Like a dog with a bone, me. And I'm glad for you. It's about time you had some luck in love." Hayes turned and looked out of the passenger window. "I'm happy for you. I mean, you know my thoughts on Walker, but I'm not the one going out with him."

Pulling up at traffic lights, Miller stared at her passenger. "And you'd be wrong. He's not a poser. If anything, he's the opposite; he has self-esteem issues. And he works bloody hard for that body, why shouldn't he show it off?"

That shut her up, Miller thought, accelerating past the lights towards Henry Curtis' place around the corner. She noticed there was a camera on top of the lights.

It took a couple of minutes to pull up outside the open gates to Curtis' home. "Why are these open?" Miller passed the gates and drove along the gravelly driveway.

"I don't know. Something's not right." Hayes opened her door as the car slowed.

Miller parked behind a car she took to be Charlotte Edwards', with the woman still in the driver's seat.

"Why hasn't Mrs Edwards gone inside?" Hayes asked, getting out of the Peugeot.

Miller switched off the engine and joined Hayes, who tried to calm Mrs Edwards. "What's going on?"

Mrs Edwards was crying as she spoke. "Something's happened. I can't get through to Henry."

24

"I told you one of us should've stayed with him last night." Charlotte Edwards waved at Hayes to give her a second or two to finish her phone call. "Thanks a lot, Richard. You've been a big help." She hung up and greeted the officers. "He's not answering his mobile. There's something wrong, I know it. Henry would never leave his gate open like that. Please, help. Can't you do something?"

Miller put her mobile to her ear. "We'll try his phone. He has a landline number, too, doesn't he?"

"I've already tried both, several times. What makes you think he'll answer you and not me? Can't you knock the door down? I know something's happened. We should've stayed with him last night, or had him stay at mine."

She would never forgive herself if something had happened to him. The longer he remained silent, the more likely it was they would find him dead inside his house. Desperate, she pleaded with the lead detective.

"I've tried both numbers. Straight to voicemail." Miller put her phone back in her suit jacket. "Shall we have a nosy round the back?"

In her state, Charlotte hadn't even thought about that. "Yeah, great idea. Henry doesn't smoke indoors. He has his cigars out on the patio." She tried his mobile for a sixth time, while following the two detectives round the side of the large house.

"Kitchen," she said to the taller detective, who tried the door handle. It wouldn't open. "Keep going. There's a patio door at the back." When Henry's phone went straight to voicemail, she hung up and carried it. They approached the rear glass door. "There it is." She prayed Henry had left it unlocked.

When she arrived on the patio, there were two thin Café Crème cigar butts in the ashtray sat atop the ornate wrought-iron garden table. His Zippo lighter was on top of his tin of Café Cremes. Seeing the lighter triggered fear. "Henry wouldn't leave his lighter like that. It's precious to him. His dad gave it to him years ago."

Miller put her hand on the sliding patio door and yanked it, as it slid to the right. "We're in luck."

"Nice. Miller, do you mind going and getting the evidence kit, please," Hayes ordered to a nod from Miller.

"Why aren't we going inside? He's probably right in there."

"In case this is a crime scene, Mrs Edwards. If something has happened to your brother-in-law, we need to document everything as we find it. We can't contaminate the area, do you understand? So, we'll wait for my partner to return with the kit, okay?"

Going out of her mind with worry, Charlotte wanted to march on in there and find him. A part of her said not to worry, that he's probably fast asleep upstairs. But the larger part thought something terrible had happened. Call it intuition, whatever.

Detective Miller returned with a bag over her shoulder. Hayes and Miller put on blue latex gloves. "If you're coming in, put these on. Touch nothing, until we know what we're dealing with."

Hayes went inside first, pulling back the net curtain. "Mr Curtis. It's the police. Call out if you're here."

Charlotte waited for Miller to enter. When Charlotte stepped inside the lounge, the television was on quietly in the background. Henry had it on Sky News.

"There's a note here." Miller read it out loud: "*Sorry!* And his signature."

"Wait! Let me see that." Charlotte stood next to her and read it for herself. Her urgency to find him increased. She wanted to rush upstairs, but she had to wait for the police officers. "Shall we go upstairs? He's probably in his bedroom, or his bathroom."

Time dragged out as they searched each room in turn. The master bedroom happened to be the furthest from the stairs, so naturally it was the last one to be searched. Holding her breath, Charlotte stepped inside her late brother's bedroom. "Through there, the en suite bathroom."

Hayes and Miller walked through first. "Oh shit! Don't come through here, Mrs Edwards. You don't need to see this."

She wasn't about to let a detective dictate to her. Charlotte barged past Miller first, then pushed Hayes out of the way, until she saw Henry's peaceful body floating in red water. His eyes were closed, his skin pallid, but apart from that he appeared serene, like he was lying in the water, having a soak. "Oh no! Please, not Henry now too."

With strong arms around her shoulders, Charlotte was escorted downstairs and out onto the patio, where a chair was pulled out for her. The detectives left her alone while they carried out their professional duties. She delved into her bag and took out her packet of cigarettes. Lighting one, she drew in a lungful of smoke.

Why Henry? Why Colin for that matter? Why hadn't she put

Henry in her car and driven him home to stay with her? Because she was selfish. The smoke made her feel nauseous, but it didn't make her put it out.

She should be crying. Why wasn't she sobbing? Her brother and now brother-in-law were both dead. All she felt was numb. Nothing. Stubbing out her cigarette, Charlotte popped a mint in her mouth. "Do you want one?"

Both detectives declined. "We've had to call in a crime scene unit, Mrs Edwards, just so you're aware. It's standard practise in cases like these, where the obvious cause of death is suicide. But we must be cautious here, okay? So, to be on the safe side, we're going to treat this as a crime scene. Do you understand?"

Charlotte nodded her understanding. "Do you think something else happened?"

Hayes shook her head. "No! It looks like Mr Curtis committed suicide, but we must be a hundred per cent sure. Our Scene of Crime Officers will be here shortly to process the area. They're going to go through the motions, just like they would at an obvious crime scene. It's called due diligence. We need to be certain."

Detective Miller grabbed a chair, sat down, and took a small notepad out of her pocket. "Mrs Edwards, we were due to discuss your brother's case with Mr Curtis this morning. Because you and your elder brother didn't know him well enough, is there anyone you can think of who knew Henry well? Maybe someone he worked with?"

"Ilya, Henry's personal assistant. You should talk to her."

25

Processing Henry Curtis' suicide took most of the morning. Hayes spoke to the coroner and asked her to carry out a full autopsy, which was routine in these kinds of cases. Chances were high that he'd sliced his own wrists, grieving over the death of his husband, but she wasn't convinced, especially in light of finding the "suicide note".

By the time her partner pulled up at the official offices of Accord FM, it was a little after two in the afternoon. She and Miller bought sandwiches and ate them in a nearby park half an hour earlier. As she opened her door and stood, Hayes saw a crumb drop to the floor. She flicked her blouse, making sure all crumbs were gone.

"Not bad for a local radio station, huh!" Miller stood admiring the glass frontage of the offices.

She wasn't wrong. There was little in the way of brick to the building, the vast majority being tinted glass. Still, it was more sophisticated than its tiny factory-turned-radio-station sister building. This was the main broadcasting station.

Hayes met Miller at the front of their Peugeot and walked

towards reception. At the doors, they had to be buzzed in. "Ilya said she's around all day."

Finally, after a couple of minutes a voice answered. The doors buzzed and Miller opened the door for her. Having a boyfriend agreed with her partner, she thought, thanking her. Inside, the doors clicked shut and Hayes sauntered over to the unmanned reception desk, which she leaned on. "This really is nice."

Everything inside the building screamed sophistication; the carpets were brand new and springy. Hayes enjoyed walking on it. The desktop was marble, the wood dark brown. There were two computers. She would be forgiven for believing it to be the reception of some high-end telecoms company.

Ilya Yashnikova opened a door and greeted Hayes with what looked like a forced smile. She stepped behind the reception desk, pressed a couple of keys on the computer and gave Hayes all the attention she could muster. "I must look a fright."

Hayes shook her head. "I think you look lovely, actually." Apart from the slight redness to her eyes where she'd been crying, Ilya brushed up great, wearing a smart suit, white blouse, and her hair up in a gorgeous display. She noticed how big and appealing Ilya's eyes were. And to top it all off, Henry's PA had beautiful, straight white teeth.

There was the slightest twang of a Russian accent when she spoke. "Oh, you are too kind. I have not stopped crying since Lottie called me. I still cannot believe he's gone, and Colin. They were both so kind to me. I would not be where I am now without them. I owe them everything I have."

"Ms Yashnikova, we'd like to talk to you about Mr Curtis, if we may. As you know, we're investigating Mr Fisher's murder, and since we can no longer speak to Mr Curtis about him, we were hoping you might have some background information for us."

"First, please call me Ilya. My surname's a mouthful in my own language. And of course, I'll tell you everything I know."

"Is there an office, or somewhere a little more comfortable?" Hayes waited for their interviewee to show them through to a plush office, complete with large desk and two leather upholstered chairs for her and Miller to sit on. They were comfortable. She waited for the pleasantries to finish. "Just to let you know I'm recording this interview, okay?"

"Can you start by giving us your name, occupation, and how long you've worked for Mr Curtis, please?" Miller sat back, notepad in hand.

"My name's Ilya Yashnikova, I'm Henry Curtis' personal assistant, and I have worked here at Accord for two years."

"And how long have you known Mr Curtis, Ilya?" Hayes hated formality.

"I would say a long time. Maybe ten years?"

"In what capacity?" Miller, straight to the point.

Yashnikova's brow furrowed. "As a friend, I would say. Why don't you ask me what you need to know, and if I know the answer, I'll tell you. I want this animal caught like you do, detectives."

Miller nodded. "Okay, Ilya, we'd like to know if there's anyone you know of who might harbour a grudge against Mr Fisher, or your boss, Mr Curtis. Have they upset anyone recently? Have there been any arguments with anyone that you know of?"

"No! Nothing like that. As far as I know, they were both happy. I see Henry once a day, and I can say he is happy, for months. If I knew of anyone like you are describing, I would tell you. But there isn't."

It didn't appear hopeful that they were going to get anywhere with Henry's personal assistant. "Have you heard the name Melodi Demirci?" And she'd hit the motherlode if Ilya's expression were anything to go by.

"Oh yes, I have, she's Henry's silent partner, a forty per cent stakeholder in the station," Ilya replied, sitting back in her seat, a look of disgust on her face.

"Partner? I didn't realise Mr Curtis had a business partner?" Miller waited expectantly for a reply from the Russian.

"Actually, Henry was in the process of buying her out."

Hayes was fascinated. "Go on, there's more, isn't there?"

"Henry offered to buy her out a couple of weeks ago, but she refused. She said she would buy *him* out. You see, detectives, Henry started this radio station using his parents' money. Years ago, it was a tiny concern, costing his parents thousands a month, but they doted on him, handed him the money no question. Until about three years ago, they told him to ditch it, to focus his efforts on other projects. Being Henry, being the stubborn man he is, he did not give up. He applied for loans from banks. In the end, he gave up trying, until an acquaintance told him that Melodi offered business loans. He went to her, offered her forty per cent, and the rest is, as you say, history."

"And Demirci gave him the money? Just like that?" Her suspicions about the casino owner were well-founded, it seemed. Hayes doubted Inspector Gillan would object to them interviewing her now, not after this.

"She jumped at it. Henry went to her with a strong proposal, a decent business model, and an even stronger hook."

"What was the hook?" Miller asked, pen poised.

"Simple. Melodi put in a million for forty per cent of the profits, which she received every month. Payments started off modest, and grew. Last month, she received three-quarters of a million. But the hook was this: if he ever wanted out, or if anything happened to him, he would let her buy him out. They both signed a legal contract to that effect."

"So, Demirci stands to gain a lot from Henry's passing, is what you're saying? She will effectively have first dibs on his sixty per cent of Accord FM?" Miller glanced at her again, before scribbling something down.

"Well, yes, but you make it sound suspicious, detective. Henry committed suicide, didn't he? At least that's what Lottie told me."

"We have no reason to suspect foul play at this time, but it does sound a bit suspect, though, doesn't it? Why wouldn't Henry give his shares to Colin, his husband? Why hand them over to a 'supposed gangster'?"

Ilya leaned forward, elbows on the desk. "It was a sweetener to secure her investment. Henry wanted to go back on it as soon as he signed the contract, but he needed the cash injection. And besides, Colin was awful with money. He had a huge gambling problem, and Henry wouldn't trust him with money."

"While we're on the subject, Ilya, is there a connection between Colin and Demirci? We've heard rumours that he owed her a significant amount of money." Hayes was keen to establish if this was in fact the case.

"I know Henry and Colin were arguing a lot recently, because Colin got himself in debt with Melodi, even after Henry made her swear to cut Colin off from using her casino. When she did not, when she let Colin build up debts in the thousands, it caused ill will between Henry and Melodi."

Melodi Demirci was all over this case. Hayes asked a few more questions. They had a lot to move on already. "Can I ask how well you knew Brandy Reid?"

"Well enough, being a regular on air here. Why? Do you think it might be something to do with her?"

"We have three murders, which gives us three sets of suspects to wade through. Do you know of anyone who might mean to harm her?"

"She's had her fair share of stalkers, yes. Then there are her ex-boyfriends, scum most of them. Even the one she's with now–"

"Dylan Oldham–"

"Yes, that's him. He's the worst. He uses her for her money to buy his drugs. I would not put it past him to offer her to his friends for money; he is that kind of man. Scum! He was always jealous of Brandy's on-air relationship with Colin. Colin almost punched him one night."

Hayes hadn't even considered it a crime of passion. Could it be Dylan shooting Fisher, Reid, and Austin in a fit of jealousy? She doubted it but had to at least entertain the possibility. "If you're here all the time, Ilya, how do you know this?"

"Henry comes by the office every day. I find out all the latest gossip from him. Like how Kurt's boyfriend went to Melodi for a business loan. It was silly. Fernando wanted to open a bicycle shop, and when the banks declined him, he went straight to Melodi. She gave him money, the shop lasted a year, and he couldn't pay her back."

And there she was again: Melodi Demirci. "What happened? We're looking to speak with Fernando, but we can't find him."

"He ran away, afraid for his life. He knows what Melodi's cousins are like. If you have not heard of them before, they're total psychopaths. They like to torture their victims in the cellar of the casino. Anyone caught stealing is punished down in that dank place. I do not know if this is true, but her cousins are her muscle. I heard a rumour that they shot and killed Melodi's dad, their uncle, at her request."

"Don't go believing everything you hear, Ilya. These stories have a way of becoming legend, and someone like Melodi Demirci will lap it up, play up to it even. I doubt there's a shred of proof in it."

"But you still think she hired someone to shoot Colin, or

Brandy. That woman's capable of anything. Excuse me, but if I didn't respect Henry's carpets so much, I would spit on them. Spit on Melodi. She's behind this, I know it."

So, there was no love lost between Ilya and Melodi Demirci. Hayes spent a further fifteen minutes questioning the personal assistant. She and Miller had so much to do, so many leads to follow up. The first thing she wanted to do was pop by Fernando Linares and Kurt Austin's apartment.

With how involved Demirci was in this investigation, Hayes doubted Gillan would put up a fuss about bringing her in. No doubt the casino owner would have a high-end lawyer, who would advise her not to talk. She and Miller needed to make her want to talk, to want to blab. It wasn't unheard of, especially on criminals with egos.

26

Luke Walker paid for his pint of Fuller's London Pride and leaned against the bar. The Round House, on Garrick Street was busy enough with daytime drinkers. Walker rarely got a chance to drink during the day with his job, but he enjoyed being able to on the odd occasion.

Half an hour earlier, he received a call from Zuccari, asking him if he would meet him for a beer, that he had something he needed to talk to him about. Reluctantly, Walker agreed, on the proviso that it was only for one beer. He had a date with Rachel.

Wiping his mouth with the back of his hand, Walker placed his pint on the bar. "In your own time, mate. Are we having a chat, or are you going to keep playing that twat machine?" He had no idea why people played fruities. They were designed for players to lose. Even when players won jackpots, they lost, because they ploughed their winnings straight back in. That was where the addiction came in. "Let's find a table, or something, yeah?"

"I'll be with you in a sec, mate." Zuccari continued pressing buttons.

Spotting a free table at the side of the pub next to a

blackboard, Walker picked up his pint and meandered through the bar. One girl caught his eye. She smiled, he smiled. It didn't matter; she wasn't a patch on Rachel. "I'll be over here, when you've wasted all your money." He was going to add, "mug" but refrained.

He'd known Zuccari for a couple of years. Walker wanted to like him, wanted to be a good friend to him. There was only one problem: Zuccari. Since his girlfriend left him a few months earlier, his colleague started unravelling. Walker had stopped Zuccari getting into two fights in pubs just like this one.

It was hard watching someone self-destruct. Zuccari had everything going for him at one time. Since the girlfriend left him with a mortgage to cover by himself, though, Zuccari seemed to have given up on life. He started smoking, both cigarettes and weed, not that he objected to the latter, it might calm his mate down.

His friend was sleeping around as well. Alcohol and pubs, chatting to people, girls, invariably led to sleeping with women. Zuccari took it to extremes, though. In January he slept with two women, who turned out to be prostitutes, unbeknownst to his friend. Zuccari threw them out of his flat, so they called in their pimp.

Zuccari ended up putting the heavily set pimp in the hospital, breaking the guy's arm, and cracking two ribs. He was arrested, but luckily the powers that be, the top brass, took it easy on him and put him on probation. The pimp was a notorious thug and hustler, so no big deal putting him in a hospital bed.

Fifteen minutes Walker spent nursing his pint, sat by himself at the table. The brunette at the bar kept checking him out. "You coming, or shall I go home, mate?"

"Keep your knickers on, bitch. I'm coming."

When Zuccari finally tore himself away from the fruit

machine, Walker saw how awful he looked. Dishevelled, unshaven. "What the fuck happened to you? Did you get kicked out of bed and come straight to the pub? You look like shit, and smell like it." He grimaced at the sweat patches under Zuccari's arms.

"I need to talk to you." Zuccari wouldn't look at him.

"Yeah? So talk! I've been here quarter of an hour already. I'm supposed to be at Rachel's flat cooking her dinner." He probably shouldn't have said anything.

"Not here, somewhere quieter," Zuccari whispered. "Please?"

What's he done now? It was becoming a regular thought. "Come on, then." He said it in almost a huff. "Let's go outside and talk. You know you're a liability, don't you!"

"You don't know the half of it." His friend followed him outside.

Out on Garrick Street, Covent Garden, Walker found a low wall to sit on away from everyone. Zuccari sat next to him with his beer in his hand. "What's up?" He had to wait a minute for his colleague to start talking.

"I've fucked up, mate." He took a gulp of beer. "I'm not talking a small fuck-up here, either. I'm talking a gigantic dump on your own doorstep, going to get my head caved in kind of fuck up. I'm in deep shit, and I don't know what to do."

Walker knew it! Being friends with Zuccari could end up being hazardous to his own health. There would come a time when he would have to walk away. "What've you done? Talk to me. I'll see if I can help."

Zuccari put his glass between his feet on the pavement and shook his head. "Not this time. You've got me out of a lot of scrapes, and I love you, I really do, but this one's above even your head. I owe money, lots of money."

"I figured. How much are we talking?"

"A hundred."

Any normal person might think he meant a hundred, but Walker knew his friend and colleague meant a hundred thousand. "What?" It was staggering. "How? How did you manage that? How's that even possible? Who staked you?"

With his head down, Zuccari paused for a moment. "Melodi Demirci."

Walker almost spat out his beer at the mention of Demirci. "You what?"

"I've been fucking her up in her office for weeks now. After being suspended yesterday, I went and had a few drinks. I ended up at the casino and she staked me the full hundred. I thought I was on a winning streak, finally."

"And you lost it all? A hundred thousand?" The amount was too much to comprehend. "Why? Why would she stake you so high? She knows what you do for a living, right? Or did you lie to her?" It dawned on him.

Zuccari hung his head. "I told her I'm an investment broker in the city."

It was Walker's turn to hang his head, but for a different reason. "Jesus Christ. You've gone and fucked yourself now, royally. You know who her cousins are, don't you? You'll be lucky if they only cut your hands off, you dumb bastard."

"Hey! Don't you think I know that? I know exactly who the Inans are. Having you point it out isn't helping. I'm in so deep, I can't see a way out. I've got a week to come up with the cash, or I'm a dead man."

His friend was right: pointing it out wasn't helping. "What do you want me to say? Does she still think you're a broker?"

"That's just it, she knew all along what I did, even before I fucked her for the first time. She played me like a right twat, and I walked straight into it."

Walker thought for a second. "But that makes no sense. Why get you so far in debt you can never pay her back? What good does that do her? She'll never see that hundred grand, not in a million years."

"I don't know. Whatever she's planning, I don't want any part of it." Zuccari stood holding his beer. "I'm doing a runner. It's the only thing for it. I want to keep my hands. I need them."

Hearing the fear in Zuccari's voice, Walker stood and put a comforting hand on his colleague's shoulder. "Don't do that! It'll only make things worse. Sleep on it. I'll see what I can come up with, okay? Just promise me you won't do a bunk on me."

With glazed eyes, Zuccari nodded. "I'm sorry. I don't know why I do these things. I'm such a fuck-up."

Walker pulled him in for a man-hug, catching glances from passers-by. "It's all right. We'll get you out of this, I promise."

He managed to convince Zuccari into staying put but how would he be able to get his friend out of this? Walker wasn't stupid with money, not by a long shot; he had a few thousand saved up, but he didn't want to waste it on Zuccari. He'd done it now. "Come on, let's get you inside. I think you could use another beer."

27

"Why are we even bothering with this? We know he won't be here." Miller pulled into a space in the residents' car park outside Fernando Linares' block of flats.

"Because it's worth a go," Hayes replied. "It's good to know where a potential suspect comes from, don't you think?"

Unclipping her seat belt, Miller checked out the block of flats through her window. "Maybe, but I thought Kurt Austin was getting paid. Look at this shithole." And she was being nice about it. The walls were covered in graffiti. Any paintwork was cracking.

Stepping out of their Peugeot, she closed her door and locked it, suspecting someone might try to nick the car if they left it for long. "A quick in and out, right? They'll have the wheels off this in no time."

"You can stay here with the car if you want? I don't mind checking it out by myself." Her partner smirked.

"And let you get all the action, forget it." She hated that Hayes knew her so well. At no point would she let her supervisor take the credit for apprehending a suspect. Having brothers forced a competitive streak in her. Miller would never change. "Let's get this over with. I might suggest wearing a peg on your nose, though."

Walking next to Hayes, she reached the main door first, wanting to use her sleeve to hold the handle. After wiping her hand on her trousers, she joined her partner at the lift and waited. The foyer smelt of piss, as she imagined it would. "Told you."

"Hit the third floor, would you?"

Miller obeyed, hitting the button three times before the metal doors slid across. "You know, we could be interviewing Demirci by now." She was a bit annoyed at wasting their time here, when their prime suspect was out there, waiting to be pulled in for questioning. "You don't think the inspector's going to give us crap, do you?"

"To be honest, I have no idea. I guess it depends if we can get her to open up. If not, her lawyer will shut us down before we even start. She'll have crazy-good lawyers."

"Arseholes, more like." And she wasn't wrong. Miller was yet to meet a solicitor or barrister she liked. There she and Hayes were trying to put criminals behind bars, and along came these bastards, whose sole job it was to free them. No, she would never get on with a lawyer. "Here we are."

Miller let her supervisor out first. Along the hallway, it still smelt of piss, only mixed in with stale cigarette smoke and body odour. Not a great combination, she thought, wrinkling her nose. "How could anyone live here?"

She felt guilty when a door to her right opened, and a young mother, probably in her late teens to early twenties greeted her pushing a buggy, two children under the age of five clinging on to the bars in front of her. "Afternoon, ma'am," was all she could say to alleviate the guilt. Not everyone had a choice of where they lived.

"Here, number twenty-six." Hayes stood to the side of the

brown wooden door. She moved closer and stuck her ear against the wood. "I can hear movement inside."

Not believing her partner, Miller followed suit, listening through the door. "Definitely someone in there. We've got probable cause, right?"

Hayes nodded. "It could be Fernando Linares, and he's wanted in connection with the murders. Try the handle first."

There was shuffling coming from inside the flat. Miller held the handle, expecting it to be locked, but it turned. "What do you know?" She turned it all the way, then pushed the door open.

A woman appeared in the hallway carrying some clothes.

Miller put her in her mid-thirties. She had long brown hair and wore jeans and a vest top. "Oh shit!"

Miller held out her hand. "Stay right where you are, ma'am."

Before she could finish, the woman dropped the clothes and sprinted further down the hall to a door on her left, which she slammed shut and locked.

Without waiting, Miller ran after the woman, arriving at the door as it locked. She cursed and started rapping on the wood. "Open this door, ma'am. We just want to talk to you. You're not in any trouble." Listening through the wood, the woman was making a move.

"Stand back, Miller!" Hayes ordered, slamming her foot against the door.

The wood cracked and the door swung open. Miller rushed into the bathroom, where the woman's leg could be seen outside. "I'm going after her."

At the open window, Miller saw the woman running along a roof. She climbed out and jumped onto the roof below. The landing stung her ankle. Hayes stared down at her from inside the flat's bathroom. "I'll get her, don't worry."

The woman ahead of her was slow, probably wondering how

she was going to get out of this. Miller used it to her advantage, running at full velocity towards her. "Stop! I just want to talk to you."

At the end of the roof, the woman stopped and stared at the ground. Miller came to a halt a few feet from her, hands out in surrender. Catching her breath, she tried to reason with the woman. "Please, you're not in any trouble. We just need to know where Fernando is, that's all. We need to speak to him about Kurt."

"He didn't do it. My brother is innocent."

Instead of turning round to face Miller, the woman bent her knees and jumped.

"No!" Miller ran to the edge, expecting to find the woman injured on the ground.

To her amazement, Fernando's sister landed on a patch of grass and ran off. "Damn it! Wait!" She took the challenge and jumped herself.

Landing into a roll, Miller got to her feet and chased Fernando's sister behind the block of flats along a path. Her quarry ahead, Miller turned right into an alley beside the block of flats. "Don't make me chase you. It won't end well."

Up ahead, the alleyway's exit growing closer, Miller had to apprehend her before she made it into the open.

The woman was too close to exiting the alley for Miller to catch her.

A white car blocked the alleyway from the right, parking across it, as Linares' sister ran into it, sprawling over the bonnet.

With an injured knee, Fernando's sister writhed on the pavement in agony. Miller stopped in front of the Peugeot. Hayes swung out of the driver's seat, ran over to the woman and rolled her onto her front, cuffing her hands behind her back. "Don't ever run from the police. We'll always catch you in the end."

Miller bent over, hands on her knees. "Good one."

"Lucky break, more like." Hayes forced the woman to her feet and put her in the back of the Peugeot. "Come on, get in. We've got an interview to do."

Wiping the sweat from her brow, Miller sat in the passenger seat. When they were on their way to the station, her mobile vibrated in her pocket. Retrieving it, she smiled at Luke's text. Using both thumbs, she keyed a reply. *I'm looking forward to seeing you, too. xxxxx.*

"Luke?" Hayes glanced over at her with a grin.

Miller nodded, smirking. "He's cooking us dinner tonight. He's over at mine prepping." She could imagine him in only an apron slicing vegetables. Or at least that was how she liked to think he cooked.

"Very nice. What's he cooking?"

"He won't tell me. Says it's a surprise, his family recipe."

Hayes glanced at her again. "Good. I'm glad you've found each other."

28

Richard Fisher closed the blinds in his office. "Shit!" The white transit van Vanu showed him was still there, seemingly with no one occupying it. His second-in-command informed him that the driver stays in the back. At first he believed Vanu was just being paranoid, but now he wasn't so certain. The van had been sat down the road from their workshop for days.

No one could see into his office from outside, or internally. His staff were all downstairs working on the Fiesta. This was the perfect time to protect his invention. At his PC, Richard clicked on the website for Neelkanth Safe Deposit. Having reserved his box, and given his nominee, Richard made the final adjustments to his application and powered down.

Vanu suggested increasing security around the workshop, which he declined, saying Vanu was paranoid, as usual. His second-in-command always thought there were people out to get him, which there weren't. Just his paranoia. However, having seen the van outside the workshop, and following him around town, Richard was beginning to think otherwise.

Picking up his mobile, Richard dialled Paula Lang's number.

"Hey! It's me. Is the car in the workshop?" When he received a positive confirmation, he pulled out his desk drawer. "Good. I'll be down in a couple of minutes."

Having hung up, he pocketed his phone and turned his attention to the contents of his drawer. He took out his invention and wrapped it in a white T-shirt he brought with him that morning. All wrapped, he picked up the rucksack under his desk.

Once the cargo was safely zipped up in his bag, a knock came at the door and Vanu walked over to the blinds in Richard's office. "If the van moves after you disappear, I'll call you straight away. Remember to keep your head down."

"I will." He dipped his head in thanks to Vanu, who nodded the gesture to him.

"Good luck. If they follow you, move around a lot, okay? Throw them off the scent. It takes longer, but at least you'll know you're safe."

He felt like an agent at MI5, or something, except he had no training. "You got it. And thanks, Vanu, I appreciate the heads-up on this."

"I have as much invested in this project as you. It has to work; the world needs it to work. And I'll be damned if I'm going to let these bastards win. Now get going."

Leaving Vanu in front of the blinds, Richard opened the office door and walked down the iron stairs to the ground floor, where Paula sat waiting for him in her Volkswagen Polo. He opened the rear passenger door.

"Lie down in the footwell until I give the all-clear, okay?"

Richard did as ordered, placing the bag in the footwell and covering it with his body, almost hugging it. With the passenger door closed, Paula started the engine and accelerated outside, after the workshop door lifted. "Nice and easy. And mind the bumps."

"Relax, I know what I'm doing."

He felt every bump along the way, until he received confirmation that they'd passed the transit van. Paula told him it appeared the van had not followed them. "Think I'd like to hear this from Vanu, to be honest." Picking up his mobile, Richard sent a text, every bump hurt. "Excellent!" He smiled at Vanu's text, saying the transit van remained outside.

Sitting up, Richard grabbed the rucksack, holding on to it for dear life. No one was going to get their hands on his baby. Checking the surrounding area for signs of being followed, Richard sat staring out of the rear window. "I can't see anyone following us."

Once on Ampere Way, leaving Croydon Valley Trade Park, Richard breathed a little easier, beginning to relax, keeping an eye out for that transit van.

The final leg of the journey to Neelkanth Safe Deposit comprised two main roads, the A236 Mitcham Road and the A235 Brighton Road. "Pull up here." He signalled for Paula to pull up near the Robins and Day Citroën showroom. The safe deposit centre wasn't far away. "I'll meet you where we discussed earlier, right?"

Paula agreed. Richard closed the door, secured the rucksack on his back, and began his convoluted walk to his destination, taking road after road, making sure he wasn't followed. Eventually, he arrived at the centre.

Keeping an eye on his surroundings, which probably looked suspicious, he was allowed entry, having to wait for various security protocols. The measures of security made him feel more confident. Only those with deposit boxes were allowed inside. The building was guarded twenty-four hours a day, seven days a week.

After passing stringent security checks, Richard walked with a guard, and the manager to his new deposit box. The manager

The Hard Way

gave him a key, which Richard put in at the same time as the manager used his, opening the door together. Without hesitation, he crammed the rucksack inside the box and closed the door, locking it using his key. "So, only myself and my sister will have access to this? No one else has a key?"

"Relax, Mr Fisher, it's all in hand. Your sister, Charlotte, and yourself are the only two people on your list. This building is so secure, even the owner doesn't have access to the vault. This should make you feel better, yes?"

"All I need to know is that it's a hundred per cent secure, that's all."

"Your belongings are safer here at Neelkanth than with any of our competitors, I assure you. So, when you go home tonight, I want you to unwind, and relax, knowing we have your security needs met. No one is getting to your locker, Mr Fisher, believe me."

Confident his baby was safe, Richard asked the manager if there was, perhaps, an alternative exit to the front entrance. The manager nodded his understanding.

"You'll be surprised how many of our customers ask the same thing." The manager and guard walked him from the room full of lockers, to the rear of the building, where there was a fire exit, complete with digital security card technology. "Thank you for your custom, Mr Fisher."

Richard shook hands with both men, stepped outside and turned to them, as the guard closed the door. With the locker key in his jeans pocket, all he had to do was to keep walking until Paula picked him up and drove him back to the workshop, where the rest of his team were waiting for him.

With his invention stashed where only he and Charlotte would know where it was, he felt safer. All he had to do was wait for confirmation of patent before he moved on demonstrating their revolutionary breakthrough. He couldn't help but smile at the thought of the expressions on journalists' faces when he showed them what they'd invented. It would blow them away, not literally, but figuratively. It blew his mind, and he invented it.

With how hectic he'd been at work, he'd almost forgotten about poor Henry. Charlotte called him earlier in the morning to inform him. She asked him to meet her at Henry's place, but he'd been right in the middle of something. He regretted not going.

Joining the human race, walking along an actual high street, and not some dark alleyway, he mingled while he walked, meandering between groups. Richard took his phone out of his pocket and dialled Charlotte. "Honey, I'm so sorry about earlier. I would've come straight over, but I was in the middle of something very important."

His sister let him have it, angry at him for not being there for her, again. He'd made a habit of disappointing her, it seemed, somehow missing everything important in her life. At least, according to her anyway. He made it to her second-born's birth, and her christening. And he made it to a couple of family Christmases, obviously without Colin. "Well, if that's how you feel about it, I'll go." He hung up.

Disappointed with himself, he thought about ringing her back, but decided to leave it for a while, to let her calm down. She was still getting over the shock of Henry killing himself. Poor bastard must have been heartbroken over Colin. Richard liked Henry. More than his own brother, actually. Which was why he went to Henry with his proposal, asking for money to invest in his project.

He sent Paula a text to meet him where she'd dropped him off. He made his way there and slumped in the passenger seat.

"Are we all good?" Paula put the Polo in gear.

"Exceptional." He sat back, clipped his seat belt in place and turned the radio up a notch. Richard was in the best mood.

Everything was in place. In less than a week the world would know his little Ford Fiesta's secrets, and Fisher Valves would soon become a household name. In the years to come, every family and business in the country would own at least one of his groundbreaking inventions.

29

"One way or another, Reyna, you're going to tell us where your brother is." Hayes was growing tired of going around in circles. The interview room so dull, she wanted out of here. "Look, I've already told you Fernando's not in any trouble, and if what you say is true, he'll be safer here in custody than out there, hiding from Melodi Demirci and her cousins. How about it, hmm? Are you going to tell us where he is?"

When Reyna Linares folded her arms and sulked, Hayes turned away from her interviewee to Miller, who stood in the corner of the room, her arms folded as well. Her partner shrugged. Hayes turned. "At least tell us what's going on inside his head." She sat on a chair opposite Reyna.

"He doesn't even know what's going on inside his own head. Ever since his bike shop went bust, he's been a nervous wreck, even after Melodi gave him more time to come up with the money. He and Kurt argued a lot about him going to her for the money, but he couldn't go anywhere else."

"Couldn't he have gone to a bank for a loan? Why go to a loan shark?"

The interviewee snorted. "You think people like us can go to banks? I am a whore, and he's married to a gay radio producer. What chance do you think we have of getting loans? No, Melodi was his only shot at achieving his dream of opening a bike shop. Stupid, having dreams in this country."

Hayes could feel Miller's temper rising. "Miller, why don't you go get us some drinks." She got up and winked at her partner. "And take your time." The last bit she whispered. "Reyna, another coffee? Tea?"

After Reyna accepted her offer of a tea, Miller sloped off.

She sat again. "I get you. I understand what you're saying. I have to confess, this country annoys the crap out of me, too. I get shit from people all the time. I get it from my colleagues, from witnesses, suspects, strangers on the street."

Reyna's face softened. "Really? Why?"

"Being a police officer. I get grief from people out on the street, even my own family and friends. I've lost friends because I chose this career. So, while it's just us, why don't you tell me why he thinks we're after him for Kurt's murder?"

"Because your lot always look to the husbands and wives first. It don't look good that he had big argument with Kurt the night before. And he was alone the night it happened."

"I see. I understand. But here's the thing, Reyna: we have to speak to him to rule him out. For every day that he remains hidden, the guiltier he appears. Please, you have to help us bring him in for questioning. Look at me, Reyna! I'm not the bad guy here. I want to help your brother. Please let me help him."

The Spanish prostitute took out her phone. "Don't know why, but I trust you. I saw you on TV not long ago; you seem like a good person."

Hayes reached out and squeezed Reyna's hand as she passed the phone across the table. "You're doing the right thing, believe me. The sooner we bring him in, the sooner we can rule him out. And we'll pay Melodi Demirci a little visit on his behalf. Nothing bad's going to happen to him, I promise."

"His address is in the book on my phone. He's staying in a derelict house not far from here with a bunch of, how you say... squatters, is it?"

"Yeah, squatters. People who move into a house with no legal right to be there." She lifted the address from Reyna's phone and jotted it down on a piece of paper. "Thank you, Reyna. You've done the right thing. Your brother won't thank you straight away, but when we sort everything out, he will, I'm sure."

"He'd better. I don't want him to hate me."

"He won't." Hayes passed the phone back across the table, as Miller entered with three mugs of steaming hot tea. She showed her partner the address and smiled.

30

Vanu Parekh turned off his laptop, folded it up, and shoved it in his rucksack. His team had all left the workshop for the day, having pulled an all-nighter the previous night. Because they had a demonstration on the horizon, a real-time demo, he and his team had to make sure it ran smoothly. Everything was at stake: his reputation, and the company's. If the demonstration failed, all was for nothing.

Since their successful fifteenth test, every further stress test had succeeded. He was as certain about its readiness as he could be. Vanu strolled over to the blue Fiesta and stroked the paintwork, admiring her, loving how to the outside world she looked like an ordinary car. But on the inside, she was extraordinary, a game changer no less. And Fisher Valves were set to become the Game Master.

Shaking himself out of his daydream, Vanu answered the call, taking his mobile out of his pocket. His wife knew he was on his way home, so why call him now? Since he'd increased his hours getting closer to completing the project, they fought, a lot. About every little detail of their lives. Their poor kids had to put up with so much.

Once the demonstration succeeded, and when everyone knew what his team had created, he would step back and give his wife the attention she deserved. He'd told her this on so many occasions, he couldn't tell her again. "I'm on my way back now." It came out irritable, which he had not intended. "I'll see you in forty minutes or so."

Didn't she realise the longer she kept him on the phone, the longer it would take him to get home? Sometimes he forgot how intelligent she was. His wife was a GP. Annoyed with her, he hung up and pocketed his phone.

Taking one last look at the Fiesta, he smiled, turned off all the lights in the workshop and left via the front door, remembering to activate the alarm. Satisfied that he'd left everything secure, he walked up to his own BMW, unlocked it and slumped in his seat.

Before he left, Vanu peeked through the closed blinds in Richard's office, only to find the van still sat there. When he reached the end of the courtyard outside the workshop, instead of turning right and heading for the van, he turned left, away from it.

With the radio playing "We Will Rock You" by Queen, he drove around Croydon Valley Trade Park, expecting a relatively fast journey at half eight in the evening. There shouldn't be much traffic on the road. He drummed his fingers on the steering wheel.

He checked in the rear-view mirror, and there it was: the white transit van. "Oh wait! No! Don't do this to me, please. Come on! Why now?" He had not been physically followed by the transit van before.

He had to be sure. At the first left available, he slowed and turned, followed closely by the van. There were two guys in the cab he could see clearly in the mirror. The driver was taller and slimmer, and wore a kind of smile. "This is how you want to play it, huh?" Vanu stepped on the accelerator.

Out of the trade park and onto a main road, he ramped up the speed, which the van matched. Every time he slowed, they slowed. Even when they could have overtaken on the outer lane, they didn't, choosing to remain behind him. Vanu was under no illusion: these guys were following.

With sweat trickling down his temples, he decided to get off the A road and travel a more scenic route home. The transit driver was trying to put the wind up him, and it was working.

When he went off the A road, the transit went left at the same time, following him onto the one-lane country road. Vanu had to shake them somehow. But how? How could he lose his BMW? It wasn't dark yet.

The road he chose was quiet. He hadn't seen another car in at least two miles. Behind him, the transit van accelerated and pulled up alongside him.

The passenger leered down at him.

Looking up, Vanu saw the passenger wind down his window.

Vanu gasped, holding his breath, when the passenger pointed a pistol at him. It had a long snout, which he realised, at the first muzzle flash, was a silencer.

There was no loud bang, merely a pop.

At first, he couldn't see. The driver's side window splintered, then shattered over his lap. Vanu had no time to think about it; he had to get away from the van, quick, before the passenger fired a second time.

Looking up at the passenger, who smiled and withdrew his gun, Vanu breathed a small sigh of relief, until the van drew closer. "No! Please!"

The BMW put up as much of a fight as it could against the heavier transit van. Vanu felt the tyres going. He didn't want to drive into the woods on his left, but the van had the power.

Trees kept whizzing past at sixty miles an hour. If he didn't slow down, his Beamer would hit one of them.

He jammed on the brakes, but the van nudged him to the left a bit more.

Vanu screamed, a tree on the outer edges of the woods speeding towards him.

He held on to the steering wheel until he knew it was too late, at which point he covered his face with his arms, bracing for impact.

His airbag failed to deploy, forcing Vanu's head to hit the steering wheel. Slamming into the tree at fifty-six miles per hour was the killer blow, not the failure of the air bag to launch. Vanu's BMW wrapped itself around the tree, crushing him to death.

31

"Cheers!" Walker clinked glasses with Rachel, happy that she enjoyed the shepherd's pie he made from scratch at the last minute. He had to apologise to her for being late, having played nursemaid to Zuccari. He didn't know how his mate got himself into such trouble; it was like he had a knack for it. "Shall we take this into the lounge?"

"You don't get out of washing-up that easily, mister." Rachel took a sip of her red wine. She smiled at him, letting him know she was joking. "That was delicious, though."

"I'll put the plates through the dishwasher for you, how about that?" He picked up their plates and carried them from the dining area to the kitchen. He scraped off the leftovers and put the plates in the machine. "All done."

"A man of many talents. What else can you do, huh?"

"That's for you to find out. I'm not giving away all my secrets." He pulled her closer. "I've got to keep you interested somehow."

He had not been seeing her for long, but from what he already knew, he liked her. Walker wanted to see where their relationship went. It might turn out that they were incompatible, but he doubted it. So far, they were very well-suited, intellectually, physically, and sexually.

In the lounge, he sat on the sofa and Rachel lay on his lap. "You didn't get to finish telling me about your day. Did you catch that guy?"

"What guy? Oh, Fernando Linares." Rachel stared up at the ceiling. "I don't know how, but Hayes managed to get his sister to talk, and she gave us the address of an abandoned house. We went, but he wasn't there. So, we stuck the local uniforms on it. When they find him, they'll bring him in."

"You don't sound too bothered," he said, stroking her belly.

"We're almost certain it's not him." Rachel leaned forward and put her wine glass on the coffee table. "We'll only be crossing his name off the list. We think we know who it is anyway. Her name's all over this case."

Walker tilted his head. "*Her* name? Anyone I know?"

"You might do. She's fairly well known around these parts." Rachel let it linger, for dramatic effect. "Have you heard of Melodi Demirci?"

He sat up, disturbing her, making her follow suit. "Really? Demirci?"

With a look of confusion, she nodded. "Uh-huh! Why? What is it?"

"That's who I've spent all afternoon and evening talking about." He piqued her interest. Walker turned slightly to face her a bit more. Her expression said, "Tell me!" "This isn't to go any further. If the top brass find out, they'll go bananas. I'm not kidding, Rachel. Not one word, you promise?"

He was half expecting her to crack wise about him calling her Rachel. She either overlooked it, or didn't mind. Rachel said she would keep the promise.

"You know I met Zuccari this afternoon... Well, when I got to the pub, he looked like shit. He spent the first half hour playing those poxy fruities, until I threw my dolls out my pram, threatening to go home. When I got him on his own, he let me have it."

Rachel couldn't wait. "And? What was it?"

"He's only been sleeping with Melodi Demirci, hasn't he? The silly bastard. He's a member of SCO19, and shagging a notorious gangster, the stupid prick."

"Really?" Rachel picked up her glass and took a sip. "Is that it? So he has a terrible choice in women. He can't help that."

"I haven't finished yet." He saw Rachel smile in apology. "So, he's been sleeping with Demirci in the office of the casino he goes to as much as he can. Zuccari's getting all comfortable, until Demirci agrees to stake him a hundred grand, which he sets about losing."

"And let me guess: he can't repay her. Am I right?"

"You got it! He now owes Demirci a hundred grand, and it increases for every day he doesn't cough up the cash. She's a nasty piece of work apparently."

"I heard today that people think she had her own dad shot outside the casino, and even hired her psycho cousins to carry it out. Is there any truth to that, do you think?"

"I guess anything's possible with that woman. I just don't get why she would get him in so much debt?"

"It can't hurt to have a cop in her pocket. You'd better watch out for him if he owes a ton of money. He'll either do a runner, or top himself." She held his hand. "I've seen it happen. One of my squad got himself into a ton of debt. He suffocated himself in his garage. He attached a hose to the exhaust and drifted off to sleep. Poor bastard only owed ten grand."

"Yeah I guess you're right. I'll keep an eye on him, as usual." He leaned back, allowing Miller to lie on him. "The arsehole's become a liability. It's getting to the point where I don't know if I can trust him anymore. And that's not good when he holds my life in his hands every day on the job."

"It sounds like he doesn't deserve to be a cop anyway." Rachel stroked his arm. "Are you going to talk about it with Sarge? See what he says. And don't forget, he might get suspended permanently after the shooting the other morning. Could be a blessing."

Walker nodded. "You're right. I might broach it with Sarge, see what he says." Walker didn't want to rat his "friend" out to his sergeant, not in the slightest, but a firearms officer with mental baggage like this wasn't a good combination. Would he trust Zuccari in a siege, or a roadblock, or anywhere? The answer was no.

"You have to do what's right for the unit, not one member."

He found the way she fussed over him endearing. Rachel was a protective lioness. There was nothing she wouldn't do to protect her family, which one day might include him. He sat there, stroking her belly, wondering why he was thinking such silly nonsense. He was having fun with her, no more, he kept telling himself, knowing he was lying. He was smitten already.

DAY 4
FRIDAY, JUNE 15TH

32

Richard switched off the engine and opened his car door. He noted Vanu's BMW's space next to his was empty. He frowned. In the three years since he'd hired his second-in-command, he'd only beaten Vanu to the workshop in the morning a handful of times.

Since they were nearing the end of their project, maybe Vanu was taking back some time? Or, God forbid, maybe he was sick? It happened, he guessed.

Picking up his briefcase from the back seat, Richard closed the door and locked it. By the cars parked, Paula Lang was the only one in so far. He stepped inside and found her tinkering with the Fiesta, putting some finishing touches beneath the bonnet. "Morning! No Vanu?"

"Not yet," she replied from inside the engine.

"He was the last to leave last night, wasn't he?" Richard walked towards the iron steps up to his office.

Paula said, "Uh-huh. I think so, yeah."

And he continued on up. "Do me a favour, would you? Find out where he is?"

"I'm on it!" She came out from under the bonnet, her dark

blue overalls covered in oil, and headed to Vanu's desk, where the workshop's landline lived. "He's probably just running late."

"There's a first time for everything, I suppose," Richard conceded. "I need to know if he's going grace us with his presence today. Thanks, Paula."

When he closed his office door, Paula was on the phone. The first thing he did was to plonk his case on the desk and step up to the closed blinds on the exterior windows. He parted a couple of slats and checked the transit van was still parked down the road. It was. "Bastards!" Of course, the van might have nothing to do with them.

If he had the nerve, he would march over there and knock on the doors, speak to the driver. Of course, he didn't, in case Vanu was right, and they *were* watching him.

Closing the slats in the blinds, Richard sighed, turned, and noticed the answerphone screen flashing. The red digital display informed him he had eight new messages. At his desk, he pressed the messages button.

He'd never had much to do with Vanu's wife in the past, yet he instinctively knew it was her desperate voice asking for help, even before she identified herself. The first message was her asking if he knew where her husband was, that he was an hour late. The next two were angry additions, scolding him for keeping Vanu from his family.

Richard ignored these messages, moving on to the next, recorded at 12:30 in the morning. Gone was her anger, replaced with sorrow. She informed him that the police had arrived on her doorstep, asking if she was the wife of Vanu Parekh. Her husband had crashed his car into a tree.

The final message was recorded at seven-thirty, asked him to meet her at the East Surrey Hospital, where Vanu's body had been flown to after cutting him out of the wreckage. There was no anger, no animosity in her voice, only sorrow. Richard sat on his chair, his head hung.

"Richard, are you all right?" Paula entered the office, gingerly approaching him. "I've tried every number I have, including his home, but nothing. His wife didn't answer."

He didn't want to say it out loud. "Something's happened." He kept his head down, not wanting to look her in the eyes. "He's gone, Paula."

Without looking at her, he only heard her approach. "What do you mean? Gone where?" She held his hand, knowing something was very wrong.

"His wife says he wrapped his Beamer around a tree." Richard could probably have told Paula in a nicer manner, but he didn't believe it himself. He only saw Vanu the previous night. "I need to get to East Surrey Hospital, now."

Paula offered to take him, saying he was in no fit state to drive. Why was she acting so normal? When he looked at her, she was pale, her eyes wide.

Downstairs, he expected to find the rest of the team. They were nowhere to be found. He followed Paula out to her VW Polo and found himself cramped in the passenger seat. Moving it back, he put his seat in a comfortable position and waited while she prepped for the half-hour journey to hospital. "Thanks for taking me."

"What're friends for?" She reversed out and drove in silence.

On the way out, Richard checked the van. No one in it. And when they passed, he checked the transit van didn't follow. "You don't think–"

"What? That van had something to do with Vanu's crash?" Her expression was incredulous. "Do me a favour, of course not. The driver probably leaves the van there in the daytime, or something. Vanu's so paranoid since we tested it successfully."

"What, you don't think there are people out there willing to kill for it?" He smiled when he said it, letting her know he was joking.

Paula kept her eye on the road. "Don't get me wrong, it is pretty special, a game changer and all that. But who would want to stop progress? It's the future. Sure companies will wish they'd invented it, but do you really think they'd kill people to prevent us from building it? Give me a break. Vanu should've taken his pills, I mean no disrespect."

"I know, I told him to remember them. And he was worse recently, especially the last couple of days." The more Richard spoke to Paula, the more she eased his mind. If Vanu had crashed into a tree, it was an accident, not because of some demonic transit driver out to murder him for the Fiesta's secrets. "Thanks. I feel a lot better."

It wasn't long until they arrived at the hospital. He exited the Polo while Paula found a parking space. Inside, he spent ten minutes trying to locate Vanu's wife, whose name escaped him, again, even after hearing it on the recording earlier.

Greeting her with a kind word, he enquired after her well-being, which was pretty stupid, given that she'd just found out that her husband had died in a car crash. The problem Richard had: he didn't know what to say to her. As luck had it, she had an ulterior motive for calling him earlier, for inviting him to the hospital.

After all the civilities were done, she pulled him to the far side of the visitors' lounge and forced him to sit next to her. "What's going on?"

"I think Vanu was right. I think someone drove him into that tree."

To Richard, she was an attractive Indian woman, not yet forty, he reasoned. "What? Why? What're you talking about? You said he crashed into a tree. What makes you so sure he didn't, hmm?"

"Because of where he crashed." Vanu's wife leaned in closer. She told him exactly where her husband died, the name of the road, everything. "He had no reason to be there. I phoned him, and he said he was on his way home. Why would he take a detour like that?"

"I don't know, but there must've been a reason." Richard wished he knew why. Dealing with her was becoming a pain; she kept gripping his arm and leaning in closer each time. "Let's see what the police say, shall we? If they think something's amiss, I'm sure they'll tell us, don't you think?"

"He died because of that thing you're all working on, and you know it. He told me about the white van outside the workshop, Richard. You can stop pretending. I suggest you watch your back from now on." Her Indian accent grew stronger the angrier she became.

He sat back, taking her hand from his lower arm. "You and Vanu are like two peas in a pod, aren't you? You're starting to sound just like him, twitching, looking over your shoulder, always thinking someone's out to get you. I've got news for you: they're not. Only people with huge egos believe people are after them."

Her voice quiet, yet angry, she said, "You know, just because he was paranoid, doesn't mean people weren't following him. You and I both know the ramifications of your project. If I were you, I'd grow eyes in the back of my head. These people are obviously serious about keeping it hidden."

Paula arrived, hugged Vanu's wife, and sat next to him. "Everything all right?"

He smiled, nodded and stared ahead. "Yeah, everything's fine. We're waiting to speak to the police and doctors." His poker face left a lot to be desired. Why was she so insistent it was the van driver's fault. What evidence did she have?

Vanu's location when he crashed did pose a mystery, he had

to admit. Not to Vanu's wife. What was his friend and colleague doing all the way over there? If he was on his way home like his wife said, Vanu had gone in the opposite direction. Having said that, Richard didn't want to countenance the obvious: he and his team were being watched.

33

"Linares is in interview room three when you're ready," Travis told her, before walking off with Inspector Gillan.

Hayes was still going through CCTV footage of Accord FM's premises. She'd tried to zoom in on the van's number plate, but it didn't appear to have one, just a blank space. "We could look for burnt out transit vans in the area, I guess."

"That's not such a bad idea. I'd burn a vehicle I used in a crime, especially a triple murder. I'm on it." Miller turned to her computer. "What about Fernando Linares?"

"Let him sweat for a bit. There's no rush. Let's face it, we both know who our prime suspect is."

"I can't believe Inspector Gillan talked her into coming in." Miller stood and stared down at her over the partition. "Are you nervous about interviewing her?"

"Nervous? No, why?" Hayes stared back with incredulity. "We both know she's as guilty as sin. If not for these murders, she's guilty of lots of other things. Nah, she's a villain through and through. I'm looking forward to sparring with her. She's not going to give anything away, I know that much. But confident suspects almost always slip up, eventually. We'll have to make sure we're there when she does."

"She's going to have the best lawyers."

"Yep. They're who I'm worried about, not her. This afternoon will end up being a match between us and the lawyers."

"I wish I was going in with you."

"That makes two of us."

"Not that there's much point, but I'll carry on looking at other suspects."

"You never know, she might not be the one we're after. I mean, it's highly unlikely, given how she's all over this case, but it's possible someone else killed Fisher, Reid and Austin. Why don't you start looking into Brandy Reid's fella, Dylan Oldham? He's bound to have form, having heard what we have about him. Do a background check on him. Like I say, weirder things have happened."

Miller agreed and sat back down at her computer.

Giving their interviewee a half hour wait in the most depressing room she'd ever set foot in, Hayes exited out of her computer and stood. "Let's go and find out what he has to say, shall we?" She put on her suit jacket. "He should be ready to crack about now, I'd say."

Her partner stood, tucked her chair under her desk and put on her jacket.

"This'll be interesting, though. With no alibi it's no wonder he did a runner," she said on the way to the lift.

"Plus he's on the run from Melodi Demirci. Sooner or later he's going to come a cropper. Guys like him always do." Miller pressed the button. "I've known dodgy guys like him my whole life. They can't help themselves, always getting in trouble they can't handle."

Hayes agreed. "You and me both. I've met my fair share of guys like him. Mostly victims through the job, mind."

"Even Luke's friend's having trouble with Demirci," Miller confided.

Hayes, surprised at her partner's candidness, glanced at her. "How's that?"

"Sleeping with her apparently, she stakes him a hundred grand and he loses the lot. Now he can't repay her because he lied to her about who he is, stupid bastard. He's worried her psycho cousins are coming after him. And Luke's the one who has to look out for the guy. I swear the sooner they ban gambling the better. No good comes of it."

Hayes waited for her partner to exit the lift first. "Yeah? Tell Luke to watch his back. Guys like his mate will do anything to get themselves out of trouble, including dragging their friends down with them. I've seen it time and again. And the government will never ban gambling, ever. There's too much money at stake."

Outside interview room three, Hayes opened the door and let Miller enter first. As expected Fernando Linares was wide-eyed and practically crying when she entered, protesting his innocence, about how he loved Kurt, and wouldn't hurt him. "Relax, Mr Linares, please. We know you didn't have anything to do with the murders."

"Really?" He seemed to calm. "When I saw the pigs, oh er, I mean police, I thought–"

Miller waved his comments away. "We're here to help you, Mr Linares, not trick you, okay? If you work with us, we'll be able to eliminate you from our enquiries, do you understand? It's our job to investigate every suspect, and right now you fall into that category, being married to Mr Austin, and having no alibi. Oh, and having a blazing row in front of a group of onlookers. Ordinarily, it wouldn't look good for you, but you're in luck. It looks like we have our prime suspect already."

Hayes found Fernando's relief interesting. "You seem surprised. Why is it so surprising that we have a prime suspect?"

His eyes opened wide. "You aren't normally this quick, are you? I've been in police interviews where I've been grilled for hours, and you lot, I mean police officers, haven't had a clue who the suspect is. I thought I was in for more of the same. That's why I ran."

"And how many police interviews have you been in, exactly?"

"A few, but you should know all that. You have my record, although for most of them I was only questioned, never charged."

"But trouble does seem to follow you, doesn't it?" Hayes had been a cop long enough to know a career criminal when she met one. "And we have read your record, yes. We already know so much about you. But, you see, Mr Linares, we're not interested in your past, are we, Miller?"

"Nope. We have to ask as a formality: did you shoot and kill Colin Fisher, Brandy Reid, and your husband, Kurt Austin?"

"No! I didn't have anything to do with it."

"Then we need to know where you were at the time of their deaths." Hayes caught his attention. His eyes widened.

"And this is why I ran. I was home alone on the night."

When he started to panic, Hayes put her palms out on display. "Shh! It's all right. We have ways around this kind of scenario." He stopped panicking and stared at her, waiting for her to continue. "Is there anyone who saw you in the flat around that time?"

"No! I thought of that. No one."

"Okay, no problem. Did you visit any shops that night? Maybe a convenience store or off-licence, to buy a pack of beer, or anything like that?" Nothing. "Do you have a dog, Mr Linares? Did you go for a walk around the block?" A shake of his head. "Order a takeaway?" Nope. "Did anyone call you that night?" No, no one. "Are you a big computer user? Were you on the computer at the time?"

He shook his head. "How will that help?"

"If we can prove you were at home between, say, ten o'clock and one in the morning, we can prove you're not the shooter. And if we can prove you were on a computer, for example, that can still count as an alibi. Just anything that proves you were at home at the time, so not a mobile phone, but if you were typing on a PC, it would work."

"Why can't it be a mobile? Each phone can be traced, can't they? You can use GPS on it, or whatever. If you did, you'd find mine was at home at the time."

"The problem with mobiles is just that, Mr Linares, they're mobile. You could leave yours at home, drive to the radio station, shoot your husband, Mr Fisher and Miss Reid, and drive home, all the while your mobile tells us you're in your house. Do you see where I'm coming from? That's why mobiles can't corroborate a suspect's whereabouts, but a PC can, because it's stationary."

"Oh hang on, what about a games console?"

Hayes shrugged at Miller. "They're connected to your broadband, I guess they can. I don't see why not. Were you playing on a console at the time?"

His face lit up. "You bet I was. From about ten until two in the fucking morning. And I played with other players. You know, with a headset, chatting and stuff."

Miller was excited as well. "Really? You talked to real people?"

"Why the fuck didn't I think of this before? Of course! Yeah, I was beating the shit out of some arsehole Yank at Call of Duty: WW2 at the time. And we got into a bit of an argument. He'll remember it."

"Will your system record all this?" Hayes knew next to nothing about video games consoles, and staring at Miller, neither did she.

"It won't record our verbal chat, but it records everything else. My console will tell you when I switched it on and off, where I paused it, and updated it. If I give you the little shit's handle, you can contact him, can't you?"

"Outstanding!" Hayes nodded. "Absolutely. If this kid can corroborate your story, you're in the clear. We'll need to confiscate your console to add verification, but if this all comes to pass, you'll be off our list of suspects."

"I don't know why I didn't think of it. I'll get you that name."

Hayes' mobile vibrated in her pocket. She delved inside her jacket and retrieved it. The digital display informed her it was the pathologist. "Hi Sheila, what's up?"

"Sorry to do this, Amanda, but you need to come down here. I'm processing Henry Curtis, and something's presented itself that I need to show you." Sheila sounded both excited and perplexed.

"Yes, we'll be right over. Listen, is this going to be good or bad news?"

"I think it depends on your perspective, but knowing you as well as I do, good news."

34

Miller pulled into East Ham Mortuary, where they were due to meet the pathologist. After parking up, Miller locked their car and walked with Hayes to Sheila's exam room, which held four examination benches, only one of which was in use. Even from a distance she recognised the corpse was that of Henry Curtis.

"You were very cryptic over the phone, Sheila," Hayes said, following the pathologist over to Henry's body. "What's up?"

"As you can see, from here all looks usual for a suicide, right? Slit wrists, and although done horizontally, and not vertically, very effective. The body almost bled dry, which struck alarm bells with me."

Miller observed the deep gashes on Henry's wrists. When Sheila prised the wound apart, Miller saw white. "Is that bone?"

"It is, very good. And do you know why it rang alarm bells with me? Slashers rarely dig that deep." Sheila put the arm down.

Hayes stepped forward. "Really? I didn't know that."

"You have to think about this logically. Anyone who is contemplating suicide is on the edge of the abyss, right? They're going to be petrified. Most of the slashers I've seen come through here have made several attempts at their wrists prior to severing arteries deep enough to kill them. Mostly, they're scared and don't really want to kill themselves. But here, there are no marks from previous attempts, no hacking practises, just two clean slices, right to the bone. In my time here at the mortuary, I've never seen two cleaner cuts."

"Right, I'm with you, but what does it mean?" Hayes raised an eyebrow. "Are you saying what I think you're saying?"

"It got me curious. I wanted to see if there were any other marks on the skin that shouldn't be there. Here, help me with the body, would you?"

Watching the pathologist and Hayes roll the body onto its side, Miller stepped closer when Sheila probed the back of Henry's head, going through his hair. "Is that a scab?" She saw a dark circle in the centre.

Sheila and Hayes rolled Henry face down. "That's from a gun muzzle."

Miller was having trouble processing the information. "Wait! Are you saying Henry Curtis was murdered? He didn't kill himself?"

"That's exactly what I'm saying. At some point, Henry's killers put a gun against his head so hard it broke the skin, leaving that mark. You said there was a letter found in the home? My guess is, if you asked a graphologist to analyse his handwriting, the results would say he wrote it under duress."

"So, you believe the killer forced him to slit his own wrists?" Miller was still having trouble believing it.

"With how cleanly his wrists were sliced, I'd say it's more likely your suspect slit his wrists. They aren't cuts of a suicidal man, detective. Like I said, they set alarm bells ringing. They're the reason I looked elsewhere on the body."

"And you're certain the scab on the back of his head is from the muzzle of a gun? You're going to write that on your report?" When Sheila confirmed she would, Hayes turned to Miller. "Smile, partner, at least now we can stop investigating Reid and Austin."

35

Charlotte Edwards opened her front door to let in her brother. When she received a phone call from Hayes that she had information about her brother's and Henry's deaths earlier, she suggested they drive over to her house. When she hung up with the detective, she immediately phoned Richard, who was driving at the time. "Oh good, you got here first," she said, letting him through.

"Tell me what the detective said, Lottie." He stood in the hallway, agitated.

After closing the door, she faced him. "What? Nothing! She told me she has news about Colin's and Henry's deaths, that she needs to speak with us. Why? What are you hiding?"

Richard seemed unduly irritable. "I'm not hiding anything."

"Then why are you so tense? I heard you talking to Henry before. I know you had something going on with him, so you might as well tell me what it is before they get here. And don't lie to me; you're a terrible liar."

Instead of revealing all, Richard went to her dining room, opened her drinks cabinet, and poured himself a whisky. "Do you want one?" When he necked a double measure, Charlotte saw his hand shaking.

"It's a bit early for that, isn't it? Are you an alcoholic, or something? It's barely midday, and you're necking it like it's squash." She watched him slam back another double. "Right, that's enough. You're not going to be pissed before the police get here."

Closing the drinks cabinet, she shooed her brother away. "What's wrong with you? This isn't like you at all; you're normally so together, so with it."

"One of my employees died last night," Richard replied, sitting on her sofa.

Charlotte sat next to him. "Oh Richard, that's awful. I'm so sorry for going off on one. I didn't know." She left a pause before asking, "How did it happen?"

"Car crash late last night. He wrapped his Beamer round a tree on his way home to his wife. I only found out this morning because his wife left several voicemails for me." He sat with his head hung. "I can't believe he's gone. I mean, first my brother's murdered, then Henry tops himself, and now my second-in-command dies in a car crash. Can anything else bad happen? It's not like I've got enough on my plate."

Charlotte was taken aback. In all her years, she'd never seen Richard cry, not once. Not even as a kid. He was always the strong, dependable one, whereas Colin was always the fuck-up, the black sheep who could do nothing right. Her place was smack bang in the middle of the two. "I'm so sorry!"

She put her right arm around his shoulder. He sobbed for the first time in front of her, his shoulders shaking. Charlotte didn't know what to say. He couldn't get any comfort from his ex-wife, so Charlotte guessed she would have to suffice. "Let it out. It's been a shit week all right." Understatement of the year, she thought.

After ten minutes, she let go of him and stepped up to the drinks cabinet. "I think we can both use one of these." She poured two double shots of whisky, had one herself, and watched her elder brother knock his back. It burned when it slid down her throat.

"Didn't the detective give anything away?" Richard's words were bordering slurred. "Why would she need to speak to us again so soon?"

Charlotte shut the cabinet door and picked up Richard's glass. "She said she has information for us, that's all. And she's only expecting to see me, not you. I called you because I thought you'd want to be here."

"I do, I want to know what's going on with Colin's case as much as you."

She thought he seemed a bit disingenuous. Her brother wasn't interested in Colin's case; he was there to find out more about what the detectives had. His mannerisms weren't right. And he'd shrugged her off when she mentioned he and Henry had something going on, which made her even more suspicious. "Why won't you tell me?" She sat next to him again, hoping the intimacy might soften him into confessing all.

"Tell you what? There's nothing to tell."

Charlotte grew up with him. If Richard didn't want to elaborate, there was no forcing him. As pig-headed as he was blinkered. She sighed. "Fine! I didn't hear you talking at Henry's." She rose from the sofa and walked over to the window, as a white Peugeot pulled into her driveway. "They're here!"

As they stepped onto the porch, she opened the door and greeted them, letting them past. "Go on through to the lounge. Richard's already in there." She flapped a little, checking the detectives didn't want refreshments.

"Honestly, Mrs Edwards, we're fine. We can't be long, we're

interviewing a suspect this afternoon." Hayes pulled a notebook and pen out of her pocket.

Charlotte thought Hayes looked so pretty in her suit, with her hair tied back in a ponytail. She was lovely-looking with a heavy tan. And her partner was attractive, in an Amazonian way, being at least six feet tall, or so Charlotte thought. "So, you said you have news about Colin's case? And Henry's?"

"We do, yes. You see, we've just come from the mortuary where the pathologist is working on Mr Curtis." Hayes paused.

"And? He committed–"

"Actually, he didn't commit suicide after all, Mrs Edwards."

Confused, Charlotte looked at her brother, and back to Hayes. "Then how? I saw him in the tub, detective. The water was red. He had cuts on his wrists."

"I'm sorry to tell you this, but he was murdered."

Charlotte gasped, placing her palms over her mouth. With shaky hands, she got up and wandered over to the drinks cabinet, pulled the door down and poured herself another whisky. "But how?" She held the glass.

"Oh for God's sake, Lottie, someone sliced his wrists while he was in the bath to make it look like he committed suicide. It doesn't take a genius–"

"That's enough, Mr Fisher!" Miller's warning was heeded. "We're here to update you on your brother's case. And now we know your brother-in-law was murdered, we have questions that need answering."

Her brother shut up immediately. Charlotte chugged the whisky back, then nodded when Miller asked her if she was ready. "Are you suggesting the same person killed my brother and Henry?" Hayes nodded. "But why? What have they ever done to anyone? They didn't deserve this."

"This is what we need your help with, Mrs Edwards. You couldn't help us much before, so we need you both to dig deep now, okay? Can you think of anyone who might harbour a grudge against your brother and his husband?"

"Or Colin or Henry individually?" Hayes waited with pen at the ready.

Charlotte closed her eyes, like it would somehow magic up a lead for them. "I'm sorry, detectives, I don't. Richard and I didn't know Colin all that well, I guess. He wasn't the easiest man to know, or like for that matter. He was very self-centred, and had an addiction to pretty much everything, which got him in trouble, all the time."

"Mr Fisher?" Miller regarded her brother. "Do you have anything you want to add? Can you think of anyone your brother or Henry had issues with?"

"What? No, of course not. They were a lovely couple." He sat back in his seat and stared up at the ceiling. "But you said you're interviewing a suspect this afternoon, so you must have an idea who's responsible?"

Noticing an exchange between the two detectives, Charlotte waited.

"One name kept cropping up during our investigation, a name who had a link to the three victims, your brother included, and now Henry." Hayes paused again.

"Let me guess: Melodi Demirci?"

"It's looking more and more likely that Demirci might be responsible, not that we can prove it. Without proof, we have nothing. That's why we're here. Did you know your brother and Henry had dealings with her?"

"Who told you that? I bet it was Henry's personal assistant, wasn't it?"

Charlotte went and sat next to her inebriated brother. "You'll have to excuse Richard, he's just found out an employee of his died in a car crash this morning." Expecting sympathy, the detectives instead eyeballed one another. "What?"

"Nothing! We're sorry to hear that, Mr Fisher." Hayes sounded genuine, except the glance she gave her partner was anything but.

"That's some bad luck, Mr Fisher. I mean, first your brother's shot, then your brother-in-law's murdered, and now an employee dies in a car crash?" Miller didn't hide her suspicions. "Did you know this employee well?"

Richard sneered. "Don't try to turn this around on me. I hardly knew him. You really shouldn't listen to Ilya whatsherface. She doesn't know what she's talking about. Henry didn't know that woman."

Why was he protecting Demirci? Charlotte gave Miller an apologetic glance. "He doesn't know what he's saying. He's slurring his words. I gave him some whisky earlier because he was upset." She didn't like the exchanges between the detectives. "Shut up, Richard! You don't know what you're saying."

"I'm afraid he did, Mr Fisher." Hayes stared at her brother. "It turns out that Henry went to Melodi Demirci for a business loan."

"Only it was far more than just a loan." Miller sat back.

"The contract Henry signed to get hold of his start-up investment gives Demirci first dibs on buying his shares of the radio station. In a few days, I'm guessing she'll be signing a contract with his solicitor giving her total control over Henry's company. I'm sure Demirci will have a CEO in place by the end of next week. And Accord FM will still be operational, with only a few days of interruption."

Charlotte saw the seriousness in Hayes' eyes. "Do you expect us to buy that? Henry was a businessman. Why would he do that?"

"And that's crap, because Henry was in the process of buying her out."

Silence filled the room, cushioning them all.

Charlotte saw the suspicion in their eyes.

"But you just said Henry doesn't know her, Mr Fisher." Miller leaned forward, awaiting a reply from Charlotte's stupid brother. "And now you're telling us he wanted to buy her out of the business?"

"Really, detectives, he doesn't know what he's talking about. He's drunk." Charlotte wanted the police officers out of her house. "I think maybe we should reschedule this for another time?" Fortunately, Hayes agreed.

"I think you're right. You know it's against the law to lie to a police officer, Mr Fisher? It's called obstruction of justice. Here, take my card, Mrs Edwards, call and we'll arrange separate interviews with you both. Oh, and they will be recorded." Hayes stood, glaring down at both siblings.

36

"Richard Fisher's the key, sir. I know it." Hayes looked at Inspector Gillan for acknowledgement. Sat in a small conference room with Gillan and Miller, Hayes' leg bobbed up and down under the table.

"And you think we should focus solely on the Fishers now?" Inspector Gillan looked at her, then Miller. "Do you agree, Detective Miller?"

"Absolutely. Richard Fisher's the key, like Hayes said. He might have been inebriated at the time, but he outright lied to us."

Gillan scratched his head. "I don't know about this. We're kind of putting all our eggs in one basket. The suspect might have targeted Reid or Austin, we don't know. I just don't like the thought of leaving avenues of investigation unchecked."

"Please, sir, I've never been more sure of anything. He knows more than he's letting on. He lied to us. Plus, we all know she's behind this; her DNA's all over it."

Hayes waited while Gillan mulled it over. He got up from his seat and strolled over to the window and looked out onto the street below. A clock hung on the wall opposite her ticked loudly. "Sir?"

"You're right. We'll make Richard Fisher and Charlotte Edwards the focus of this investigation, for the time being. This might change over the course of the next few days, though, is that clear?"

"Crystal, sir. Thank you."

Gillan turned to Miller. "Miller, while we're in with Miss Demirci, I want you to gather as much information as you can about the Fishers, that includes Charlotte Edwards, and Henry Curtis. If this family is at the epicentre of this case, I want to know everything about them. Look into the businesses, Accord FM, and I believe Richard Fisher owns Fisher Valves, if my memory serves me. We'll get to the bottom of it. Amanda, you're with me."

"You've got it." Miller rushed out of the room.

Hayes stood and regarded him. "I know he's the one. You had to be there."

"You can stop the sales pitch now." Gillan gathered up his paperwork, then stared at the door. Gillan eyed her with suspicion. "Before we go, is Miller dating Luke Walker going to be a problem for us?"

"What? No, of course not. Why would it? She's great company because of him and if they break up she'll go back to being a pain in my arse."

"Fine, I'll not make it an issue for now, but if it causes any problems in the field, you let me know. Understood?"

"Of course. If it's a problem, I'll break them up myself, how's that?" Hayes smiled, letting him know she was joking, yet serious at the same time. "Are you ready?"

Inspector Gillan marched to the door and held it open for her.

"Let's go and introduce ourselves to Miss Demirci, shall we?" Hayes stepped out into the corridor and waited for her supervisor. As much as she promoted strength in her walk, she had butterflies in her tummy for the first time. Why should interviewing Melodi Demirci make her nervous?

37

"Remember what I said: do not antagonise her. Her lawyer's a pain in the arse."

It seemed Inspector Gillan was terrified of Demirci's lawyer, a guy in his fifties with a full head of white hair, not grey, white, wearing an expensive navy suit.

When Hayes closed the door behind her, Melodi Demirci sat next to her oh-so-expensive legal man, with a smirk. Hayes took her seat, waiting for Gillan to commence proceedings.

After making their introductions, Gillan started the camera, which recorded every nuance of the meeting. He asked Demirci's criminal solicitor to say their names on film, which he did. Inspector Gillan introduced himself, then left it to Hayes to say who she was.

Their interviewee was well-dressed, in a grey suit, not unlike hers, only more expensive, and tailored to her curves. With long, dark shiny hair tied back in a ponytail, Hayes thought Demirci pretty, in a bad-girl sort of way.

"I've seen all your interviews on the news." Demirci leaned forward. "You're the bravest cop I've ever met going up against that suitcase killer. Shame we should be meeting over a table like this."

Hayes glanced over at Gillan, who nodded. "Why, thank you, Miss Demirci, I appreciate that." Her nerves were getting the best of her. "Now, why don't I start by telling you why you're here this afternoon."

"I'll save you the bother! I have a busy schedule, and in my line of work, Friday nights are the second busiest of my week. It's imperative that I get back to the casino at a reasonable time."

"Be our guest." Gillan took control.

"It was terrible what happened over there at Accord, tragic. But you have a triple murder to investigate, and no doubt my name's been mentioned a couple of times, am I right? So, you've brought me here to account for my whereabouts between ten o'clock on June eleventh and two o'clock on the twelfth."

"And can you? Account for your whereabouts?" Hayes knew an alibi would be established almost straight away.

"Absolutely. If you give me an email address, I'll have my man send over CCTV footage from inside my casino that will support my alibi. He's waiting to send it. I'm seen walking the casino floor every hour, on the hour, as I do every night of the week. I would have my croupiers and pit bosses robbing me blind if I didn't."

Giving Demirci her email address, Hayes took out her mobile, waiting for the message to ping. When it did, she pocketed it again. "I don't suppose your cousins are on this footage, are they?" She said it in a nonchalant manner, an add-on, but judging by Demirci's scowl, an unexpected comment.

"My cousins? They don't have anything to do with my family's business." Her eyes narrowed, a frown forming.

"Unar and Yasin Inan, your cousins from your mother's side. Not nice guys from our records. It's not like you're going to do the heavy lifting yourself, is it? So, if you were going to have, say two radio presenters and a producer shot and killed, you would need men like your cousins to do it for you, wouldn't you?"

The solicitor objected, but when Demirci shut him down verbally, he shrank back in his chair. "I really can't speak for my cousins' whereabouts, Detective Hayes. I know they weren't at the casino because I've banned them from the premises."

"That's a shame. Because until we can vouch for them, you're still right at the top of our list of suspects. In fact, you're our prime suspect."

"Prime suspect? Me?" Demirci didn't laugh, or smile.

"For one reason or another you knew each of the victims. Kurt Austin's husband owed you money. You've had poor Fernando Linares scared out of his wits for weeks, frightened that your cousins would put the squeeze on him."

"No, you're right. Fernando does owe me money for his failed venture. I gave him a loan when he needed it the most, which is more than the banks would do. I consider myself a bit of a philanthropist, detective. I hand out loans when one wouldn't be forthcoming through other, more mainstream avenues. A last chance saloon, so to speak. And nine times out of ten I see an RoI on my investments. But sadly not on this occasion."

"And you threatened physical harm on him if he couldn't find your money, didn't you?" Hayes' hands were shaking, adrenaline spiking.

"Of course not. Why would I? And what does all this have to do with the three murders anyway?" Demirci ignored her lawyer's pleas for quiet.

"Well, maybe shooting his husband, Kurt, was a way of making him pay you? Maybe if he thought you're psychotic enough to have his husband killed to make a point, you'd get your money back quicker."

"You don't have to answer that–"

"No, it's fine, Inspector Gillan. I'll answer any question she has for me, and do you know why? Because I'm innocent of these crimes. And I know you don't have any real evidence, or you'd have arrested me by now. So, I'll tell you what, I'll give you access to everything. If you want to scour through my company's accounts, or you need to interview my employees, just let me know and I'll have the documents shipped over, and my staff available. You see, inspector, I need these murderers caught as much as you do."

Hayes decided not to seize on the words "these murderers", for now. "Since you're being so generous, would your generosity extend as far as giving us access to Accord FM's accounts?"

A look of confusion wedged itself between them. Demirci glanced at her lawyer, who shrugged. "Why would you ask for that? I don't have anything to do with Accord."

"Oh, so you're not currently in conversation with Henry Curtis' solicitor regarding buying the rest of his shares of the company? We know you already own forty per cent, Miss Demirci. And now, after Henry Curtis' untimely passing, you stand to gain a hundred per cent ownership."

"I don't want it to be public knowledge, is all. And the way you're talking, you make it sound like I wanted Henry to kill himself."

A quick look at Gillan, then back at her interviewee. "Did I? I didn't mean to say that, because he didn't commit suicide, did he?"

"What? What do you mean? He slashed his wrists and bled to death in his bathtub. His PA told me."

"No, he was murdered. We found a mark on the back of his head that matches a muzzle from a pistol. Someone forced him at gunpoint to write a sloppy suicide note, then marched him to his bathroom, where they sat him in his tub and slashed his wrists so deep the blade touched bone. You're right about him bleeding out. That's how he died, and you stand to gain sixty per cent more of a profitable enterprise. That's some motive to want Henry Curtis out of the way, wouldn't you say?"

Stunned silence.

Hayes waited while Melodi Demirci whispered with her lawyer. She was expecting the lawyer to say the meeting was over, that they'd answered enough questions. Demirci sat back and eyed her.

"I had no idea Henry was murdered, detective, and in light of this, I've decided to give you everything you ask for. Of course you can look at Accord's accounts. It goes without saying. If these files can lead you to the killers, then I want you to use them. I will have my company's accounts sent over this afternoon, along with the radio station's."

With her mouth hung open, Hayes felt a nudge from Gillan. Snapping herself out of it, she thanked Demirci. "Um, the sooner we get them, the sooner we find those responsible." This was highly unexpected, like a confession from a cold case killer.

"If I'm prime suspect number one, I want you to find these bastards as much as you do. It's not easy, you know, having people believe you do these horrible things when you don't. I help people; I don't hurt them."

Hayes wasn't buying Demirci's holier than thou routine. What a load of bollocks. But was she telling the truth about not being Henry's killer? Her fingerprints were all over the investigation, yet Demirci was giving her access to all the accounts? Puzzling. "If you say so."

"It's a stereotype, that's all. People think because I own a casino that I have my cousins going around making collections for me. It's all crap. The gambling industry's so heavily regulated now that I can't get away with anything. It's not like the seventies, we're not in Las Vegas. This is the UK. I run a tight ship, with a tight stranglehold over my employees. That's how

I've turned the casino around, not by hiring muscle to break legs if I don't get my money."

Hayes wanted to get started with the accounts. She questioned Demirci for a further half an hour, asking about her relationship with Colin Fisher. She got the impression there was nothing in it. Reluctantly, she and Gillan let Demirci and her solicitor leave.

38

Charlotte parked up outside the main office of Fisher Valves, the company her clever elder brother started all those years earlier. When God had been handing out brains, she and Colin were bypassed in favour of Richard. It wasn't fair!

The receptionist was busy behind her desk. Charlotte couldn't remember the last time she drove to the factory outlet to speak with Richard, but with how she'd left it with him earlier, Charlotte had to fix it.

After the detectives left her house, she argued with Richard about why he lied to them, and so brazenly. Her brother was a horrible drunk, which his ex would attest to as part of the reason she left him. The row grew until it reached critical mass, and Richard launched himself out of her front door.

Looking at the dash, Charlotte noted it was late afternoon. Some of Richard's staff were leaving for the weekend, probably looking forward to after-work drinks. Gathering up her mobile and bag from the passenger seat, she opened her door and got out.

Why was she here? Would Richard even talk to her? Would he remember what happened earlier? With these unanswered questions, and more, she walked through the reception doors, and up to the desk.

"Hi there! Can I help you?" The receptionist was young, brunette, pretty.

"I was wondering if Richard's in?"

"I'm sorry! We have four Richards here. You'll need to be more specific."

Charlotte felt terrible. She should visit him often enough for his receptionist to recognise her as his sister. "Um, Richard Fisher. Could you tell him his sister's here, please?"

The receptionist smiled. "I didn't know he had a sister. I'll check his office."

Way to lay on the guilt trip. The brunette replaced the phone and pulled an apologetic smile.

"He's not in? I just came on the off-chance. Thanks anyway." When Charlotte turned to leave, the brunette spoke.

"He's at our other site. If you're quick, you might catch him." She scribbled an address down on a piece of paper and handed it to her. "I knew he had a younger brother. I wonder why he didn't mention you."

She ignored the rhetorical question and read the address. "I didn't know about another site. When did the company take this on?"

"A little over three years ago, I believe. I wasn't here back then. I would've been taking my GCSEs. But as far as I know, they hired it for a special project. Everyone's a bit excited around here, as Richard's going to fill us all in next Thursday, before a press conference on Friday." She made a funny, excited squeal noise, her hands pressed together.

Charlotte almost laughed at her exuberance. Bitch. So young, with the rest of her life in front of her. She thanked the whipper snapper and walked to her car, mumbling to herself about being ignored by Richard.

The Hard Way

In Friday afternoon traffic, it took her forty mumble-filled minutes to arrive at the Croydon address the receptionist handed her. The units in front of her were closed, the metal shutters down. She hoped they had not all gone for the day.

"I wonder what your little project is," she muttered, pulling up in front of the reception door. There was only one other car there. Richard's wouldn't be because his was still in her driveway from earlier. "What're you hiding, Richard?"

Wandering up to the wooden door, she tried the handle and it opened. "Hello?" Charlotte found someone tinkering with a blue car in the centre of the workshop. The tinkering continued. "Erm, hi, I'm here to see Richard?"

Up closer, she heard the faintest hint of music, and realised the woman in blue coveralls was wearing headphones. Right behind the woman, who had her head inside the engine, Charlotte tapped her on the shoulder.

The woman screamed, making Charlotte jump.

The short woman turned, letting out a huge sigh of relief, telling her not to sneak up on people like that, that she almost gave her a heart attack.

Charlotte apologised for scaring her. "I didn't think. Do you forgive me?" She gave the woman her most genuine smile. "I'm Charlotte, Richard's sister."

Shaking her hand, the woman introduced herself as Paula, one of Richard's team. "It's funny, but I've been here three years, and haven't seen you before. I almost forgot Richard had a family. I always thought he was a robot."

With a laugh, Charlotte agreed with Paula. "You're not the first person to say that. That's one of his ex-wife's biggest complaints, that he's always working." Charlotte took a good look around the workshop. "So, what's the big secret? What exactly are you doing here? I've just come from the factory, and the receptionist told me there's this big reveal next week, or something? Is it big news?"

Paula nodded. "Oh, the biggest."

"But you're not going to tell me, are you? Have you invented some new valve, or something?" It was the only thing she could think of.

"Something like that, except this 'valve' will literally change the world as we know it. Let's put it this way, over the next year or so, Fisher Valves will become a household name. This valve is so big, it's going to change the automotive trade forever."

"A valve can do all that?" Charlotte hid a disbelieving grin. "Wow!" Cuckoo sprang to mind. "Is he about?"

"Richard! Your sister's down here!" Paula bellowed, making Charlotte jump.

She thanked Paula and stared up at the room on the mezzanine level. "There you are! Surprise!" Richard stood at the top of the iron stairs glaring at her.

"What the hell are you doing here? How'd you find this place?" He started walking down the steps.

"I went to the factory, but the receptionist informed me you were here. It's okay for me to drop by like this, isn't it?"

"Not really, Lottie, no." He met her by the car, took her arm and started walking her towards the front door. "You shouldn't be here. Go on home. I'll call you later, but you can't be here, okay? It's not safe."

She took one last look around the workshop, before stepping outside. "What do you mean it's not safe? It looks plenty safe to me. If I didn't know any better, I'd say you're trying to get rid of me."

"No! Really? What gave you that idea? You're out in the car park, now please go home, would you! I'll call you later. Oh, and turn left when you leave. Whatever you do, don't turn right."

Stood by her car, Charlotte opened her door. Her brother

turned to walk towards the workshop. "You're such an arsehole sometimes, do you know that? And to think I actually came here to apologise." She stuck two fingers up at him.

With his back still to her, he said, "Go home, Charlotte. I'll call you later to explain." At the door, he turned. "And remember what I said, left out of here. It's not safe to turn right."

Wanting to ask him more questions, her brother disappeared inside. Charlotte put her car in gear and reversed out. At the end of the car park, she looked both left and right. Remembering Richard's order, she turned right and set off on her journey home.

Who was he to be throwing orders around? He wasn't the boss of her. Almost immediately, she came across two white transit vans, which she noticed because she had to wait for cars coming the other way. They weren't on the pavement enough for her to pass. She beeped at them, and when ready, passed them, extending her middle finger at the two vans, even though there were no occupants. "Wankers!"

At the roundabout from Beddington Farm Road onto Ampere Road, she was surprised to find one of the two transit vans behind her. Or at least she thought it was one of them. Charlotte tried to get a good look at the driver. Two men sat in the front.

On her way home, she kept studying her followers in the rear-view mirror. For forty-five minutes the van was there, the driver and his passenger watching her. The transit drove past her house when she turned left into her driveway.

39

Luke Walker took his pint from the bar. He tried to make his way through the throng of customers waiting to buy a drink and bumped into a guy who made him spill a bit. It went over his T-shirt. "Don't worry about it, mate." Sarcasm oozed over every syllable.

The guy who'd bumped him shot him some daggers. Instead of rising to the bait, which would have been so easy, Walker continued on his way to the Sarge and Vodicka, who already had drinks. Friday nights in Bar Boho were packed, manic affairs that Walker hated.

Wanting nothing more than to spend the evening with Rachel, he was intent on getting this chore over with. He carried his pint outside, where the Sarge and Vodicka were sat on a pub bench. "It's fucking packed in there. I could've twatted some guy who spilled beer over me." He placed his drink on the bench and wiped his T-shirt with his hand, like it would somehow help.

To his annoyance, they laughed. "What's so funny?"

"You! You're whining like a bitch," Vodicka said, sucking her drink through a straw. "Hey, Sarge, maybe we should've found a nice cosy pub for him, with a lovely open fireplace." She laughed, then winked at him.

"Yeah, how about it, Skywalker? Shall I bring you your slippers and dressing gown?" The Sarge took a gulp of his lager.

"Or maybe he wants Miller to do that?" Vodicka winked again.

Walker sat opposite them, playing along, taking it all in jest. "Fuck the both of you. Who really likes it in places like this anyway? Soho's such a shithole."

"It wasn't last week if I remember correctly. I seem to recall you getting some last weekend from a place just like this." The Sarge picked up his pack of cigarettes and lit one. "So, what's she like, this Miller?"

This was the part of the evening Walker dreaded. Every time he got with a woman, the Sarge would start asking questions. What's she like? He was basically asking what she was like in the sack? With a woman he'd slept with and left, he'd go along with it, for the sake of keeping up appearances. Not with Rachel, though. He wouldn't risk it. "She's great. Thanks for the interest, Sarge. I appreciate it."

"Come on, man, have you sealed the deal yet, or what?"

He had all eyes on him. "I'm not telling you that. Piss off."

"Ah, I get it, he likes this one, Sarge, he's gone all coy on us."

"Fuck off, Voddy, and drink your drink, will you?" Walker took a big mouthful of beer, hoping they'd back off about Rachel.

It was always like this; his team would rib him until he'd had enough, then roll it back. "And there's something I need to discuss with you both anyway. The reason I suggested we meet up tonight."

"Wait! You mean it wasn't for our scintillating company?" Sarge smirked.

"I feel so used, so dirty," Vodicka said with a grin.

"You'll get over it."

"I can tell it's something serious, Walker, so what you got?" The Sarge lost all joviality, his craggy face serious. "This have something to do with Zuccari, by any chance? I saw him this morning and he looked like shit, worse than shit."

Walker nodded. "He's in a bad place. He's gone and got himself in way over his head. He's in so deep, I just don't see a way out for him. He's talking about doing a runner, but I don't see how that's going to help."

"He's gambling again?"

Walker nodded to the Sarge, who shook his head in disgust. "And it's bad."

"How bad? Who's he owe money to this time?"

With his head hung, Walker muttered, "Melodi Demirci." He heard Vodicka gasp, and the Sarge groan. He lifted his head up to find his boss staring skyward, his hands on his head, exasperated. "And you don't want to know how much he's into her for."

"Whoa! Don't even think about holding out on us," the Sarge growled. "If we're going to help Zuccari out of this, we need to know what we're dealing with. You say it's bad. How much is bad in your book?"

"A hundred grand." Walker waited for the frowns to appear. A few thousand was bad enough, but a hundred grand was not easy to come by.

"How the fuck did he get that much credit in her casino?" The Sarge was confused, livid. "I couldn't get half that."

"He lied to Demirci, told her he was some big shot investment broker, or something. He lost money and kept asking for credit. Oh, and he was fucking her. As it turned out, she knew he was a cop, and offered to stake him a hundred grand and he took it. Then he lost it all. Now he's got a week to pay her quarter of it, or her cousins will take it out of him a piece at a time."

"Her cousins, Unar and Yasin Inan, they're a nasty pair I hear." Vodicka, face grave, stared at the Sarge, then him. "If they want their pound of flesh, they'll take it."

Walker wanted the Sarge to take action, or at least tell him that he would sort it somehow. The thought of Zuccari getting beaten and tortured by the Inans filled him with dread. Rachel told him to involve his supervisor, that he would know what to do. "Sarge? What do you think we should do?"

"Leave it with me. I'll look into these Turkish thugs. They'll leave Zuccari alone, don't worry, but both of you be ready, in case I need help with them, okay?"

40

Miller lay on the sofa with the TV on, not that she was watching anything. It was a noise in the background keeping her company, nothing more. Luke sent her a text at least an hour earlier saying he was on his way over. If he didn't hurry, she would go to bed without him. "Where are you?" She got up and went to the kitchen.

She spent all afternoon on the computer, finding out as much as she could about Colin and Richard Fisher, and Charlotte Edwards. After hours of research, she and Hayes concluded Colin Fisher was the intended target, not Brandy Reid or Kurt Austin.

Hayes filled her in about the interview with Melodi Demirci and her solicitor, telling her that Demirci agreed to give them access to all her accounts. She thought it odd that the prime suspect in this investigation would willingly give up so much information. Her partner still believed she ordered the murders, and the murder of Henry Curtis, although they were both stuck as to a real motive.

According to Hayes, Demirci made a valid point: why hurt or kill people who owed her money? She would never see a penny out of them if she knocked off every non-paying loanee. Plus, the death count in the capital would be huge. Despite this, Hayes still believed Demirci was behind it.

While sat at their desks, they discussed the interview with Richard Fisher and Charlotte Edwards earlier, and why Richard lied about Henry knowing Demirci. There was no need for it, although Richard Fisher could claim no knowledge of it through intoxication. That was how he would get away with it.

At about four in the afternoon, Demirci's accounts came through, and ten minutes later, Accord's accounts pinged into Hayes' folder. There was so much data, it would take days to check it all out. Inspector Gillan managed to speak to a judge about obtaining Henry Curtis and Colin Fisher's accounts, both joint and separate.

As a last resort, they would request to see Charlotte Edwards' accounts, although they had no reason to suspect she was involved at all. If nothing came of it, they lost nothing. Covering all their bases was the important thing.

Miller kept coming back to thinking it might not be anything to do with Richard Fisher, Colin Fisher, Henry Curtis, or Charlotte Edwards. It might still be about Brandy Reid, or Kurt Austin, or their other halves.

Charlotte Edwards telling them about one of Richard's employees dying in a car crash piqued her and Hayes' interest. So far, they had three bodies in the radio station, Henry in his bathtub, and now Richard's employee wrapped around a tree. If only they could find a connection between them.

The doorbell rang. "About bloody time." Miller strode into her hallway and up to the door. A peak through the peephole told her it was Luke. "Hey, you!" She gave him a long kiss before inviting him in. "Are you sober? I expected you to come home swaying."

"Nah, I wish. I was too busy trying to convince the Sarge not to go after Melodi Demirci and her arsehole cousins, wasn't I? He and Voddy are talking about taking care of them, saying how the world will be a better place without them."

Miller took him through to the kitchen. "They're kidding, though, right? I mean, they wouldn't go through with something like that, would they?"

"Yesterday I'd have said no." Luke went into her fridge and took out a can of lemonade, rather than a can of Carling. He yanked the ring pull. "But now, I don't know. You should've heard the way they were talking. They sounded serious to me."

"What did you say to them? Please tell me you didn't go along with it." Miller took out a lemonade for herself. "You did, didn't you?"

"What did I just say? I was too busy trying to talk them out of it."

She could imagine him going along with his Sarge. Since getting to know him, Miller had noticed Walker's lack of self-esteem, as hard to imagine as it was, given his looks. It took courage to go against the grain, to go against the status quo. "Well, good, because the last thing I want is you getting in trouble because a so-called mate can't keep it in his pants, and lies about who he is to get credit in a casino. Remember, Zuccari's in the wrong here."

She stepped up to Luke, put her arms around his neck.

"You don't need to worry about me. I'm fine." He kissed her, putting the can on the counter behind him. "I can handle the Sarge. And we have more important things to discuss."

"Oh really? And what might they be, hmm?" She loved his face, loved his dimples, and the way his left central incisor bent ever so slightly over his right, giving his teeth an almost-perfect appearance.

"We've only done it in your bedroom, you know. How about we christen some other rooms?"

"I think it would be rude not to."

DAY 6
SUNDAY, JUNE 17TH

41

Paula Lang dropped the cutlery into the dishwasher's holder. Placing the plates in their slots, she closed the door and switched on the machine, listening out for the whir. On two separate occasions, she neglected to and ended up with dirty dishes in the morning for which her husband chided her. "Is there anything else out there that needs rinsing?"

"A couple of glasses, I think." Her husband went into the dining room, bringing them back for her to hand rinse. "I think that went really well, don't you?"

What her husband was really getting at, was that she hadn't fought with her sister for once. Only because she'd been separated from her for the duration of the family barbecue. "Yeah, sure. It went okay." Even with her German accent, her husband caught the sarcasm in her tone.

He was such a turd. It defied belief sometimes that she married him. Looking at him now, with his massively receding hair, big cheeks and round glasses, he was such a pretentious arsehole. And a massive nerd. All she needed to do was sit him in front of *Star Wars*, *Star Trek*, anything with Star in its title, and he was happy.

For the past year she'd been counting down the days until Fisher Valves went public with their project. Because as soon as Richard showed the world what they had to offer, the company's coffers would be full, and her contract kicked in. She had her solicitor poised to start divorce proceedings.

When they married, before they said their vows, he made her sign a prenuptial agreement so that she couldn't touch his earnings. Another dick move, by a turd of a man, she thought, washing a wine glass by hand, just the way he liked. He actually thought he was the breadwinner. She omitted to inform him of the contract she'd signed when she started on the project at Fisher Valves.

As and when the project went into production, she would start receiving a six-figure pay out, as stipulated in the contract. Paula wouldn't need her husband anymore. She couldn't wait to see the look on his face when he opened the letter.

Her five-figure salary during the project had helped, but she was certain he wouldn't lay a finger on her money once her contract changed. Richard told her last week that the press conference was imminent. Now she knew it was on Friday. "Here, you dry." She handed her husband a tea towel.

The doorbell rang. "You're not expecting anyone, are you?"

He shook his head, said no, carrying on with the drying up.

"I guess I'll get it, then, shall I?"

Honestly, sometimes she just wanted to lamp him, he was so lazy. Yanking a tea towel from the oven handle, she walked through the hallway to the front door. When she peered through the peephole, two guys in suits stood outside waiting. "Who is it?"

Through the thick wooden door, she heard one of them say they were detectives. He held up an ID wallet that said he was with the Metropolitan Police. "We just want to ask you some questions about a colleague of yours, Mr Vanu Parekh. May we come in?"

"It's a bit late to be calling now, isn't it?" She stood back, hoping these guys would disappear.

"Who is it, honey?" Her husband stood behind her.

"It's okay, darling, they say they're detectives."

"Then what the hell are you making them shout through the door for?" He unlocked it. "I apologise for making you wait out there. Please, come on in, detectives. What can we do for you?"

All Paula wanted to do was scratch his eyes out. Those glasses made them appear twice as big as they really were. She smiled at the detectives, one taller and slimmer, the other shorter, butch, scary-looking. Both suited, both showed their ID. "Great! You're in. Why don't you come through to the lounge?"

She led them through. "So, like I was saying, it's a bit late for questioning people, isn't it? I thought your lot would stop at a decent time."

"Can I ask what this is about, detective?" Her husband sat on an armchair, while the detectives chose to sit on the sofa.

"One of your wife's colleagues was involved in a fatal motor vehicle collision, Mr Lang. We're just carrying out routine questioning."

When her husband glanced up at her, asking her what this was all about, she had to get away from him. "I was about to make a cup of tea. Would you both like one?" She received two nods from the detectives. "Great! Let me go and get them."

"I think I'll come with you, if you don't mind," the taller detective said, standing. "I'll give you a hand bringing them in."

In the kitchen, Paula busied herself preparing four mugs of tea. "So, this is about Vanu? It's such a shame. He was the nicest man I ever met, and the smartest."

"We're after any information you may have, Mrs Lang.

Between you and me, I don't believe he lost control of the vehicle. My partner and I believe he was run off the road."

The thought had occurred to her, although she poo pooed any assertion by Vanu and Richard more recently. Paula wasn't stupid; she knew the ramifications of the project she had spent three years working on. There would be people, companies, governments out there who would pay large sums of money to prevent its existence, such was its global environmental impact. "You think he was murdered?"

"It's a possibility, yes." He stood back, his arms folded, as he leaned on the kitchen table. "I don't suppose you'd know why someone might want him dead, do you?"

There was something about these detectives she didn't trust. It was too late to do anything about it now. Putting the milk and sugar into the four mugs, she spoke without looking at him, while placing the mugs on a tray. "No, I have no idea."

"What is it you do over at Fisher Valves?"

"We're working on a revolutionary car valve," she replied, hoping she hadn't said too much. She picked up the tray and turned to him. "Shall we go back to the lounge?"

Paula heard a noise in the distance. She carried the tray through the hall and turned in the doorway. "Here we are, four mugs of–"

She gasped at the sight of the squat detective holding a bag over her husband's head. Her husband was desperate to breathe, but the bag sucked in and out, preventing him.

Dropping the tray of mugs, Paula made a break for the front door.

"Where do you think you're going?"

Managing to open it, she found herself running along the gravelly driveway in bare feet, the stones cutting into her flesh.

A bang preceded a force so great it knocked her to the ground.

Sucking in, trying to breathe, her back and legs felt numb. Her biggest fear was being unable to get a lungful of air. She sobbed.

Strong hands grabbed her ankles and pulled her along the gravel to her house, up and over the step into the hallway, and along the carpet into the lounge. "There! We wouldn't want you to miss this, Mrs Lang."

The taller intruder lifted her into one of their dining room chairs.

In front of her, the squat intruder put a plastic bag over her husband's head again, only this time he didn't take it off.

His body thrashed about as much as the rope tying him down allowed.

After a minute and a half, her husband's head dropped. "You bastards. Why are you doing this?"

"You know why, Mrs Lang. You're not working on 'some valve' in that workshop. You know it, we know it. But you won't be around long enough to see the rewards." He grabbed her hair and yanked her head back.

"Wait! Please."

He let go of her hair, and a moment later she couldn't see through the plastic bag over her face. Panicking, she thrashed about with her arms, but they were held back by something, hands. Squat guy must've come over to help. She couldn't move her legs.

She couldn't breathe. Everything was getting dark around her. The bag kept sucking in, blowing out, with every breath. When she called for help, it came out muffled.

Paula Lang didn't want to die; it wasn't her time. She had so many memories to make, people to meet. Tears rolled down her cheeks inside the bag, as she thought of all the opportunities that life had to offer, cut short by these two killers, her killers.

42

"Excuse me, gentlemen, while I take this." Melodi Demirci smiled at her captive before stepping outside of the barn. Out in the blackness, she put the phone to her ear.

"It's done," a male voice said. "We had to go ahead and punish the husband."

"Too bad for him. Make sure they're never found, like we discussed." She hung up, smiled, and put her mobile in her bag. Turning, she opened the barn door wide enough to creep back inside, closing it behind her.

"You told me I had a week to come up with the money. Please, I'll get it."

She nodded at Yasin, her cousin, who gagged Zuccari. "Everyone here knows you can't come up with the cash. How can a police officer earn enough to save twenty-five grand, hmm? No, you got yourself in way over your head, and now you're paying the consequences of your actions. It's a shame, because I like you, I really do. I liked fucking you, too." Her cousin, Unar, stepped up to Zuccari carrying a handheld electric circular saw.

With her captive lying on a bench, Melodi stepped up to him and grabbed his hair. "Lying to me about who you are, though, very stupid. Never lie to me, do you understand? I'm going to show you what happens to liars."

Her voice was almost drowned out by the combined noise of the saw and Zuccari screaming. Yasin held Zuccari's left arm out while his brother walked the saw closer to Zuccari's hand. "Just take a souvenir, yes? A couple of digits will do."

Added to the deafening mix of the saw and screaming was the sickening sound of metal going through flesh and bone. Melodi held Zuccari's wrist, and before her cousin sawed off Zuccari's little and ring fingers, she made sure he didn't ball his hand into a fist.

A little blood sprayed over her face, which she enjoyed, it not being hers. "This will act as a reminder, won't it? Don't ever lie to me again, understood?" Her victim sobbed, bleeding heavily from his severed digits. "You know what to do."

Yasin Inan, the elder of the brothers, stepped up to Zuccari with a red-hot poker, stabbing the stumps of his missing fingers with it, as Zuccari screamed, a feral, high-pitched sound penetrating the airwaves. "Such a drama queen. We don't want you bleeding out on us, do we? No, I've got a special assignment for you. Something you can do to help me, and help you pay off your debt. You're mine now, little piggy."

Looking at the pathetic lump sobbing, Melodi wondered how she could have found him attractive to begin with. "What was I thinking? I must have been desperate, is all I can think." But he had been good in the sack, fucking her on her desk that first time. He'd initiated it, the dirty pig. "Not the cocky guy now, are we? Look at you! It's pathetic."

Letting go of his wrist, she walked around the bench, stood in front of him. Crouching, she met his weeping eyes. "As part of repayment to me, you're my new source inside the Met, do you understand? You're going to keep me informed regularly on what's going on in the Fisher case, yes?"

Zuccari nodded through the tears. "Whatever you want."

"I hear one of your team is dating the taller detective woman."

"Luke's fucking Miller." He nodded, trying to make her feel better about it. "I'll do whatever you ask, but please can I have my fingers back. They might be able to save them." He held out his other hand.

Spotting his fingers on the straw-bound ground, she picked them up, took out a handkerchief and wrapped them, putting the parcel in her bag. "These are my keepsakes, I'm afraid. Like I said, you need a reminder not to lie to me, or go behind my back."

"I'll get you whatever you want." He sobbed again.

Melodi pulled a disgusted face, turned and left her cousins with Zuccari. "Make sure he gets home safely, okay?" She didn't wait for a reply from Unar or Yasin. They knew what they were doing, the way she liked everything done.

DAY 7
MONDAY, JUNE 18TH

43

"Show me what you've got so far." Inspector Gillan sat on one side of the table next to Travis, while Hayes and Miller stood in front, working a projector. "Do you still think this is all about the Fishers?"

"We do, sir." Hayes pressed the button on the remote control, as a picture of a bank account appeared. "We've highlighted interesting transactions in yellow, as you can see here. These are Melodi Demirci's accounts, and as you can see highlighted is an amount paid into her account from Accord. It's a hefty amount, that accounts for forty per cent of the company's profit."

Miller stepped up to the whiteboard. "And if you go back, month on month, you can see the amounts get smaller the further back you go."

"Right, so we've established a link between Demirci and Henry Curtis. You're not showing me anything I didn't already know." Gillan sat back and folded his arms.

"This is a copy of the agreement signed between Curtis and Demirci at the start of their arrangement. Demirci invested a cool million for forty per cent of the profits. And highlighted is the addendum, the added clause that stipulates once the debt has been paid back, one will have the right to buy the other out."

"And you still believe Melodi had Curtis murdered for that extra sixty per cent, is that it? You think that's a big enough motive to have him killed?"

"Sixty per cent of a growing, future multi-million-pound business is, sure. Think about it, sir, there's no risk involved. With her casino, she has hundreds, maybe thousands of customers a week trying to break the house, right? It's a risky business because luck plays a part. But not with the radio station – it has a massive audience, and it's growing every day. They had a falling out, apparently, when Henry tried to buy her out."

"I agree her DNA's all over this, but we need more proof. Melodi even said to us in the interview that she wouldn't have someone killed for owing her money. And Henry didn't. What makes you think she went through with it? She thought he was the best man for the job of CEO."

"Sure, that's what she said, except that she knew he wanted her out of the business altogether, that he wanted Accord to himself. Knowing she would stand to inherit his shares, that's one big motive right there. You wait, I bet she has someone lined up, willing and raring to go in Curtis' place. Because she ordered his murder."

"You make a convincing argument," Travis volunteered. "But like Inspector Gillan said, where's your proof of all this? You can show us accounts, money exchanges, but there's no plot to murder that I can see, just one person loaning another for a percentage of profits, and the other paying them back. I'm sorry, but I'm just not seeing it."

Hayes sighed, looked at Miller and handed her the remote. She was certain of Demirci's guilt, even if they weren't.

"We did find something else interesting." Her partner pressed the button, and another page of accounts came up.

"Henry Curtis' accounts here. The figure you see highlighted was transferred from his joint account with his husband, Colin Fisher, to Richard Fisher's company account, Fisher Valves. Just a cool million jumping from one account to the other. We'd like to know what that cash injection was for."

"You know, it seems to me that Richard Fisher's the epicentre of this case, not Melodi Demirci, as much as we all think she's a villain. I'd like you to interview Richard Fisher, find out what's going on. First his brother, and now his brother-in-law."

"And let's not forget his employee dying in a car crash on Thursday night," Hayes added for good measure. "Most probably a coincidence, but it could be something."

"It can't hurt to look into it." Gillan stood and stared down at her. "Go and find Fisher, bring him back here and interview him. If you can't find anything on him, widen your search again. Focusing on the Fishers might not have been the best move after all."

"Uniforms have been interviewing people of interest over the weekend. And so far everyone's alibis have checked out. They've spoken to Henry Curtis' employees. They still haven't located Dylan Oldham, Brandy Reid's other half. He's still out there."

Miller stepped up to the table. "We're not dealing with some psychopath on the loose here, though, sir, are we? With how accurate the gunshots were, we're dealing with someone in the armed forces, either present or ex-Forces. It could be that this was a guy, and we'll find him through our investigation, but it's more likely that someone hired him. It's going to make catching him that much harder."

"You do what you have to do, of course, Detective Miller. But we've apprehended hired killers before. They often make as many mistakes as common or garden shooters do. They almost always leave trace. How did forensics go with the footprints on Colin Fisher's chest?"

"Much the same as the glove prints found at the scene. They have records, but no match to any former crimes, sir. We have the suspect's shoe size and print. Most of the trace came back negative. Demirci's prints turned up in Colin Fisher's dressing room, though, which we thought was strange." Hayes turned off the projector, and began gathering her paperwork together.

"There could be a hundred reasons why her prints were in his room. Follow up with the brother, interview him, see what you can get. In the event it's nothing, we'll widen our search. Let's go!"

Hayes picked up her papers, waiting for Gillan and Travis to leave. "I thought we had them on our side."

"Same here." Miller met her at the door and walked with her. "Let's go get Fisher and see what he says. You never know, he might still be the key to all this."

44

Richard was the first person to arrive at the workshop for the second day in a row. He shook his head, unable to believe Paula wasn't there. After Friday, he hoped she was okay. Taking his mobile out of his jacket, he phoned her landline, which went straight through to an answer machine. "Where the hell are you?"

Figuring she must be running late, he tried her mobile, which also went to voicemail. He hated leaving messages, so he hung up, thinking she must be in her car on her way in. By the dash clock, it said: 09:36. She really was running late, abnormally so.

At the wooden door to the workshop, Richard let himself in, disabling the alarm on his way, which he so rarely had to do, he was surprised he could remember the code. After switching on the lights, the Fiesta sat there, glinting in the bright white overhead lights. "Morning, baby," he said, stroking her paintwork with affection. "Friday's the day. Everyone's going to know what you are."

With Vanu gone, and Paula currently AWOL, he wondered where Yurika and Nathan were; they should be there by now. He strolled over to the main PC on Vanu's desk and switched it on, readying the workshop for productivity later. They still had some last-minute checks to run through before the press conference.

According to Vanu, the normal day saw Yurika arrive shortly after Paula, at around half eight. Then, at quarter to nine Nathan would arrive. It was now 09:45, so even Nathan was a full hour late. Where the hell was everyone?

After trying both Yurika Ishii and Nathan Stewart, Richard gave up. Straight to voicemail every time. Richard hated leaving voicemails, so instead he hung up and made himself a mug of coffee. While he drank it, drumming his fingers on the kitchen counter, he wondered where they were. Paula, Yurika and Nathan, none of them stressed they were going to be late that morning.

Up in his office, he turned on his own computer and sat in his chair, waiting for it to load, when his mobile went off in his jacket pocket. Looking at the caller ID: Yurika. *"I'm sorry! They know everything. If you are in the office, get out now!"*

Richard blinked twice, the information not registering in his brain. The second he read the message, police sirens, multiple, rang out in the courtyard below. When he jumped up from his chair and went to the window, there were five pandas and two plain police cars down there. "Oh shit!"

In that second he realised he was screwed. Vanu was right to be paranoid; they were here to destroy his project. Whoever hired them never wanted it to see the light of day. His blue Fiesta, with its secret to tell would be silenced forever, his company discredited somehow. Sweat ran down his forehead.

He had to do something. Richard needed time to think, damn it! As he watched uniforms exit their vehicles, he remembered the key. He ran to his desk, yanked the drawer out and picked it up. "Now, where to hide you."

In a Eureka moment, he decided the best place to hide the key to the safe deposit box was down the drain in the centre of the workshop. "Perfect." With sweat pouring down his face, he took a white envelope out of the drawer, then ran down the iron steps, his feet barely hitting the stairs, until he was on the ground floor.

Outside, he heard voices calling his name.

Richard had seconds before they came flooding in and arrested him on some fictional charge. He ran to the Fiesta, opened its driver door, took out the key and bunged it in the envelope with the locker key.

With seconds to spare, he ran back to the drain, scooped down, and struggled to open the small lid, placing the envelope inside. He then replaced the lid and stood.

Pulling his phone out of his pocket, he sent Charlotte a quick text saying, 'Key in drain in workshop. Being arrested. Come get key. Important!' Then he sent it, with his back to the front door.

"Mr Richard Fisher?" a voice called.

"Yes?" He deleted the message to his sister, before turning to find a workshop full of mostly uniformed cops in front of him. His hands shook with adrenaline. The two suits who spoke were detectives by the look of it. "Who the hell are you, and what are you doing in my workshop?"

The taller of the two detectives explained that they were National Crime Agency officers, and he was under arrest for being in possession of offensive images of children. They were investigating a huge child exploitation case, and they had evidence he was involved. In addition, the suit told Richard that every computer in the workshop, office at the factory, and his home would be checked for images of child pornography.

He was being set up. Richard knew that Vanu wasn't in any car accident; he was run off the road, murdered for his involvement in the project. Suspecting foul play had befallen

Paula and Nathan as well, he turned and allowed the suits to cuff him while they read him his rights, just like in the TV programmes and movies he watched.

From her text, it sounded like Yurika had made a deal. Bitch!

Oh bugger! He hadn't told Charlotte what the key was for, or what locker it opened. He figured he would use his one phone call to tell her. It was risky, though. He didn't want to get her in trouble, because whoever wanted him out of the way was dangerous. They'd already murdered his brother, Henry, Vanu, and possibly Paula and Nathan, too. If he went to prison, there would be no one left to carry on his work.

45

Hayes pulled up outside the Fisher Valves factory office. "I preferred the Accord office." It wasn't the most pleasant of buildings to look at, although the receptionist she saw through the glass seemed attractive and smiley.

"Let's hope he's in." Miller unclipped her belt and opened her door. "I know he was lying. He knows more than he's letting on."

She had to agree. There was something off about Richard Fisher, something, dare she say, fishy about him. "I'm with you on that." After opening her door, Hayes climbed out and leaned against the car. "I know he was drunk, but his lie was so blatant."

Meeting Miller on their way to reception, she held the handle of the glass door, and let her partner through first. They were greeted by a set of perfectly straight white teeth in the form of a huge smile.

"Welcome to Fisher Valves. How may I help you this morning?" The youngster, no more than twenty studied Miller, then her.

Holding up her ID wallet, Hayes smiled back. "Hi! We'd like

a word with Richard Fisher, please. And before you ask, we don't have an appointment."

"He's not here, I'm afraid." She picked up a scrap of paper from her desk and scribbled on it. "This is the address of a workshop we own in Croydon. He spends most of his time there these days. I don't know, maybe I should be there, not here. Shall I let him know you're coming?"

On a TV at the back of reception, Sky News' crime correspondent stood in front of a car park full of police cars, the lights still flashing. Miller noticed it first. "What the hell?" Underneath the picture, words scrolled horizontally, 'Fisher Valves Boss Arrested in Child Pornography Ring'.

Hayes heard the receptionist pick up her desk phone. "Is that Richard being taken to a car?" In the distance she saw a man who resembled Fisher being escorted by uniforms. "Oh shit! It's an NCA bust."

"So? What does that mean?" Miller awaited her answer.

"It means they won't give us the time of day. If it falls under National Crime Agency jurisdiction, we can all go swing as far as they're concerned. They won't let us speak to Fisher now."

The young receptionist put the phone down and came out from behind her desk, walked up to the TV and stared at it. "This is bullshit! Richard didn't do this. He's not a paedophile." She burst into tears and ran into the ladies' restroom next to her desk.

Turning to face her partner, Hayes sighed. "I'll go and talk to her."

"Don't take too long. We need to get over there."

Hayes opened the restroom door to find the young receptionist crying, sat on a toilet in a cubicle with the door open. "Knock, knock. Do you mind if I come in?" She pulled a roll of toilet paper, broke the link and handed it to the teary-eyed girl. "Here."

"They're lying. He didn't do any of those things. I know he didn't."

"I don't believe it either," she replied, stroking the girl's hair. "I met him the other day, and he didn't strike me as the type."

"He's not. He's kind and gentle, not like they're trying to make out."

This wasn't a girl crying over her boss; she was crying for a much more personal reason. "But then again, can you ever truly know someone?" And her comment raised the girl's mascara surrounded stare. "I'm not saying anything here."

Standing abruptly, the receptionist stormed over to the sink. "What would you know? Richard wouldn't do those things they're saying. He's a lovely man, perfect. He's smart, funny, kind and generous."

"And you love him, right?" Hayes stood behind the girl, staring at her in the mirror on the wall above the sink. "Does he love you?"

"He says he does, although he's been preoccupied recently, what with the press conference coming up on Friday. He says he'll find time for me when the product's out."

Acting nonchalant, Hayes asked, "What product's that? It sounds important."

"Oh, it is. Groundbreaking, he says. Richard told me it's so environmentally important that we'll soon have every car manufacturer and consumer coming directly to us. He says Fisher Valves will be bigger than British Steel, in its day."

"I don't doubt it. Richard's a clever man." But she was no nearer knowing what the product was. "So, are you going to tell me what this magical product is?"

"Oh, I don't know that. His team in the workshop never come here. I asked Richard once, but he wouldn't tell me. He was due to give us a glimpse on Thursday. But I guess that's not happening now, not if he's in prison." She burst into tears again.

After calming the youngster, she helped her back to her desk. Hayes signalled for Miller to meet her at the door. "We're on our way over to the workshop now. Are you sure you're going to be all right here?" Given the green light, she marched over to Miller, rushed through the glass door and marched up to their waiting Peugeot. "This is about something Richard's working on. He's due to go public with some groundbreaking new product, something that will make Fisher Valves, and I quote, 'bigger than British Steel'."

Miller sat in the passenger seat beside her, closed the door and clipped her seat belt in place. "So, what's the product?"

"The receptionist's sleeping with Fisher. Even *she* doesn't know." Hayes started the car and reversed out of the space, turned and drove to the main road. "Whatever it is, though, it's big enough to murder for."

"You think this product's the link?"

Turning onto the main road, she sped up. "It was something in the way that she spoke about the product, like it was the next big thing, going to make the company billions or something. I'm willing to bet that when we find out what the product is, it'll explain these murders. Although I can't see how two radio presenters and a producer link to it."

Miller regarded her. "Are you still thinking Melodi Demirci's behind this?"

Hayes glanced over at her before turning her attention back to driving. "I don't know. We have to find the link between Colin Fisher, Henry Curtis, and Richard's employee, the one in that collision."

"You think he was murdered now?"

"This is all linked somehow, I know it is. I think the suspect murdered Colin Fisher, Brandy Reid, and Kurt Austin together to throw us off course." Her partner nodded. "Then, they went for Henry."

"And? Why?" Miller waited for her response.

"I don't know. I've no idea why they would murder Henry Curtis. If they ran Richard's employee off the road, it was to silence him because he worked on the product. Which would mean the rest of Richard's staff at the workshop are in danger. We need to find them before it's too late."

46

Charlotte finished her run on the treadmill, sweat dripping down her cheeks. Picking up her towel, she wiped her face, before sitting on the rowing machine. Rowing was the most laborious part of her ritual morning workout, but the gains were immeasurable. Next to swimming, she believed rowing was the best form of exercise: low impact and heart rate increasing. "Here we go!"

She leaned forward, took hold of the handle, and pulled back, the front wheel acting as a fan spinning away. After ten, or maybe eleven pulls she heard her mobile bleep, signalling she had a text. It could wait until she completed her workout.

Still mad at Richard, she had mulled over their row for days. He was such a pig sometimes, she wondered how they were related. How were Richard and Colin related, for that matter?

For the whole weekend she tried to get hold of Richard, wondering what he meant by it wasn't safe to be at the workshop. He told her he would call, but he didn't. Every time she phoned him, it went straight to voicemail. Richard must have known his actions would freak her out.

When she told Sam what happened at Richard's workshop, and about the van following her, he thought she was joking. And now that she had not seen a transit van all weekend, she wondered if it was just a coincidence. Maybe it wasn't one of the two vans she passed down the road from Richard's place?

After five kilometres on the rowing machine, she stopped, replaced the handle, feeling the wind in her face die down. Even the fan didn't stop her sweating. Standing, she dried her face for the third time, then walked over to the windowsill where her phone lay.

"Now you want to talk?" Seeing her brother's name on her text list, she replaced her mobile. "Arsehole!" Charlotte decided to read it after her workout, or perhaps after lunch, to make him wait, like he'd made her wait all weekend. Why was he such a pig?

Fifteen minutes on the exercise bike later, she stepped off and dried her face. Taking deep breaths, she sauntered over to the windowsill, picking up her phone. Charlotte wanted to leave it, to let him wait, but curiosity defied her. *'Key in drain in workshop. Being arrested. Come get key. Important!'* She read it three times.

Arrested? Her brother wouldn't hurt a fly. What could the police possibly arrest him for? She ran into her bedroom, whipped off her training clothes and changed into jeans and T-shirt. It was warm outside, so she ran downstairs, put on her flip-flops, and headed out the front door.

Richard was a good man. He might be an arsehole to her, but overall his heart was in the right place. If the police had evidence of wrongdoing, it was falsified evidence. On the road, Charlotte headed for the workshop. She thought having the radio on might help calm her nerves; it didn't. She switched it off.

Forty-five minutes later, she pulled up in front of the courtyard where police cars parked in every direction prevented her from getting in. On the way there, the two white transits sat doing nothing. "Shit!" There were so many police cars, their lights flashing.

Parking on the opposite side of the road, further up, Charlotte got out of her car and started walking towards the entrance to the courtyard. Before she reached it, two uniformed officers erected a cordon. "Oh shit!" She would have to jump the tape or go under it somehow. She had to see Richard.

"I'm here to see my brother, Richard Fisher," she told one uniform, who blocked her way. "Let me pass, please. I need to speak to my brother."

"Not this morning, I'm afraid, ma'am. Your brother's under arrest. He's being taken to a police station any minute now."

She screamed at him, asking him what Richard was under arrest for. "Let me through; you don't know what you're doing. He's a good man." The officer stood in her way, moving with her each time she stepped left or right. "Get out of my way! I have to see him."

Eventually she gave up, stepping back, until the uniform walked over to his colleague, talking to her. Spying Richard's hung head in the back of a panda car, she made a run for it, jumping over the cordon, the uniform calling after her.

"Don't let her through!" the uniform shouted to his colleagues.

Charlotte dodged every police officer, managing to stop outside Richard's window. When he saw her, he started shouting something. After a couple of seconds, it sounded like 'get key from drain'.

"I know, I got your text. I'll get it," she shouted through the glass.

It was only a few seconds until she felt hands on her shoulders dragging her back towards the cordon. Charlotte didn't listen to the officer telling her off; she didn't care. Richard was all she cared about. By the way he sat in the rear, his wrists were cuffed. "I'll get you a good solicitor, Richard. Don't worry, we'll have you out in no time."

"I don't fancy your chances, ma'am. Not with what he's being charged with."

Behind the cordon once more, she regarded the officer. "Why do you say that? What's he being charged with?" She didn't like his disgusted expression. "What?"

"Distributing indecent pictures of minors, for one," the uniform replied.

"And that's just for starters, eh, Sarge?" the female uniform added.

"Yeah, one sick puppy, your brother. I'd love to put him down."

No. It couldn't be, not her brother, not her Richard.

"I don't think you'll need to, Sarge. They don't like nonces in prison. The inmates will do it for us." The female officer gave her daggers, like she was Richard. "He deserves what he's going to get."

Charlotte thought about the text. *'Key in drain in workshop'*. Somehow, she had to get into the workshop, find the drain, grab the key, and get out without the police seeing. Vowing to wait for as long as it took to get that key, she turned and walked away from those opinionated, hateful police officers.

Repeating the lapel numbers of the officers to herself, she crossed the road to her car and sat inside, the doors closed. In her mobile's notes app, she typed the numbers of the lapels, telling herself she would report them to the IOPC, or whoever. "Judgemental bastards!"

In the rear-view mirror, Charlotte saw a white Peugeot pull up outside the cordon. Turning in her seat, she saw Hayes driving with her partner in the passenger seat. Charlotte still had Hayes' card somewhere.

47

Miller got out of the still running car, walked up to the uniforms in front of the cordon and showed them her ID wallet. "We're here to speak to Richard Fisher." As she put the wallet away, the uniforms glanced at one another. "What? Don't give me weird looks. What is it?"

Beside her, Hayes waited for them to speak. "We're not going to, are we?"

"Not unless you outrank the NCA officers dealing with him, no," the male uniform replied. "They've given us strict instructions not to let anyone inside the cordon."

"Like you're going to stop us." Miller turned and raised an eyebrow at her partner, grabbed the tape and lifted it. Expecting an argument from the uniforms, she handed it to him. "If you've got a problem with this, make a complaint in writing." The smile she gave was in complete contrast to her actions. "Thank you!"

Hayes walked by her side. "Thanks for doing that; I was about ready to punch him. There he is!" She pointed out a sorry-looking Richard Fisher.

Noticing the suits walking out of the workshop, Miller knew

they would have only a short window with which to speak to Fisher. She sped her walk into a run. Arriving at Fisher's window, she tapped on it. "Mr Fisher, we need to talk to you."

When he looked up, his eyes widened. "I'm being set up. They're going to plant pictures in my computers. Help!" He tried to find the window controls.

Hayes tried to open the door. It was locked.

"You! Take your hand off the car!" A suit's walk turned into a run towards them. "Just what do you think you're doing? Get away from the car."

Miller looked past the two suits at the police officers carrying items from the workshop. She pulled out her identification, not looking at them. "Detective Sergeant Rachel Miller, and my partner, Detective Inspector Amanda Hayes, Metropolitan Police."

"I'm afraid you'll need to hand Mr Fisher over to us," Hayes added. "He's a witness in a triple murder. So please, go on about your business and we'll take Fisher to our station and interview him, okay?"

She had to grin at Hayes' bravado, at the suits' faces turning redder with each word she said. Miller thought the taller suit was about to explode. He puffed out his chest, produced his ID. Reading it, she grinned at her partner.

"National Crime Agency? Why, I must apologise most profusely. Had I known it was you..." Hayes even curtsied at them, like they were royalty, the sarcasm draped over every word. "Now, if you'll open up, we'll be on our way."

The taller suit stepped up to her partner, looking down on her. "The only place you'll be going is our holding cell for obstructing justice, Detective Inspector Hayes." He grinned at the shorter suit. "Fisher may be a witness in your case, but he's one of the prime suspects in our child exploitation case. We'll be sure to let you interview him after we're done with him, okay? We'll call you."

"I'm not sure he'll be of much use to you by the time we're done with him, mind," the shorter suit said, laughing with his partner. "I'll drive."

"We'll be sure to take it up with your supervisor," Miller shouted, as the suits got in the front, with Fisher cuffed in the back. "Corrupt pieces of shit. How many kiddy porn pictures are you going to plant on this poor bastard's computers, huh?"

Hayes put her hand on Miller's shoulder, pulling her back. "Leave it, he's not worth it. We'll go over their heads at the agency. You'll be at the Job Centre by this time tomorrow."

"You have a great day now, ladies." The taller suit laughed, closing the door as their car attempted to get through the throng of panda cars.

"Let's take a look around the workshop, shall we?" Miller watched the uniforms faff about trying to move their cars for the NCA officers' car.

"Yeah, you never know, we might get lucky. The rest of his staff might be inside. It's about time we had some luck on this case."

Waiting outside the front door, a couple of uniforms carried computers and monitors. The last officer to leave told his sergeant that there was nothing left. Miller waited for him to step out of the way, poking her head around the door frame, spotting the blue Ford Fiesta in the middle of the workshop, and feeling a hand on her shoulder.

"We're locking up now, detective." A uniformed sergeant stared at her. "Don't make this any harder than it needs to be."

"Detective Hayes, you need to move your car, the NCA officers can't get out," a female constable said apologetically.

Miller stayed put while Hayes ran off to move their car. She regarded the sergeant. "What do you make of all this? It's a bit suspect, isn't it? Did the NCA get an anonymous tip-off about Fisher, or what?"

He checked there was no one listening. "I don't know for sure, but I think so. At the briefing this morning, that taller NCA officer said they'd been investigating Fisher for months, as part of an ongoing child exploitation investigation, but I don't know. When I pressed him for more info he was hesitant. The shorter officer didn't even know where the offices were for Fisher Valves, like he'd only just heard of Fisher. I didn't tell you this."

"Of course not. Goes without saying. Fisher told me he's being set up, that the NCA are going to plant pictures inside his computers."

"Nothing would surprise me with these guys. Anyway, I've got to go. Remember what I said, we didn't speak about this, okay?" He gave her a stern look, then took off towards the main road.

Miller cursed when she tried the locked door. Walking back to the car, she noticed Hayes across the road talking to someone in a car in front of their Peugeot. Her partner leaned on the open window. Intrigued, she double timed it, made sure the road was clear and ran across, arriving at the car in front of theirs. "Hey, what's going on?"

"Look who it is," Hayes said, leaning back and letting her see.

"Mrs Edwards? What're you doing here?" It might be a stupid question, Miller thought, when Fisher's sister stared at her.

"She received a text from her brother just before he was arrested. He's left something in there," Hayes informed her, pointing to the building.

"What is it? What's he left you?"

"He said it's a key, but he hasn't told me what it's for. He said he left it in a drain in the workshop, said it's important."

Miller opened the passenger door and sat, while Hayes leaned in. "We spoke to the receptionist at his other site, and she told us he's working on a groundbreaking new product that's going to change the world. You wouldn't happen to know anything about that, would you?"

"Anything you know, no matter how small, will help, Mrs Edwards. Please, your brother needs us to work together."

"I don't know anything about it. All I know is I heard Richard telling Henry that something was ready, then when I entered the room he clammed up, wouldn't say anything about it. I came by here on Friday and spoke to some woman working on a Fiesta in the workshop, and she told me they were bringing out a new valve that would change the world. I remember thinking, 'cuckoo'. It's just a valve; how life changing can that be?"

Miller looked up at Hayes. "A valve?" She concurred with Mrs Edwards. How groundbreaking or life-changing could that be? "It has to be something else."

Mrs Edwards opened her door. "We won't find out until we get that key."

She grabbed Mrs Edwards' shoulder and pulled her back in. "Where do you think you're going? We're not breaking into that building; not unless you have a key?"

Charlotte shook her head. "No, I don't, but you're detectives. It's my brother's place. I give you permission to go in there and look around. Don't you have little lock-pick devices like I see in the TV programmes?"

With a tut, Miller grumbled as she lifted herself out of the passenger seat.

"No, we can't risk anyone seeing us go in there. We'll wait until it's dark," Hayes suggested. She stared at Miller. "You're not going to get all Girl Guide on me, are you? We need to find out exactly what we're dealing with here, and getting hold of that key is vital."

"You know how many laws we'll be breaking if we do?" When she received pleading looks from both Hayes and Mrs Edwards, she sighed. "Are we ever going to have an investigation where we don't have to break the law to do our job?"

Hayes grinned. "Probably not. It's the price we pay, I guess."

"Fine! We'll come back here tonight. But if we get caught, it's on your head, understood?" She only half meant it. "What are we going to do in the meantime?"

Taking her phone out of her pocket, Hayes asked Miller to get her notepad and pen. Hayes spoke to the receptionist, introducing herself. "Listen, we need your help. We're at the workshop, and we can't see any of the staff here. Could you look on your system and give me the names of all the employees registered as working here, please."

Miller leaned on the bonnet, her pen poised. 'Vanu Parekh', 'Paula Lang', 'Yurika Ishii', and 'Nathan Stewart'. Her partner thanked the receptionist and hung up. "Good going. We've got some tracking to do this afternoon."

"They're doing a proper number on your brother. Whatever he's been making in there, it's costing people their lives."

Mrs Edwards stood and regarded Hayes over the roof. "I don't know how. Valves are valves. Why would someone want to murder another person over one. Now, if my brother invented a new kind of energy, or new breed of phone, I'd understand, but this?"

Ignoring their chatter, Miller walked to their car, sat in the passenger seat and entered 'Vanu Parekh' into the PNC. There weren't many, funnily enough. "I've got it. Not much info though. He lives a few miles away. Will take about an hour or so to get there."

"Great idea. Good work." Hayes sat in the driver's seat, started the engine.

Leaning outside, she waved at Mrs Edwards. "We'll see you tonight. Hayes will let you know what time we're getting here."

With the woman out of earshot, Miller turned to Hayes. "Let's hope it's not Mr Parekh who was run off the road."

48

Walker pulled up behind a Honda Civic at a set of traffic lights. The radio crackled in the background, with Vodicka playing with it. "I'm worried, though. I haven't heard a thing from him since I saw him at the pub. I told him to keep in touch. I even went over to his on Sunday afternoon. He wasn't home. I hope he hasn't done a runner."

The Sarge sat next to him in the passenger seat. "I hope not, too. He's still got to pass his psych evaluation and survive the inquest. He's not safe yet, and it won't look good if he does a runner."

Walker studied Vodicka in the rear-view mirror. "What's up, Voddy?"

"It's pretty quiet, how about we drive over to Zuccari's now? He might be in, you never know." She leaned forward, waiting their approval. "It's only ten minutes out of our way. No one'll miss us for half an hour, will they?"

"What do you say, Sarge? Shall I go for his house?" Walker accelerated when the light went green, spotting a good turning point up ahead.

"Let's go find him," the sarge ordered finally. "See what

trouble he's got himself into. He's such a fuck-up. I'm not sure my nerves can take the beating."

Walker drove the BMW X5 cruiser through the capital's streets until he turned onto Eastern Avenue, then onto the A12 towards Brentwood, where Zuccari had a tiny flat. They all listened out for the radio in case they were called to an incident. So far, the day had been quiet.

It took another fifteen minutes to arrive outside Zuccari's block of flats down the road from the Slug and Lettuce pub on the High Street. They passed The Gardeners, Zuccari's regular drinking hole. Walker parked on the pavement outside the building.

"Wait here with the motor, Voddy," Sarge ordered.

Walker would have suggested himself. Their vehicle housed several weapons, a battering ram and rocket launcher. If scumbag locals got their hands on their cruiser, there would be hell to pay. At least Vodicka would put up a fight if someone came along. And she would win. "We won't be long. I just want to make sure he's okay."

Acting like they were on duty, a pistol holstered on his hip, and his carbine in both hands, Sarge next to him, Walker made his way to the front doors. It always surprised him to see the level of degradation people put up with. The flats were beyond scruffy; they smelled too. The lift reeked of piss. "He's on three."

Holding his breath as much as he could, Walker joined Sarge on Zuccari's floor. He strolled towards his front door, stood, knocked.

A noise came from inside.

He waved, knowing that Zuccari used his peephole. "Come on, mate, open up. We've come to see how you're getting on." Nothing. "Open up, I mean it."

The door almost sighed, opening slowly. Zuccari's swollen

face appeared in the crack. "Look, I'm fine. Just leave me be, please?"

The Sarge took one look at Zuccari, then barged his way inside the pokey flat, putting his arm around Zuccari's shoulder and walking him through to the lounge. The big guy sat the flat owner on the sofa and stood looking down at him. "The fucking state of you."

"Gee, thanks, Sarge, you say the nicest things."

Walker could read through the bravado. His colleague and friend was petrified. He noticed Zuccari hiding his left hand, sitting on it. "Show us your hand." He could see a white bandage that had turned almost grey.

"What? Fuck off. You'll be asking to see my dick next."

"Ah no, that comes after dinner." Walker leaned over and grabbed Zuccari's arm. His little finger and ring finger were missing. "What the fuck! Who did this to you? Where are your fingers?"

Whipping his arm back, Zuccari sat on his hand again. "I had an accident with a saw, is all. They couldn't sew them back on, so the nurses disposed of them."

"It was those Turkish gangsters, wasn't it?" Sarge said.

Zuccari broke down. "They blindsided me, bundled me into a van and took me to some barn out in the middle of nowhere. They beat on me until she arrived. That's when they took out the circular saw and sliced off my fingers. Melodi's demanding I pay it off in part by keeping her in the know on your girlfriend's case, that triple murder."

"She wants a cop on her payroll, Zuccari. If it wasn't you, it'd be someone else." The Sarge's eyes flared, angry. "This fucking bitch and her thug cousins are going to get what's owed them. Where are your fingers really?"

"Melodi wrapped them up in a hanky and put them in her bag, then she left and the Inans beat the crap out of me, bundled me back into the van and dropped me off outside a hospital. I don't remember much about the latter part; I passed out, woke up in a hospital bed attached to tubes this morning. I only got home quarter of an hour ago."

"Why's she interested in Rachel's case? Why that one specifically?" Walker couldn't understand the specificity of it. "I mean, having a cop on the payroll makes sense, but why earmark a certain investigation?"

"I don't know! Maybe she had them killed and she wants to keep an eye on how the investigation's going? You tell me! You're shacked up with Miller, you must know more about it than I do." Zuccari's eyes were wild, darting all over the place, scared. "Help me, please. They said if I don't come up with the goods, they're going to take my hand next."

Sarge bent down and helped Zuccari to his feet. "You're coming with us. If you're in our custody the whole time, they can't touch you. Luke, get the door, would you?"

"Where am I supposed to stay? They'll find me."

"Not at mine, they won't." Sarge helped him out into the hallway. "And while you're recovering, we're going to pay the Inans and Melodi Demirci a little visit, aren't we, Luke? They can't get away with this kind of crap, not on one of my boys."

Walker closed Zuccari's door, cursing. He had an inkling Sarge wasn't all talk on this one; he meant every word. The fact one of "his boys" had been hurt by the Inans was a slight to his name personally. Walker was positive Sarge would find a way to repay the favour, with interest.

49

Charlotte couldn't motivate herself at home knowing Richard was being grilled by the police, the NCA, or whoever. Since arriving home, she tried to put her efforts into cleaning the house, which she failed to do, never wanting to stray too far away from her landline phone in case he called her on it. "Ring, you bloody thing, ring!"

Sat on the third stair up, she took out her mobile and checked she didn't have a missed call from him. Hopes dashed for the fifteenth time, she sighed, got up and went to the kitchen, switching the kettle on. The stress of it made her want to smoke.

In her handbag hung on one of the kitchen chairs, she reached in and felt around the bottom. "There you are!" She continued rummaging, until she found what she was looking for: a lighter. "I shouldn't, but sod it."

Carrying her packet of cigarettes outside, she slid out a Silk Cut and put it between her lips, the familiarity comforting. Back when she used to hide smoking from Samuel, she'd kept an ashtray hidden by the side of the shed. Charlotte retrieved it, sat on a patio chair, and lit her cigarette.

And boy was it worth the wait. The smoke harsh but lovely

on her lungs as she inhaled for the first time. Stupid, really, given how into exercising and eating healthy she was. Why would she smoke? It was barbaric in this day and age, yet so enjoyable. With no one else around to scorn her, she tilted her head back and drew on her "cancer stick". "Why did I ever give you up?" She knew why.

Her landline phone rang. Charlotte sat up, choked, waved away the smoke, before getting up from the white plastic chair. And when she did, the head rush kicked in. It was heaven. Woozy, she made her way through the kitchen, to the lounge.

On the sixth ring, she answered. "Richard, it's you! Are you all right? Where are you? Is the solicitor with you?" She didn't wait for him to answer.

"Lottie, I love you, but please shut up. This is important." His voice was hushed, but angry, like he was trying to be quiet, and talk. "I haven't long. They're probably listening to us right now, but I don't have a choice. That which I showed you earlier will fit in Neelkanth Safe Deposit, okay? When you go, shake off anyone following you. No one but you can open the locker, not even me now. Everything will be explained when you see what's inside the locker. I'm sorry I got you into this."

The line went quiet. "Richard? What? Neil what?" She wasn't expecting him to come out with such a vast amount of information; she was scared she didn't hear it all. "Richard?" Nothing. She hung up.

Deciding to do some investigating, Charlotte picked up her laptop. After waiting for it to load, she clicked on Google, typed in Neil Safe Deposit, and waited. "Well, shit..."

On screen came her entries; the second one down made her heart light. Google had filled in the missing word for her. Neelkanth Safe Deposit, and when she clicked on its website, one address was near Richard's workshop.

Thinking back to Richard's one comment before he so

abruptly hung up, he said, "That which I showed you earlier will fit in Neelkanth Safe Deposit." What did he mean by "that which I showed you earlier"? He didn't show her anything earlier, unless he meant the text. Glancing at his earlier message, it clicked: the key.

Her brother had hidden the key in the drain to prevent anyone from taking it, then he had to give her a cryptic clue as to what the key would fit. She had it: she would snatch the key from inside the drain, then drive to this Neelkanth place, pick up whatever he left in the locker, and that would be that. Why had he apologised to her?

Since she wouldn't be sneaking into the workshop until after dark, she wouldn't be able to use said key to open the safe until the morning. Charlotte picked up her phone, found Hayes' card, and phoned the number. "Yeah, it's Charlotte Edwards. I know where we need to go with the key once we've got it."

After a short conversation with the detective, Charlotte hung up. In a few hours she would know why her brother's and her lives were imploding. She would hopefully know why Colin and Henry, Brandy and Kurt had been murdered.

50

"This is the card the police officer gave me." Mrs Parekh handed it to Hayes.

"Thank you, Mrs Parekh. I appreciate this, I really do." Hayes exchanged sorrowful glances with the grieving wife. "I understand how hard all this is, believe me. And I know you have your suspicions about how your husband died." She sat on the sofa next to Miller, who remained uncharacteristically quiet throughout the interview.

"The truth is, Mrs Parekh, we've been having the same doubts as you." Miller's first words made Parekh take note. "You told us earlier that he'd driven out of his way?"

With tears rolling down her cheeks, the dainty Indian woman studied Miller. "I phoned him when he said he was on his way home. When I found out where he'd crashed, I couldn't get over why he would be there. It's in the opposite direction. There was no reason, unless–"

"Unless he was chased," Hayes finished. "That's what you were going to say, isn't it? You think he was run off the road?"

Her interviewee nodded. "I'm not one for conspiracy theories, detective. I'm a level-headed woman; I have to be in my line of work. Vanu could be quite paranoid at times, to the point of him scaring me, but he was very good at his job, and he told me one night how important his work at Fisher Valves was, about how when their project was complete, it would change the world as we know it, and how we'd be set for life."

Hayes regarded Miller. "Mrs Parekh, please tell us what he's working on."

"I can't do that. I don't even know myself." She sniffed. "But I know my husband, I know my Vanu; he wouldn't just make that up. And I think that project is what got him killed. He was talking about being followed, all the time, about vans following him from the workshop. My guess is, the project's almost complete, time to erase everyone associated with it. I saw on the news they picked up Richard Fisher for child pornography. They're cleaning house, that's what they're doing."

"We'll see about that." Hayes took her mobile out of her pocket and dialled the number on the card Mrs Parekh handed her. She introduced herself to the inspector. "Yeah, I'm calling with regards the Vanu Parekh collision." She listened to him, said, "uh-huh" a few times. "I see. Can I trouble you for the photos?"

When she hung up, she gave Mrs Parekh a soft smile. "He's emailing me the photos. He says they found two sets of tyre tracks on the approach to the collision site. They're looking into the possibility of the car having collided with another vehicle, only he thought it more likely a hit-and-run. He's not in full receipt of the facts."

"Why didn't he tell *me*?"

"I can't say, I'm sorry. Maybe he wanted to get more evidence."

Miller interrupted. "We ought to get going. It's getting late, we should go see the tyre tracks for ourselves, if they haven't been washed away already." She turned to Mrs Parekh. "I don't suppose you met, or knew any of your husband's colleagues, did you?"

"Only Paula, we were quite good friends, actually," Mrs Parekh replied. "Why?"

"I was just wondering if you had her address? The one we have for her might be old." Miller followed their host to a bureau. "Thank you so much; this is a big help."

"Is she the only one?" Hayes checked. "You never met Yurika Ishii, or Nathan Stewart?" When she received a negative, she nodded. "Okay, we have enough to be getting on with. Thank you, Mrs Parekh, you've been a huge help. And we'll be in touch when we know more." She waited for Miller to leave the room, then followed her out.

Outside in their Peugeot, Hayes sat in the driver's seat. The email came through from the inspector she'd spoken to. "Look, clearly two sets of different tyre tracks. I think that says it all, don't you?" She slid the key in the ignition and turned over the engine.

"Let's see what Ms Lang has to say, shall we?" Miller looked at her.

As she drove away from the kerb, Hayes mused, "So, I wonder what they're working on. It can't be just a new valve, surely. How can a valve be society-changing?"

"No, it has to be something bigger than that."

"Let's hope Charlotte Edwards finds something good in that deposit box." Hayes turned into a road on their right.

"Fingers crossed, huh!" Miller stared out of her side window.

Hayes drove them to Paula Lang's huge, secluded house. It was surrounded by acres of land, its nearest neighbour a quarter of a mile away. "Nice digs," Hayes said to Miller, who whistled at the decadence. "Look at the garden. Wow!"

"If she's been bumped off like Parekh, we can't hope for neighbours to have seen anything, can we? Look around."

Ignoring her partner's negativity, Hayes got out and joined Miller as they walked along the gravel to the front door. There were two cars on the drive. She stepped up to the wooden door and knocked.

Nothing.

She tried a further three times, each knock louder than the last, until she smashed the knocker. Trying the handle, it turned, the door opening. Hayes checked with Miller, who stood to the side and let her take the lead. Her cosh was in her hand extended before she realised what she'd done. An automatic reflex. Miller also had her metal baton out. "Paula Lang? I'm Detective Inspector Amanda Hayes. Please shout out if you're here."

Nothing.

Stepping inside, nerves on edge, Hayes walked through the house room by room. With no sign of life, no sign of a struggle, she cleared the downstairs, proceeding up to the bathrooms and bedrooms, where she expected to find someone, dead or hiding. Miller followed her upstairs.

Upon clearing the fourth and final bedroom, bathrooms included, Hayes breathed a sigh of relief at not finding Paula Lang and her husband dead. She'd found victims this way before. "There's something not right about this. Their cars are here, the front door's unlocked, her handbag and phone are on the kitchen counter, and I saw a wallet and mobile on the coffee table in the lounge."

"Shall we call it in?" Miller retracted her cosh and put it back in her suit jacket. "Although, what do we call it in as?"

That was a good question, Hayes thought, putting her own cosh away. "I don't know. Maybe we should look at their phones, call some of their friends and see if they've heard from them, but I don't think they will have."

"Do you think they're dead?" Miller asked.

Staring at the huge unslept-in double bed, Hayes agreed with Miller's question. "Like Mrs Parekh said, they're clearing house. They've tried to make Parekh look like an accident, and Richard Fisher look like a paedophile. Personally, I don't think we'll ever find Paula Lang, or the others. They're erasing all connections to the project."

"We're going to have to bypass their passcodes somehow. We need a tech head in here who'll open the phones for us." Miller led their way back downstairs, where Hayes picked up Mr Lang's phone with gloved hands.

Two hours later, Miller joined her in the kitchen after the IT guy they called in opened both phones in no time at all. SOCOs were busy dusting for prints in their coveralls. "Nothing?"

Miller said, "Nope."

"I managed to speak to Paula's sister, who said she was here yesterday afternoon having a barbecue with the family. She last saw or heard from her sister in the evening, but she did say they weren't close."

"Most of Mr Lang's contacts are work related. Although, when I spoke to one colleague, he did say he's not expecting to see Mr Lang until next Monday. He's on holiday this week. Is there any chance they had three vehicles and are on holiday?"

"Wishful thinking, Miller," she said. "Who goes on holiday and leaves their front door unlocked, and phones and wallets on tables? Nah, they're missing. If only this place had CCTV, or something."

51

"What the fuck are we doing here, Sarge?" Walker sat in the driver's seat of the black VW van. He knew full well what Sarge had in mind but didn't want to acknowledge it himself. "We've been here for hours. They're obviously not coming."

"Ah, they'll be here all right." Sarge leaned back in his seat.

Vodicka leaned in between them, sat on her knees in the back. "This is where they come every Monday night. I trust my guy. If he says they'll be here, they will. Be patient. I know how much you want to pay them back for Zuccari."

In front of them, on Walker's right, was a kebab shop, the owner of which owed protection money to Yasin and Unar Inan, Melodi Demirci's cousins. Being quiet on a Monday night, very few people were out walking along the high street, which was fortunate.

"Of course I do, but it doesn't look like they're coming, does it?" He wanted to be anywhere but here. Walker had no intention of getting involved in giving the Inans a beating; it wasn't why he joined the police force. He tilted his head back. If he had the balls, he would tell Sarge and Vodicka he was out.

"There they are!" The sarge was excited. "I brought these along."

Walker stared, dumbstruck, at the balaclava his superior handed him. "What the fuck's this? I'm not wearing a mask." He threw it back at Sarge, who glared at him.

"You'll wear it if you want to be a part of this, Luke." He handed it back. "I'm not going in that shop showing them my face and making myself and my family targets. No, we're going in there, we're going to bundle these pricks into the back of this van, we're going to drive them out to a farm I know, beat the shit out of them, and drop them off in the woods somewhere, got it? It's too late to back out now."

Reluctant, Walker sighed, put the mask on his head as a beanie hat and nodded his understanding of the situation. "And that's all you're going to do? Just beat the shit out of them, nothing more? You're not planning on taking fingers, or anything like that?"

His sergeant looked at him like he was an alien. "I'm a fucking police officer, Luke, not a thug. If I did that, I'd be no better than them. No, I'll leave it up to Zuccari to decide how far we go, though, but it won't be further than beating them up, okay?"

Alarm bells rang in his head. "Zuccari? Where is he?"

The sarge gave him a strange, "You know where" look. "He's with the others, picking up Melodi. Tonight's going to be a lovely little family reunion for them."

Vodicka, her mask as a beanie, patted him on the shoulder. "Give us a minute, then pull up outside the shop, got it? Let's go get these bastards!"

How had this all happened so quickly? Only this morning they picked up Zuccari in his flat. How was he now sat in a van waiting to hurl two psychopathic Turks into the back, ready to cart them off to God knows where to give them a hiding they wouldn't forget? Sarge gave him no time to think; he came and found him in the changing room earlier and gave him instructions to meet at his house. "Oh shit!" He stamped his feet, watching Sarge and Vodicka approach the kebab shop.

If it had been anyone other than Vodicka with Sarge, Walker would have offered to go in their place, but he knew just how tough she was. If one of the Inans gave her trouble, she would drop them before they knew what happened. "Shit, shit, shit!" He banged his hands on the steering wheel, watching his colleagues go inside.

He switched on the engine. With visions going through his mind of Vodicka drop kicking one of the Turkish brothers, while Sarge had the other at his disposal, Walker saw the shorter Vodicka tying one of the thug brothers' hands behind his back while the Turk was forced over a table. Sarge had the other one on his front on the floor, tying his wrists behind his back with plastic cable ties.

Walker got out of the van, pulled the mask over his face, and slid open the van's side door. He stood waiting for his colleagues. The first out was Vodicka; she used all her core strength to fling the Turk into the back of the VW van. Then she climbed in after him.

The Sarge came out second, wrestling with the enraged Inan brother. "Get the fuck in that van!" He punched the thug in the face, kneed him in the balls, then bulldozed him into the rear of the van, where Vodicka kicked him in the face. "Go! Go! Go!"

Walker slammed the side door, yanking it shut with brute strength, showing his colleagues how pissed off he was. "Jesus fucking Christ!" He kicked the side of the van, before hopping on the driver's seat. "Which way now?"

He followed his boss's directions out of the city, along dual carriageways for about an hour. Every now and then he would hear Vodicka keeping the brothers quiet with brute force. She was brutal, he thought, hearing one of the thugs cry.

Sarge turned to his captives in his seat. "You're in trouble now, boys. You've made a career of hurting people. Now you're going to know what it feels like." He turned back to Walker. "You're right, though, they're pussies. Bullies, huh?"

Another punch for the Inans was Vodicka's reply. Walker never wanted to piss her off, ever. Vodicka was without a doubt the toughest woman he'd ever met, in every way, emotionally, and physically. He wanted to say Rachel was, but he suspected that the shorter, squat Vodicka would have Rachel for breakfast, and the leftovers for lunch.

"It's this turning here," Sarge said, as Walker indicated left.

He drove them along a country lane, until Sarge ordered him to take another left up an even thinner track. There were potholes everywhere. Fortunately, the farm, their destination, wasn't far along the track. Walker parked outside a barn.

"Let's get these bastards out of here." Sarge jumped out of the van.

The farm's owner joined them. He opened the barn door and switched on an overhead light. "Good to see you, brother." The farmer hugged Sarge.

Walker wanted to know what Sarge's name was. The whole unit wanted to know. They'd all tried everything to find out, but their boss wanted it kept quiet. He liked the title too much to end it. Opening the side door, Walker grabbed one of the brothers' ankles, yanked him out, grinning when he landed on the dirt with his face. When the Inan brother cursed him, he accidentally kicked him in the balls. "Shut your fucking mouth."

Vodicka pulled the other brother along the dirt into the barn. When everyone was inside, the farmer closed the barn door. Walker stood back, not wanting to get involved, as much as he desired to. His mask shielded him from reprisals.

52

Charlotte saw the headlights coming a few seconds before Hayes parked up behind her. When she arrived, she saw the police cordon tape across the entrance to the courtyard, and decided to park across the road from the workshop instead. With excitement mixed with fear, she opened her door and rose slowly. The two detectives joined her. "How are we getting in?" she asked Hayes.

"With this." Hayes held out what looked like a straight paperclip.

"So you do have a pick-lock thingy. I asked you earlier and you looked at me like I was mad." She took the thin metal slither and held it. "Is it hard to do?"

"Not once you know how to use it."

"Can we do this and get the hell out of here, please?" Miller walked away.

Charlotte followed Hayes, who followed her partner.

Miller held the cordon up, allowing her and Hayes under without bending too much. Charlotte kept her eyes open for approaching cars, of which there were none. "Let's get this done as quick as we can. It gives me the creeps being here."

Miller stood to the side, allowing Hayes access to the thick wooden door. Charlotte glanced from left to right several times in the time it took the detective to open the door. "Good work," she said in genuine amazement. "I'll have to get me one of those."

Inside, she waited for the detectives to join her before she closed the door behind them. Miller brought out a pen flashlight, which lit up parts of the large workshop at a time. Charlotte was surprised to find the floor space empty. "I see they've taken everything, even the Fiesta."

Hayes took charge, using her own flashlight to find the drain in the centre of the floor. "Your brother must've put it in there. It's the only drain I can see."

Crouching, Charlotte opened the small drain cover with a bit of bother. She lifted the cover and took the torch from Hayes. "There it is!" A white envelope.

Handing the flashlight back, she tore open the envelope. "What's the second key for?" She held it up to the torchlight. "Ford. It's the key to the Fiesta. I wonder why he stuffed this in here too?" She held the locker key.

"Right, let's get out of here before someone sees the lights in the window." Miller turned hers off, headed for the door, with Charlotte following.

"Go now, go," Hayes ordered, as she followed them out onto the courtyard.

Charlotte walked fast, her shorter legs struggling to keep up with the Amazonian Miller. With an eye on the entrance to the courtyard, she saw the coast was clear and made a move towards her car.

The road was bathed in white light, as headlights lit them up.

Charlotte froze, deer-like, in the lights. "Oh shit!"

"Run to your car, Charlotte, we've got your back," Hayes ordered.

When Hayes and Miller ran, Charlotte shot into hers, fumbled with her keys, and turned on the engine. Up the road, the headlights kept her well lit.

Looking through her rear windscreen, she saw Hayes making gestures with her hand to go.

Charlotte put her foot down, hearing the tyres screeching, and shot off along the road, Hayes and Miller's car directly behind.

With adrenaline kicking in, she drove as fast as she could without crashing, until she was on Ampere Way, and then the A23, Purley Road. Then she opened up the throttle, watching the Peugeot behind swerve, blocking the van from overtaking.

53

"What're you waiting for, man? You're in this, too." Vodicka punched one of the brothers on his chin, snapping his head to the left sharply. She stood up straight, stared into him. "Well?"

With Sarge's eyes on him, Walker stepped up to the other brother – he didn't want to know which one – brought his fist back and punched his cheek, the flesh breaking, claret pouring down his face. He forgot he was wearing a ring. He gasped when he saw the welt he'd created. "Oh man! I'm so sorry!"

Sarge, Vodicka and the farmer laughed, hard. Mainly at him apologising, but also partly at Yasin Inan's bloody face, his expression solemn. "Good job. Couldn't have done it better myself. But I think now's the time to start proceedings."

Vodicka's phone rang. Walker listened, knowing the new information wasn't good. How could it be? Zuccari was on his way here with the rest of the unit. "And?"

"Five minutes, and your darling cousin's going to be joining you," she said to the gagged prisoners, who'd both received quite a beating already. "And we've got a surprise for you two. You're going to love it." If her mask were off, they would have seen her grinning from ear to ear.

"It's time." Sarge took a knife out of his pocket, walked behind the Inans in turn and cut the cable ties. "You boys want out of here, you've got to come through us."

Walker saw the fear in their eyes; they weren't getting up.

"But here's the rub, if we catch you, we're going to hurt you, do you hear me? And it won't be a subtle beating. No, it won't be as soft as that. So, who's going to get up first? Huh?" Sarge kicked the brother on the left. "No? What, you're not a tough guy now?" He kicked the other one. "I heard you're big tough guys like me, but clearly you're not."

They sobbed at the thought of being beaten up. One screamed into his gag.

Stepping up to the one on the left, Sarge picked him up, withdrew his fist and punched the Turk so hard, he sent him flying over a bench, onto the hay-strewn floor. "Where do you think you're going?" He found the prisoner and kicked him in the face. "That felt good. You should give this a go, Luke. It's cathartic. Should've done it a long time ago."

"Come on, man, he's had enough, look at him." Walker just wanted out of this nightmare. He wasn't some vigilante wannabe cop. He joined the police to help people, not beat the crap out of them.

"I say when they've had enough, not you." Sarge stepped up to the second brother, still sat on a rickety wooden chair, and punched his cheek. "Come on, don't just stand there looking pretty. Kick him in the head or something."

Walker stared down at the semi-conscious Turk. "I'm sorry!" He swung his boot forward and cracked the guy's face. "There, happy? It's done. Let's put them back in the van and dump them somewhere, yeah? No harm done."

"Don't be an idiot. Help me put them back in their chairs for their cousin's arrival." Sarge stooped over, grabbed the thug, and put him in the chair with little effort.

The farmer opened the wooden door, bathing the barn in white light.

"See that, you piece of crap? Your cousin's here. Now we can start the reunion." Sarge spat at the brothers.

Walker made out people in silhouette form, one pushing another, until he saw the one being pushed was Demirci. And Zuccari had already had fun with her; she was bleeding.

"There! Sit down on this chair, love," Zuccari said through his mask.

Walker glanced at the farmer, the only guy not wearing a mask, who looked nervous. Zuccari's stance and demeanour was intimidating. Walker noticed his "friend" was wearing gloves, but nothing could disguise the fact two of his fingers were missing on his hand. "Take it easy." He was ready to jump on Zuccari.

"Easy? You want me take it easy when these fuckers are here?" Zuccari's eyes blazed at him through the holes in his mask. He reached behind him and produced a pistol.

The atmosphere in the barn changed.

Sarge, Vodicka and his two other colleagues gasped, before Sarge tried to intervene. "What the fuck're you playing at? Put that away before you get someone killed, you sick maniac."

Zuccari whipped round and pointed the pistol at Sarge, who froze. "I won't be needing this anymore." He pulled the mask off. "Or these." One by one, he pulled his gloves off, training his pistol on Sarge. "You thought we're here to beat these bastards up? Oh no, we're here for a lot more than that."

Melodi Demirci stared up at him. "You're police officers. Do something!"

"Hey mate, how about you put that gun down, huh?" Walker stepped closer to him from behind. His charge turned to face him, the pistol pointed at his chest. "I know you're pissed off with these two, and I get it. But please don't do anything you'll regret. We're not past the point of no return yet."

"Oh no?" Zuccari marched forward, put the muzzle of the pistol against the Inan brother on the left, and pulled the trigger.

The Inan brother fell backwards in his chair, a red mist hanging in the air.

Stunned silence filled the barn.

Zuccari spat on the corpse of his tormentor. He raised the pistol at Sarge once more. "He took my fingers with a circular saw. He deserved it."

Everyone present, including Walker, knew they were in shit, accomplices to murder. Angry, Walker rushed Zuccari from behind, grabbed him around his neck and put him in a stranglehold, making sure he grabbed his gun hand with his free arm. "You fucking psycho." He crushed Zuccari's windpipe until his colleague collapsed unconscious on the hay-covered ground.

"You killed my brother." Yasin Inan glared at him. "You're bent coppers. Murderers. You're all going down for this."

"Yasin, do us both a favour and shut the fuck up." Demirci tried to kick her cousin, but her restraints prevented it. "Don't listen to him. We won't say a word about this, ever. I'm a businesswoman. Let's talk terms and conditions, yes? We all want to get out of this alive, and not in prison, don't we?"

Sarge took the gun from Walker. He stepped up to Demirci. "Do you really think we're taking advice from the likes of you? You're scum! We decide what happens from here."

"You know what happens from here," Walker shouted. "We have to call this in, right?" He didn't like the glares he received from his team. Sarge whipped his mask off. "Sarge? What're we even thinking about this for? Call it in!"

"Don't be so fucking stupid, Luke. How can we? We're all a

part of this now. We're all equally as guilty as Zuccari. What we have to do is damage control."

There was a long silence.

Every free person in the barn glanced at the others expectantly.

"There's nothing for it, Sarge, we have to get rid of them."

Walker couldn't believe how cold-hearted Vodicka sounded, nonchalant, like it was "no big deal". "Voddy, no. You don't mean that. You're a cop, for fuck's sake."

"We don't have a choice, Luke, do we? We can't let them go. We can't call it in, or we all go down, and I for one, am never going to prison, especially not for someone else's mistake. I like Zuccari, but I'm not going to prison for him, got that?"

"Then we make a deal with them, never to take this further, right, Melodi?"

"Yeah, absolutely. Anything to help the situation."

"Fuck that!" Yasin growled. "Fuck you, Melodi. No deal. I fucking kill all of you."

"Yasin, shut up! What did I just tell you. Either shut up, or I swear I'll kill you for them, and make a deal for just myself."

Walker spent the next fifteen minutes trying to talk Sarge, Vodicka and the rest of his team out of killing them. The only person on his side was the farmer who hadn't expected dead bodies on his property. Sarge took the farmer aside, gave him a talking to.

When the Sarge returned, he whispered in Vodicka's ear, who held the pistol to Yasin Inan's forehead and pulled the trigger.

As his brain's sprayed the air, Yasin's head slumped forward.

"I'm sorry! I had no choice." Vodicka held the pistol by her side.

54

Hayes swerved to the left, keeping the transit van behind them. Mrs Edwards drove at speed in front of her, but on a winding country road, they would all come a cropper eventually. She had to do all she could to give Fisher's sister a chance to slip away. Miller held on tight next to Hayes. "Hold on."

She slowed, while swerving from left to right, keeping the van in check, watching as Mrs Edwards' car vanished. Behind her, she could sense the driver's growing frustration by how he kept trying to get by her. "Oh shit!"

The van sped into the back of her, as their Peugeot veered to the left, giving the transit the chance to pull up beside her.

Glancing to her right and up, the passenger window wound down and a pistol appeared. "Down! Get down!" Hayes screamed.

A bright flash preceded her side window smashing into tiny shards. Hayes looked away, trying to concentrate on the road ahead, which became an embankment.

"Look out!" Miller screamed.

Before she knew what was happening, Hayes drove their car

along the embankment, narrowly missing trees and bushes, until she managed to slam on the brakes.

"Holy shit! That must've been what happened to Parekh," Hayes observed, unclipping her seat belt and opening her door. "Are you okay? You're not hurt?"

Miller was up and out before Hayes received a reply. "We're in trouble. They've pulled up over there. Come on, we've got to get out of here."

Listening to her partner, Hayes stared into the distance, observing the rear red lights of the transit. "Oh crap!" She instinctively went into her pocket for the cosh, which she extended. "Let's call for backup."

"It's too late for that." Miller took her butterfly knife and bottle of mace out of her suit jacket pocket. "Here, you take this. I've got the knife and cosh."

"Right, let's move!" Miller took control, unsheathing the blade.

They made so much noise running through the woods, hoping the van occupants wouldn't catch up with them. If they did, Hayes knew they would put up one hell of a fight. The fact their pursuers had guns didn't bode well. "Stop! Shh!"

In the blackness, she listened to twigs snapping and bushes rustling. Hayes knew which direction their aggressors were heading: towards them. "Quick! Behind this tree." She snuck behind a tall, wide oak. "If we keep running, they'll win."

"We make a stand here, now," Miller agreed.

With her partner stood next to her, Hayes listened to them approaching. They weren't the brightest of assailants, which was probably why they left the door open at Paula Lang's home, together with their mobiles and wallets. Stupid. And why one of them stuck the muzzle of a pistol in the back of Henry Curtis' head. Dumb.

"They're around here somewhere. Split up."

Hayes waited as one walked off in a different direction. The moonlight was enough to make out Miller's features. The remaining pursuer was in front of them, right by their tree; she could hear him breathing. She took a step out.

A twig snapped beneath her shoe. "Oh sh–"

Raising her bottle of mace, she aimed it at the guy's face and pressed the button, liquid firing in his face. He fired the gun wildly a couple of times.

While he screamed, Hayes stepped forward, and kicked him in the balls, using the cosh to force him to drop the pistol.

When he pitched forward, Hayes used the cosh to sweep away his legs, putting him on his back. Stood above him, she whacked his legs a couple of times with the cosh.

Miller jumped on him, turning him over onto his stomach. She read him his rights while cuffing him.

The cuffed assailant screamed that his eyes stung, his voice loud, high.

"You're not going anywhere."

A bright flash in the distance preceded a dull thud in the tree next to her. Hayes instinctively looked for the gun their cuffed guy had, but couldn't find it. She heard Miller make a move. "What are you doing?" Her whisper was angry.

Before Miller replied, her partner ran into the darkness. "Over here, dickhead."

"Miller, no!" She wanted to go after her partner, but she couldn't leave her captive. His legs weren't bound, so he could still be a menace. "Stay where you are."

Sweeping her flashlight over the ground, as she heard another gunshot. "Miller!" Worried, Hayes found the pistol, and when she turned around, heard a scuffle, as her bound assailant ran into the woods.

55

"We don't have to do this, Sarge." Walker took a step towards his boss. "Look, she's just a woman. We can do a deal with her, yeah? No one else has to die tonight."

Sarge had a pistol pressed against Demirci's forehead.

"Oh, and we all live happily ever after, is that it?" Zuccari shouted from behind.

Walker turned and pointed at his "colleague". "You, shut your fucking mouth! You've already done enough damage. You really won't be happy until they're all dead, will you?" He received a defiant stare from Zuccari. "Yeah, well, you'll be digging three graves yourself, you piece of shit. Don't be expecting my help."

"Enough, Luke." Sarge glared at him. "None of this matters now. We have to do this. She can't live, not after tonight. And besides, this is no worse than she's done to others. This bitch has had more people killed than I've had hot dinners, haven't you, love?"

Demirci shook her head. "Not me, uh-uh. I've not had one person killed. Why would I? I'm a businesswoman, not a gangster. If someone owes me money, I don't have them killed.

Where's the sense in that?" She tried to lean forward, to grab his attention. "I play up to that image on purpose. It never hurts to have people running scared of you, but I swear I never had my cousins kill anyone."

"And what about his fingers?" Walker noticed her close her eyes. "Your cousin sliced them off, and Zuccari says you wrapped them up in a hanky and put them in your handbag before you left him with these psychos."

"I never said I'm Mother Theresa," Demirci said, leaning back. "I said I've never had anyone killed, not that I've never hurt anyone. It comes with the turf, but I've never had to order anyone's death because everyone pays, sooner or later. How quickly they pay back determines how many body parts they walk away with."

Sarge raised his eyebrows. "You see? Would this world be any worse off without her?" He pulled back the hammer, his finger on the trigger.

"Hang on, Sarge, let Luke do it," Zuccari suggested. "I don't trust him, and I won't until I see his hands bloody. Give him the gun, let him do her."

Walker threw his hands up, took a couple of steps back. "Hey, no fucking way am I doing that. Forget it! If you want to blow her brains out, one of you can."

When he took another couple of steps back, he bumped into Vodicka, who glared at him. "Or let one of them do it. I'm not touching that gun, got it?"

Sarge turned the pistol on him. "You'll do as you're damn well told. I'm the sarge here, not you. If I say you're blowing her brains out, you'll do it, or we'll bury you with her, Luke. Am I clear? You either put a bullet in her, or I put a hole in you."

"This is fucking ridiculous. Look at you all, acting like the thugs you swore to protect the public from. I'm ashamed of you,

Sarge," chirped the farmer. "And when this is dead and buried, I want you all off my property."

Turning the gun on the farmer, Sarge ordered him to shut up. "You won't see us again after this night, ever. But we need to finish it." Sarge handed Walker the pistol. "Take it! Shoot her in the forehead, or I'll put one in *your brain*, got it?"

"You don't need to do this, Luke. It's not too late to let me go." Demirci's eyes pleaded with him not to kill her.

Walker narrowed his eyes, unable to believe how his evening had turned on him. He was now accessory to a double murder, about to commit his first. He'd have laughed if someone told him he would murder someone tonight. He took hold of the pistol.

"For fuck's sake, just kill her already," Zuccari hissed. "Put her out of her misery, before I do it for you."

When he raised the gun at Demirci, she cried. Her eyes begged him not to kill her. His hand shook. Every particle in his body defied him, preventing him from pulling the trigger, knowing he was committing a damnable offence. And just because he didn't go to church, didn't mean he was a non-believer. Thou Shalt Not Kill, simple as that.

"Please, you don't have to do this. You're better than them."

"Shut up, you scum," Walker growled, pulling the hammer back. "You had those radio presenters killed, didn't you? You had the owner murdered."

With tears streaming down her cheeks, she shook her head again. "I didn't. I needed Henry Curtis. He was making me lots of money; why would I have him killed?"

Walker was confused. "Then why have Zuccari on the payroll snooping around Rachel's case? Why the interest in it?"

"Because I'm their prime suspect. It pays to have ears close to an investigation when you're that deep into a case. I needed to know what was going on. I didn't pay to have them killed, Luke, you have to believe me."

Confused, the gun started shaking in his hand.

"This is boring, give me that," Zuccari hissed. He grabbed the gun out of Walker's hand and stepped towards Demirci. "Lights out time, bitch!"

Walker rushed at Zuccari, too late, as his "colleague" pulled the trigger and the shock of it made Melodi Demirci's body fall backwards. "No!" Too late, he stared down at the dark red mark in the centre of her forehead, and the blood pooling around her head.

"Now that's over with, can we get on with burying these scumbags? I've got plans tonight." Vodicka grabbed a shovel off the wall of the barn and launched it at Walker. "You've done nothing to help so far, get shovelling."

He couldn't believe only half an hour earlier, he'd have laid his life on the line for her. Now? He wanted to pummel that face. Respect to hatred in the space of a night. How was that even possible? His whole unit were now accessories to a triple murder.

56

Breathless, Miller stopped and leaned against a tree in the dark, the woods lit by moonlight only. Sight wouldn't do her any good here, hearing was her best friend. Picking up rustling behind her, she held her breath, listening.

A twig snapped. Her attacker mumbled a curse.

His footsteps grew louder.

With her butterfly knife in one hand, and cosh in the other, her weapons wouldn't stand for anything if he managed to fire his pistol. Talk about bringing a knife to a gunfight!

When she thought he was close enough, she followed him around the tree, until she stood behind him. Seizing her chance, Miller pulled the cosh behind her, ready to swing through him, when he caught her off-guard with a back kick to the chest.

Being thrown back, and falling, the shock made her drop her knife.

On the mud on her back, she readied herself for his assault.

Deep, fast footsteps caught her attention.

Her assailant stared down at her, his pistol trained on her.

The fast footsteps made him look up. "What the hell is–"

Miller swung her cosh along the ground, as it caught his

shin. A loud groan preceded a body leaping through the air, landing on her assailant. She got to her feet in record time, only noticing the bound hands behind Shin's back. It was the other assailant!

"Miller!" Hayes' voice reached her before her partner did. When Hayes arrived, she was out of breath. "Are you okay? I was scared there for a minute." Her partner stepped up to the fallen duo. "Drop it! Don't even think about it!"

Beneath Bound Guy, Miller's assailant dropped the gun. Hayes stepped in and kicked it out of the way. "Right, does one of you want to spill why you're trying to kill us? Come on, don't be shy. Because one way or another, we're getting answers from you two geniuses. Honestly, Miller, how thick can you get?"

"Fuck you!" spat Bound Guy, who lay on top of the other. "We're not telling you shit!" He yelled in the other's face, until Miller's assailant rolled him off. "Let us go, or we're going to fucking kill you."

Miller glanced at Hayes and smiled. "Yeah, I don't know if you're keeping up with current events, but you're in no position to bark orders at us." She took out a second pair of cuffs, bent down and put them around his ankles roughly, making sure they hurt. "You big dummy. Whoever hired you to kill all these people, I hope you gave them a discount; you're the worst hitmen ever."

Bound Guy told her to fuck herself once more.

With a sigh, she said, "And you set the bar for originality so high as well. Come on, Hayes, let's take these two geniuses back to base." She bent over and helped Bound Guy up. With cuffs around his ankles, he walked slowly, which gave her partner time to get her assailant to his feet. "Easily the dumbest suspects we've ever seen."

"I sure can't think of any dumber," Hayes agreed behind her.

"Why do you keep calling us dumb anyway?" Ankle Cuffs asked.

Miller pushed him towards the upcoming road, keeping his gun trained on him. "It's like this: if you're trying to off people, making it look like they've disappeared, don't leave their mobile phone, wallets and bags lying around the house."

"And remember to lock the door," Hayes added.

Miller stepped sideways when Ankle Cuffs turned around. "I told you to lock that fucking door, you idiot!" He tried to hurl himself at his partner in crime.

Whipping out her cosh, Miller swung the metal bar at his shins, putting him on the earth. "Don't try any tricks. There's nothing you've got we haven't seen before."

Hayes' captive stared down at his partner. "I did lock that fucking door."

"No, you didn't." Miller bent down and helped Ankle Cuffs to his feet again. "Oh, and another thing: don't stick your gun in the backs of victims' heads either. It leaves a mark, one that pathologists can identify as gun muzzles."

Hayes' assailant regarded her, then his partner. "Hang on. I didn't put my gun to the back of anyone's head."

"No, but your partner did. When you murdered Henry Curtis, you left an imprint of your muzzle. Our pathologist noticed the circular mark in his hair. I mean, considering he was supposed to be committing suicide, that was a big clue for us. That and the wobbly handwritten suicide note."

"And don't forget the cuts," Hayes chirped.

Miller reached their car, opened the rear door, and helped Ankle Cuffs inside. Once he was secured, she went round and helped Hayes seat her assailant. "Seat belts, boys. The next stop's a cell for you two."

Taking the keys from her partner, Miller started the engine, reversed out of the woods their attackers forced them into, and accelerated onto the country road. The hitmen in the rear seats were secure behind a metal grid partition. In the mirror, all she could see were two dark blobs, with mesh in front of them. "That was a sloppy job."

"You were saying, about the cuts?" Ankle Cuffs asked.

"They were too deep, too clean," Hayes stated, turning in her seat. "The pathologist knew almost immediately Henry Curtis didn't kill himself, like you wanted us to believe. She said slicers never cut that deep. You cut him to the bone."

Breaking her concentration, Miller swerved when Ankle Cuffs launched himself at his partner in the back of their car. He kept saying how he told him not to cut so deep. Ankle Cuffs' partner retaliated, saying at least he didn't stick his gun in the back of Curtis' head. She smiled at their argument, enjoying it. The more they argued, the easier it would be to get a confession out of one of them, officially, not in the back of their car.

"Will you two please shut up!" Hayes turned to face the windscreen. "I've only known you five minutes, and already you're grating on my last nerve. Stop talking!"

To Miller's surprise, they followed orders. Ankle Cuffs went back to his place.

"You don't know why we're here, do you?" he asked finally. "All this superiority you think you have over us, and yet you don't know why we're here. Calling us idiots, yet we know what you're after."

"We know enough," Miller retorted, focusing on the road ahead.

"If you knew what it was, you wouldn't be bothering with us. You'd be going after the real villains." He leaned in closer to the security grate.

"We're investigating the murders of two radio presenters and their producer," she said into the rear-view mirror. "We have you both in cuffs. Tomorrow morning ballistics will test your guns, and when they prove to be the weapons used to shoot Colin Fisher, Brandy Reid and Kurt Austin, you'll be going to prison for a very long time."

"Yeah, and who paid us to kill them? But more importantly, why? I can't wait for you to find out why we're doing this, because then you'll have to alter your perception, believe me. This is so fucking huge, no one will believe it."

"I wish you'd shut up." Miller glared at him in the mirror. "In fact, get back! I'd advise you to shut up now, before you incriminate yourself any further. We'll have plenty of time to discuss all of this tomorrow. Right now, we have our suspects in custody. That's enough for one night."

It was getting late. All Miller wanted to do was get to the station, process these two morons, go home, and wait for Luke, who was due to stay over again. A good night's sleep would do wonders. Tired, she pulled into the police station car park.

DAY 8
TUESDAY, JUNE 19TH

57

Walker opened Miller's front door quietly. As he closed it, he thought maybe he should have gone straight home. He couldn't get the images of the Inans being shot out of his mind, or the look of shock in Melodi Demirci's dead eyes. He wouldn't get any sleep tonight.

Having dug a hole deep enough and wide enough to bury their three victims, Zuccari and Sarge filled it in, forever covering their murderous secret. The Sarge told everyone to relax, that it wouldn't come back on them, it couldn't. At least he had some help digging from the farmer, while the rest of the squad chatted amongst themselves.

The scariest thing about the whole experience was Vodicka's change of personality. In one night she went from being a jovial, fun member of the team to his least favourite. He didn't need to be psychic to know she wanted him to join the Inans and Demirci. Her evil eyes haunted him more than anything else.

In the lounge, he found Rachel lying on the sofa, asleep, her mouth open enough for the smallest of snores to escape. He held the TV remote and switched it off. When he turned back, she was smiling up at him. "Hi! Sorry I'm so late."

Rachel sat up, patted the cushion behind her, and he wedged her between his legs. She settled into him, his arms wrapped around her. "How was your day?" He needed something, anything to take his mind off his awful night.

"Eventful." She stroked his hand. "We caught the shooters."

The news was big enough for him to force her to turn and face him. "How'd you manage that? And how do you know they're your shooters?"

She filled him in on their brush with danger in the woods, how the shooters waited for them outside Richard Fisher's workshop. Rachel also filled him in on the fact one of them wanted to sort out a deal; apparently, he was worried for his own safety, that his employers would want him dead now that he was in custody.

"Wait! You're not, though, are you?" He thought he could tell by her expression that she had no intention of dealing with him. But he didn't know her that well; they'd only been seeing each other for a week. "You can't deal with them. They're your shooters."

"Relax, no way! The only problem we have is we still don't know what this is all about. The shooter says when we find out what it is, we'll know why they've gone to such measures to silence Fisher. He knows what it is."

Knowing full well how hard getting a confession from suspects was, Walker didn't bother continuing. "So, where do you go from here? Is it case closed, or what?"

"Inspector Gillan will want us to carry on the investigation, but Hayes reckons the superintendent will insist on closing us down, since we have the suspects in custody. We'll wait on forensics and ballistics to come back to us tomorrow. And we'll find out the shooters' names, too. They haven't even given us that."

"Sounds like you've got a couple of hard cases there."

"Yeah, and dumb. You wouldn't think it to look at them, but they're hitmen, like real, as God is my witness, hitmen. I thought they'd be smarter." She smiled at him. "What about you?" Rachel rubbed her eyes. "Here's me going on about my day? How was yours?" The question lingered between them.

"Fine!" He lay back and stared at the ceiling, Rachel between his legs, lying on him. "Pretty quiet, actually. Nothing major to report."

He should tell her. It affected her every bit as much as it affected him. Rachel was dating a triple murderer; well, accomplice to a triple murder at the very least. He held her tight, stroking her arms. She smelt amazing. He could tell she'd showered and washed her hair.

The scariest part of this whole mess wasn't Vodicka's stare. It was the thought of losing Rachel. But he always thought negatively when he liked a woman, always thought something bad would happen to spoil it.

58

Richard Fisher lay on the only bed in the small cell, listening to the ominous prison noises. When he woke up that morning, prison was the last place he would have guessed he would be staying overnight. No one could have prepared him for being locked in a room against his will. And he wasn't even in a real prison; it was a holding jail for suspects awaiting trial.

Since being arrested earlier in the morning he'd been questioned, grilled for hours about his involvement in a child pornography ring, a paedophile ring. The National Crime Agency officers showed him vile photos of vulnerable children. They made him want to be sick, but apparently they were located on the PC in his workshop office. What a coincidence, yet they said not. According to the two lead officers, they'd had him on their radar for a couple of years, and it took them this long to act on solid CI testimony.

The NCA officers finally relented, disappeared. Then the interrogation room door opened and in walked two more suits. Neither identified themselves, except to show him the documents he'd uploaded to the Intellectual Property Office's portal. They asked him where the prototypes were, but he refused to answer, knowing this was all about his product, not some smokescreen kiddy fiddling ring. They were trying their best to smear his name in case the prototype found its way into the public sphere. And what better way than to make out he was "into children"?

Richard couldn't do hard time like some common or garden thug; he was a scientist. He used his brain, not his limited brawn. No, he had to get out of there. The problem was, he didn't know where he was.

He could hear the other inmates shouting. Lying on his back, in prison issue blue trousers and blue shirt, he heard someone calling to him, saying they were going to bash his paedo brains in. "Wait until breakfast, we're going to eat you alive," the voice called.

If he didn't get out of there soon, he believed every word the con said. If he was getting this kind of treatment now, in a holding prison, what would his life be like in a bona fide category A prison? Hell.

An observation slat opened. Two eyes stared at him through the hole for a couple of seconds, before the slat closed. Suicide watch. They were afraid he might try to kill himself. But he wasn't about to do that, and how could he if he wanted to? There was nothing he could use, no ceiling beams to tie his bed sheet to; no knives or sharp pointy objects he could stab himself with.

The voices outside grew in intensity and volume. Richard listened. It sounded like a riot going on outside. When he heard the lock in his door, he stood and waited for the door to open. Fight or flight? He wanted to flee.

"Remember what we said," the guard said in the doorway.

When the guard stood to his left, two muscular prisoners stepped inside his cell, both had bald heads, and nothing by way of necks to speak of. Their prison-issue shirts were unbuttoned because they were too small for them. "No! Guard, you can't leave me in here with them, please." His plea was ignored.

The door slammed shut, the guard locked him in. "Good luck, Fisher. You're going to need it." His laugh ricocheted around the small cell. "He's all yours, boys!"

He had nowhere to go. Richard backed up against the wall, his eyes darting from left to right. He couldn't have been more afraid if he tried. "Please, you don't have to do this."

"It's nothing personal, old man. Stand still, and this will be over quick. If you fight us, we'll make sure it hurts, bad." The taller of the prisoners was convincing.

Colin once told him, when outnumbered in a fight, go for the biggest one first, that way, if you were lucky enough to knock him out, the others would back off. When they were within arm's width, he lunged at the taller meathead, his fist connecting with the guy's already-broken nose. "Ow!" He hurt his hand.

The shorter of the intruders grabbed him and put him on his front. Richard lay with the muscular prisoner's full weight on top of him. "Please, we can talk about this."

"Grab the sheet!"

The prisoner whose nose he'd hit whipped the sheet from his bed, scrunched it into a long thin rope and handed it to his partner in crime.

Richard felt the sheet around his neck, as his attacker – his murderer – twisted the sheet, which squeezed his neck. He couldn't breathe. The pressure inside his head unbearable, Richard flapped his arms in the air, trying to find the sheet.

The prisoner kept winding the sheet, the tougher it became, the harder he wound it. Richard tried screaming, but nothing came out. The pain in his neck grew to such intensity that he wished he were dead. *Please let it be over!*

"One last twist," said the prisoner on his back.

The last thing Richard Fisher heard was the prisoner

mopping up his own blood, laughing. It was a sinister, deep, bragging laugh. At the next suicide watch, the guard who'd let his killers in would find his body attached to the sheet, which would in turn be tied to the door handle. It didn't matter, though, his death would never be investigated, or even called into question. His suicide would be seen as admission of guilt, that Richard Fisher, the scientist, inventor, engineer, liked the company of little children.

59

Miller awoke to Luke's comforting arm around her. She lay on her side, her arm draped over his chest. When she looked up to see his handsome face, he was awake, his eyes open, staring up at the ceiling. "Hi!" She put her palm to his cheek.

When he failed to reciprocate her smile, she sat up and stared down at him, his eyes avoiding hers. A single tear rolled down his cheek, which he wiped away, as though the act itself might erase it from her memory. "Luke, baby, what's wrong?"

Luke sat up quicker than she could pull him back. He turned away from her, bent over, and picked up his artificial toes. Wrapping her arms around his shoulders, she kissed the side of his neck. "Baby, please tell me what's the matter? Is it something I've done?"

He turned to her, his eyes sad. "It could never be you. You're perfect."

Perfect wasn't a word she would use to describe herself, but who was she to argue? "What then? Tell me. I might be able to help."

Turning his back on her again, he sniffed. "We're done for, all of us."

She didn't like the sound of his voice, the tone. "What do you mean? Who's done for? Why?" Did she want to know?

He whirled round, faced her, took her hands in his. "It's so unfair, after we've just met. Babe, I'm going to be going away, soon, and for a long time. I'm so sorry!"

"Luke, I'm confused. Going where? Why? With who? Who's we? Talk to me, please. I'm a great listener." She could tell he wanted to tell her.

"I can't tell you, I'm sorry. They'll kill us both."

"Now you have to tell me." She put both palms on his cheeks. "Something happened earlier, didn't it? That's why you were late. Just tell me, Luke, I can help."

"How? Nobody can help me? We killed three people tonight."

Miller felt her mouth open. "Huh? What do you mean? How? Did a job go wrong? If it did, the inquest will exonerate you, surely? You'll be suspended until then, but–"

Luke stood up. "No, you don't get it. My team, we executed three people tonight, in cold blood. They were tied to chairs, for fuck's sake; they had no way of defending themselves. Zuccari just let the first have it, shot him in his forehead."

Not knowing how to react, Miller recoiled at this fantasy. "What? No, this is some sort of bad joke, right? Haha, Luke. Very funny. Your sarge, your friends, they wouldn't risk their jobs by executing people. Good one, you almost had me."

"It's the truth, Rachel, believe me. Zuccari shot one of the Inan brothers. Then Vodicka shot the other brother, and the Sarge tried to force me to shoot Melodi Demirci, but I couldn't do it. I dropped my gun, and Zuccari did it for me. Then Voddy threw me a shovel and I dug a grave big enough for all three of them."

The Hard Way

Stood on the other side of the bed, Miller felt like she'd been punched in the gut. Her boyfriend was an accomplice, a complicit participant in a triple murder. If he wasn't joking, she had a murderer in her flat.

"Rachel, what're you doing?" He rushed around the bed towards her. "Baby, don't run off, I need your help. I'm in deep shit." He grabbed her shoulders, stared into her. "Please, baby, help me. What am I supposed to do?"

Feeling hemmed in, naked in front of him, she looked into his tearful eyes. "You have to tell your superintendent." She saw the sorrow in him. "You're telling me the truth, aren't you? This isn't a joke?"

"I promise you, it's no joke. They're dead. Buried on a farm somewhere. Sarge, Voddy, Zuccari, they're all going to get away with it."

"Promise me you had nothing to do with it, that you didn't execute one of them yourself." Somehow just knowing that put her mind at ease. "Please, Luke, promise me."

"I've already told you, they tried to force my hand, but I couldn't pull the trigger. Zuccari swiped the gun from me and shot Demirci in her face. I'll never forget her dead eyes. And I can't go to my Super, the team are going to be keeping an eye on me from now on. Voddy wants me out of the way, I can tell. And only yesterday we were talking about going to France for a weekend. I can't believe how quickly things can change."

Miller's head was spinning. "Luke, go and wait in the lounge, would you? I need time to think."

"Please don't leave me, Rachel, I'll do anything. I love you!"

She moved to the bathroom, closing and locking the door.

He loved her? Sat on the toilet, she realised he meant it. And on top of that, she loved him, too. How cruel life was. They'd only been seeing each other for a week; how could she love him so quickly? It made no sense. Sense or no, there was no denying her heart. Luke Walker was the man for her. But how was he going to get out of this?

Underworld gangsters or not, Luke and his team wouldn't get away with murdering Demirci and her two psychotic cousins. It didn't matter that the Inans had severed Zuccari's fingers on Demirci's behest; squads of armed police couldn't run around executing villains, no matter how evil they were. There was no room for vigilantes in the nation's capital, or any other city or town for that matter.

Miller sat on her loo for fifteen minutes, thinking to herself. "Luke, I know what you need to do." She stood, walked into the lounge to find him lying on the sofa, staring at the ceiling. "Did you hear me? I know what you need to do."

"I'm listening," he replied, eyes straight up.

"You need to report your team to the IOPC." Miller expected him to put up a fight. When he didn't, she sat on the couch with him. "You can report them online, ask them to be discreet when they call you in. It's the best way. We can do it now, use my computer." She wasn't expecting him to do it.

He sat up. "Fuck it! Let's do it!"

60

Charlotte awoke, startled. It took her a few seconds to acclimatise to the fact she was sat behind the steering wheel of her car. Hidden by a hedgerow on a country lane, she'd parked in a field, hoping to escape the van driver who chased her and the detectives.

After the van stopped chasing her, and after she lost sight of the detectives' Peugeot behind her, she'd carried on driving, not daring to go home, in case someone was following her, or worse still, knew where she lived. Paranoid, she'd turned left, then right, then left, until she had no idea where she was.

Wiping her eyes, Charlotte looked around her. In the dark, she'd failed to notice the cows grazing in the field. "Where the hell are we?" Why she was talking to the cows, even she didn't know.

Her mobile lay on the passenger seat. Picking it up, she checked her messages. There was a missed call from Hayes, several actually. A voicemail lay in wait for her, so she dialled the appropriate three-digit number and listened to the playback.

Hayes informed her that they had Colin, Brandy and Kurt's shooters in custody, as well as Henry's murderer. Although the initial threat was over, Hayes believed Charlotte was still in danger, that Richard's invention was still worth killing for. Hayes urged Charlotte to call her, so that they could establish what her brother's invention was.

She had no intention of calling Hayes. Charlotte was going to pick up the package her brother left her. All she had to do was figure out where she was, then drive to Neelkanth Safe Deposit, grab what was inside and leave without being seen. And that was when she realised she needed help.

What if these shooters were listening when Richard phoned her to tell her where the key was from. They had Neelkanth in the conversation. Colin's killers might be in custody, but what if there were others? Hayes thought she was still in danger, and Charlotte believed her. There was a lot more to this case than anyone would dare admit.

Before she did anything, Charlotte decided to phone Neelkanth Safe Deposit to book a time to visit. She remembered the website stipulating that clients were required to book slots to avoid customer crossover. They didn't want any customers bumping into one another by mistake. Security was paramount.

"Really? That's the earliest you can fit me in? And there's no way you can squeeze me in before that?" The manager, a steadfast man, stood his ground. 15:30 was the first available appointment. "Well, if you can't help before, I guess I'll see you then."

What the hell kind of place had such a rigid schedule? Whatever Richard had left for her was hers to take; she shouldn't have to wait. On the other hand, at least she knew when she went there, she would be the only customer inside.

Thinking about Richard made her sad. Charlotte dared not think where he was right now. The NCA had him holed up somewhere, and she had no clue where to begin looking for him. The police were useless. Remembering the desperation in

The Hard Way

Hayes' voice, Charlotte picked up her phone again, found the detective's number and called.

"Yeah, it's me. I didn't feel safe at home last night, so I phoned Sam and told him to take the girls to a hotel for a couple of nights... No, he doesn't know what's going on... Sure, I'll meet you outside Neelkanth Safe Deposit... Uh-huh... Please try to find Richard. He's in a bad place right now, I know it. I can feel it... If we don't get him out soon, I'm afraid we might never get him out. Thank you so much. When you find him, call me, okay? I'll see you outside Neelkanth, half three. Yeah, bringing backup might be a good idea. They could be anywhere. See you later, and thanks for your help. I really do appreciate it."

Knowing the detectives were on the case felt better. Without their help, she might never see Richard again. The charges were bullshit; they had to be. The elusive enemy were doing a good job of burying the product, but she wasn't about to let that happen.

The first thing she had to do: find out where she was. Then, she would drive to a service station somewhere, pick up some breakfast, go to the loo. Charlotte was counting down the minutes until she opened the safe.

61

Hayes held out her hand, as Inspector Gillan handed her two files, one for each of their suspects in custody. Her supervisor grabbed the nearest chair to him and wheeled it over to her. She took the top file and flipped it open. "Brendan Marlowe. Born March 31st 1986." She read the boring general information about him, noting the photo on his record was an arrest picture. When she turned the page over, large swathes of writing were blanked out.

"This looks like a special forces job if you ask me. It seems our suspects might have extensive military backgrounds."

Turning her attention to the main doors, she noticed Miller rush in, flustered, flapping. When her partner reached her desk, she apologised for being late, mouthed that she would explain later, and went about getting her things together.

Hayes held out the second file. "Here, take a look through this for me. We now know our suspects are ex-special forces."

Miller pulled a face that told her she didn't believe it. "Those guys? Not a chance. They're both dumb as a post; there's no way they're special forces. Do you think we'd be able to take them down just like that?"

"I don't know what I'm supposed to say, Miller, but we did. Look, the insignia on top of the form's blacked out, but I can tell you what it says. 'By Strength and Guile', and below it reads, 'Special Boat Service'."

Reaching over, Miller took the file. "I don't believe it! He's in the SBS? That's ridiculous. But we took him down so easily."

"He is ex-special forces. Maybe he wasn't very good?"

Gillan got up. "My guess is, he's into something altogether different now. Special forces don't have their files redacted, as a rule. No, someone else has reached out and requested this. I think it's time to go talk to your guys, what do you say?"

"Wait! What've you got in that other file, Miller?" Hayes waited for her partner.

"Jason Nye, born January 16th 1988," Miller read. "Grew up all over the place by the look of it. His dad was in the marines. He grew up with four brothers; he was the youngest." She turned the page, stopped, and turned the folder around so she could read the writing.

"I'm sorry! I don't know what that's supposed to say." Hayes shrugged.

"Look closely, you'll be able to read it."

"I can read the numbers 63, and UKSF, but that's it. Sorry!"

"This guy was a member of the 63 Signal Squadron," Gillan clarified. When she shrugged again, he continued. "Signal Squadron are the top of the top in communications, far in advance of the army. That means he knows his way around comms."

"So? Why is that important?" Hayes looked to Gillan for guidance, feeling stupid for not knowing. But why should she? She wasn't ex-army. "Please help me fill in the blanks here. Don't make me beg."

"There's no earthly reason why these two should be together, okay? The SAS, the SBS, Signal Squadron, they're all part of

Special Forces. But they hate each other. An SAS guy would like to think they would eat an SBS guy for breakfast, right? Do you get it? They assist one another on the surface; deep down they loathe each other."

"Exactly, like they tried to tear into each other in the back of our car." Hayes thought back to the previous night. "So, why were they tailing us together in the van, then?"

"That's the million-dollar question," Gillan said, hurrying them to follow him. "Travis, I'm helping Hayes and Miller in an interview."

Following Gillan and Miller into the interview room, the first thing Hayes noticed was how handsome he was in the daylight. She hadn't even noticed the previous night. Brendan Marlowe was a looker, with a head full of dark hair, a strong chin, and all over stubble. He looked like he worked out. She closed the door behind her.

"It's about bloody time! What the hell are you lot waiting for?" Handcuffed to the table, which in turn was screwed to the floor, Hayes and Gillan were taking no chances with him. "I've already told you I'm ready to deal. What more do you want?"

"You're SBS, yes?" Miller sat on a chair opposite him.

Marlowe smiled. "You've read my file, huh? I mean, what you can read of it. I should imagine that's not a lot."

Hayes stood at the back of the room, observing. She wanted to give Miller the chance to lead for once. "Just answer the questions, okay?"

"Yes, I'm ex-SBS." He rolled his eyes. "Look, the longer you keep me here, the more likely they're going to send someone in to execute me. You need to get me into witness protection, or something."

"Answer me this, Mr Marlowe, if you're ex-SBS, why were you with Jason Nye? Huh? On what planet would you be working with a member of Signal Squadron?"

He grinned. "Ah, so you really don't know what's going on at all, do you? You have no idea the shitstorm that's about to rain down on you." He leaned back in his chair. "It's going to cost you: get me in a safe house somewhere, and I'll tell you everything you need to know. I've been covering my arse since I started with The Company. I have enough intel on them to put them away. If you get me into witness protection, I'll show you where that intel is, and you'll be able to bring them all down. What do you say?"

Crossing her arms, Hayes was getting restless. "First, tell us what Richard Fisher's product is. What is it you're trying to destroy, hmm?"

"You want me to do your job for you, is that it? If I give you all this intel now, what do I get, huh? Nothing. Screwed, that's what. No way! You get me a deal, and I tell you everything, or we go our separate ways."

Miller turned and smiled at Hayes, before turning back to Marlowe. "Go our separate ways? No, you're going to prison for the murder of four people, that we know of. In a couple of hours ballistics will confirm your gun was that used to shoot Colin Fisher, Brandy Reid, and Kurt Austin. Then we have the comparisons of your boot sole impression, which I'm sure will match those found on Fisher's chest. We have trace all over the place in Henry Curtis' home. The muzzle mark on the back of Curtis' head will match your pistol, or your partner's. Basically, all this adds up to a bad diagnosis for you."

Glad to see the fear in his eyes, Hayes stepped up to the table. "You're going to have to give us something pretty big if you want our help. Right now, we have our suspects. You guys go to prison, we've done our jobs; we've brought two murderers to justice. I'm happy with that. Are you, Miller?"

"Oh, I'm ecstatic. I don't understand why we're even talking to him. He's already confessed. This is a slam-dunk case if ever I saw one."

"You'd better give them something, Mr Marlowe," Gillan chirped. "I've seen them like this before. They'll just walk out any minute if you don't start helping us."

"What is the product you're trying to destroy?"

"You'll have to find out for yourself, won't you? But when you do, be sure to come and find me, and I'll tell you what you're up against. Shit, the way you're going about this, you'll be lucky to live past lunchtime. Give me a deal and I'll tell you now."

Hayes turned at a knock on the door. Travis poked his head in, gestured for her to join him outside in the corridor. Making her excuses, she stepped into the hallway, closed the door, then waited for Travis to speak.

"I've just heard, Richard Fisher's dead."

She gasped. "What? How?"

"According to the NCA officer, he committed suicide using his bed sheet and the handle on the cell door. He died of asphyxiation. I'm sorry! I know this is a blow to your case."

Not knowing how to feel, Hayes stepped back into the interview room. "Richard Fisher's dead. He committed suicide in his cell."

"What? No fucking way! Don't you see? How can you be so blind? The Company's just had him killed. How did he commit suicide?"

"With his bedsheet tied to the door handle."

Marlowe laughed. "And you believe that? You must be dumber than you look. They sent someone in there to silence him. It's what they do; it's how they operate."

"Right, I'm sick of this! You tell us what you know, or I swear we're going to throw you in prison and leave you there to rot, you horrible piece of shit." Hayes glared down at him, hands on the table. "What's The Company you keep mentioning?"

Marlowe sighed. "Okay, I'll give you this in good faith. Me and Jay, we're both ex-special forces, hired by The Company to carry out various tasks. Every member of The Company is ex-armed forces, and we're put into units. There are six units of six in total. The colonel chooses the operations, we go where the money is. Is that enough for you?"

"So, you're mercenaries? Is that what you're saying?" Miller looked her way.

"Hired guns, mercenaries, whatever. It doesn't matter now, does it? I'm a dead man. My best chance of getting out of here is a deal with you guys. So, please, I've told you what you're up against. You've got ten 'mercenaries' out there looking for that product, ready to take out anyone, and I mean anyone, who gets in their way. These guys won't hesitate in taking out a cop, trust me. They'll shoot you where you stand, leave your brains sliding down a wall, and be gone before your body hits the ground."

"Why only ten? I thought you said there were thirty-six of you?"

"There are, but the colonel only assigned two units to this operation. The rest are overseas on other ops. But, if the colonel sees this op going south, he won't hesitate in deploying the entire Company. Bottom line, the colonel doesn't lose."

Hayes unfolded her arms. "Guess what? He's going to have to learn. This colonel of yours isn't going to get away with this."

62

Walker kept an eye on Vodicka in the rear passenger seat. She was busy on the comms, working the radio, while his front passenger, Sarge, sat stony faced next to him. It was lunchtime, the streets were quiet, or so it seemed, yet he caught Vodicka's stare every so often. Nothing was said about the previous night/that morning.

Walker left Rachel's place under the illusion of having reported his team to the Independent Office of Police Conduct. While he'd gone as far as typing out his report, Rachel went to the toilet as he'd finished typing. Instead of hitting "Send", he'd clicked on the X, then lied to her that he'd sent it. She kissed him in praise of his bravery.

What the hell kind of guy was he if he went and snitched on his own people? It was bad enough having covert informants on the streets, ratting everyone out for a step up the ladder, without police officers squealing on one another. As he hit the "X", he vowed to finish this his way, and on his time. He couldn't let them get away with it, and he couldn't go getting the IOPC involved either. There had to be a better way.

All morning he'd driven the BMW around the capital, going

from one dodgy area to the next, looking, craving for some action. It seemed action wasn't in their immediate future, though. The radio was quiet.

There was an eeriness inside the car as well. Sarge had barely said a word to him, or Vodicka all morning. The rest of the team were in their BMW.

"Left here, Luke," Sarge ordered.

Walker slowed the car, indicated left, and followed the main road around, noting the youngsters all out on the street playing football. They stood back, let them through, recognising the yellow dots on their windscreen, knowing they were heavy. He had to admit to enjoying the adrenaline rush of being an armed response officer.

63

Charlotte parked her car in a side road, a two-minute walk away from Neelkanth Safe Deposit, on Allenby Avenue. When she drove past the safe depository building she didn't see Hayes and Miller's white Peugeot, or any armed response vehicles nearby. Switching off the engine, she glanced at her watch: 15:31. They were late. "Shit!"

When she opened her door and got out, she heard a woman behind her. Upon turning, Hayes beckoned her over. Looking around, she couldn't see anyone suspicious, no vans, or cars out of place.

How she hadn't spotted it, she didn't know, but five cars behind hers sat two armed response vehicles, BMWs, and between them was Hayes' white Peugeot. "Aren't we walking there?" Was she being naïve?

"Erm, no, we're not. Get in the back, we'll get a move on."

She said hello to Detective Miller as she got in the rear, her bag slung over her shoulder. "You don't think they're going to try to do something out in the open, in broad daylight, do you?"

"We're playing it safe, okay?" Hayes nodded to Miller, who pulled out after the first armed response vehicle. "Before we get out, check you have everything you need. We don't want any last-minute surprises."

Charlotte checked her bag. The two keys were in one pocket, the locker key and the Ford car key. She had her passport as proof of identification, which she'd retrieved from home before heading to the workshop, just in case. "I've checked and double-checked." She felt the car swerve to the left, slow and park outside the building.

"Wait until the response team are ready," Hayes ordered, her hand on the door handle. "Here we go."

Charlotte had to wait for Hayes to open her door, as the child locks were on to prevent detainees escaping. Once out of the car she noticed the stony faces of the armed police officers, all six of them. The drivers remained in their seats.

The manager of the facility met her, Hayes and Miller at the brown wooden double doors, under the green sign with white writing. Blue blinds in the front windows kept nosy outsiders at bay. After a brief introduction, Charlotte showed the manager her passport, telling him she needed to open her locker. "I hope it's not too much trouble, but my brother has asked me to collect what's inside."

Reassuring him that they will retain the locker for future purposes, he relaxed a little, as he walked them through the rooms until they came to one room in particular, which was home to hundreds of lockers. "This is it?"

When she retrieved her key, Charlotte and the manager unlocked the safe deposit box together, using two keys. She peered inside: a bag of some sort. Taking out the rucksack, she placed it on the floor, knelt, then opened it. Above her, she could feel the detectives' excitement.

"Well? What is it?" Miller demanded to know.

Uncovering a black plastic object, she lifted it out of its bag and held it. Whatever it was it weighed next to nothing. Its lightness surprised her. "I've no idea. What do you think?" She held it up.

In her hands was an object she was no nearer saying what it was now than ten minutes earlier. "The only thing I do know is it's no valve."

"Is there anything with it? Anything that explains what it is?" Hayes asked.

Charlotte rummaged around inside the rucksack. Empty. In one of the outside pockets, however, she felt a thin oblong lump. After unzipping the pocket, she took out a USB stick and smiled up at the two detectives. "Let's go and find out what this thing is, shall we?"

"Even now, looking at it, we're still none the wiser." Frustration was evident in Hayes' voice. "Right, pack it up and let's get out of here."

"I'm with you on that." Charlotte placed the black plastic object back in its bag, the word "Prototype" emblazoned on its side. Charlotte put the bag on her back and followed Hayes and Miller out of the building.

With all the testosterone nearby, when she stepped out of the safe deposit building, she half-expected to hear the crackle of gunfire. Charlotte ducked inside the white Peugeot, closed her door and sank in her seat, barely able to see out of the window.

It was the first time she'd been in a police car. Miller put the lights and siren on, following the armed vehicles' lead. She held on tight to Richard's bag. "Did you find out where they're keeping my brother?"

Silence invaded the car.

"Well?" She didn't like the quiet, not one bit. "Detective Hayes?"

The detective turned in her seat, so that she was pretty much facing her. "I've got some bad news, Charlotte. The NCA officer informed us this morning that Richard committed suicide in the early hours of this morning. I'm so sorry!"

No! It couldn't be! Richard couldn't be dead. "But I only saw him yesterday. He was fine. I mean, as far as he can be when he was arrested, but he wouldn't kill himself."

"There are those who believe he didn't commit suicide, though, Mrs Edwards." Miller stared at her in the mirror. "There are some who believe he was murdered in prison for whatever that thing is you're holding. Now, I'm not saying they're right; I'm letting you know it might not be as simple as it first appears."

"How did he kill himself?" No way did he off himself, she thought, hugging the bag even tighter. "You said he was in prison at the time."

"Yes, a holding prison, a place people go when they're charged and awaiting trial. He was in a cell there, apparently. He died of asphyxiation. They found his bed sheet rolled up, one end tied around his neck and the other to the door handle. I'm sorry!"

Charlotte knew her brother. Richard wouldn't kill himself. She was still numb after the deaths of Colin and Henry. Lifting the bag, she unzipped the main compartment, stared at the white writing: Prototype. "You'd better be worth it. Both my brothers and brother-in-law died for you, whatever you are."

She sat in silence all the way back to the station, where the armed police escorted her, Hayes and Miller upstairs to their office. Hayes offered Charlotte a chair in front of a computer. "You want me to put the USB stick in?" She uncapped the metal connector, sliding it in the main terminal.

There was a crowd behind her, as the computer came to life. With Hayes to her left, Miller to her right, stood behind her were two officers.

"Oh, Charlotte, this is Inspector Gillan and Detective

Sergeant Jackman. They've been helping us on this case, so I asked them to be here."

Not feeling the need to introduce herself, she said hello, then turned back to the monitor. "There's a video here, shall I?"

The video showed her brother talking about test number fifteen. She recognised the woman she saw working on the blue Fiesta, the car her brother got into. The footage was now inside the car, as it left the workshop. She and the police officers watched it to its conclusion. Charlotte was none the wiser as to the significance of the test.

"What else is on the stick, Charlotte?" Hayes asked.

The first file she opened was what appeared to be a schematic. Within a minute, she heard murmuring from the officers surrounding her, except she still didn't understand what it was she was looking at, until it stared her straight in the face.

"Oh my God! It's a fucking car battery," Miller clarified, hands on top of her head, elated. "Do you know what this could do for the environment?"

Staring from Miller, back to the screen, she read more. "A dual-celled, self-charging car battery. So? What does it mean?" She went to Hayes for clarification.

"Let's put it this way, Charlotte, if I'm reading that right, it means your brother's team have just invented the world's first self-charging car battery. It means that while one cell is being expelled, the other is charging."

"So? What does that mean?" The officers surrounding her were so excited, muttering to one another. Only Hayes gave her the time of day.

"It means the blue Fiesta in that video will carry on driving forever, the literal battery bunny. It doesn't need petrol, doesn't need charging with electricity like electric cars do now; it will outrun everything on the road. Basically, your brother has invented the world's first carbon-free electric car that doesn't require topping up, do you get the importance of it now? He's solved the world's car crisis with this little invention. In ten to fifteen years' time, every car on the planet will be fitted with one of these batteries. Petrol, hybrid, diesel, and electric cars of today will be a thing of the past."

"He's done all that?" All she saw was a big ugly black box with a funny-looking thing underneath. "How does it work?"

Hayes moved to a different file. "It looks like they've found a way to harness the energy from the wheels, amplify it and store it in the empty cell, like a dynamo. Yeah, that's what this thing here's for. It clips under the car, draws energy from the wheels like so. You don't remember dynamos, do you? The lights that used to work more the harder you cycle? Remember? That was a dynamo, utilising energy from the wheel going around. That's what this battery is doing, only in a much more sophisticated manner."

"And both my brothers are dead because of this?" Charlotte didn't understand, couldn't. What was so important?

The police officers went quiet. She went to Hayes for support.

"This will piss off a lot of companies," Gillan said. "Your brother has made a lot of powerful enemies inventing this, Mrs Edwards."

"What? Why? It's just a car battery."

"Oh, it's so much more than that. This mere car battery is going to change the world for the better for everyone. Richard and his team are heroes, don't you see?"

"The only problem is petrol and diesel companies are powerful, the owners rich, and they won't want this seeing the light of day. When their customers hear of a petrol-free or diesel-free car, they'll bite the owner's hands off to get one. Just think how much the average driver spends on petrol per year, imagine the saving," Travis informed her.

"And you think these petrol companies hired someone to kill my brothers?"

"We don't think, Mrs Edwards, we know." Miller stood. "We have two of the assassins they hired in custody. They tried to kill us last night, after we left you."

"Oh God. But that's good, isn't it? You caught them."

"Unfortunately, they're not working alone. They're part of a group of mercenaries paid to eliminate anyone who's had anything to do with this battery. One of them told us that there are ten more of their colleagues out there, and their superior can order the whole company of thirty-six to join them if they don't get the results they need."

64

Miller glanced at each of her colleagues in turn. "We need to talk to Marlowe. He has all the answers we need." She turned to Mrs Edwards. "We need you to stay right here, okay? It's too dangerous for you out there until we've cleared this up."

Hayes, Gillan and Travis joined her in walking to the lifts, where they all got on, and off on the interview room floor. Within two minutes, she was in the room with the bound Marlowe, who looked angry. "Right, you're going to tell us everything."

"Not without a deal I'm not." He turned his head to the side, pretending to be snooty. "Count yourself lucky I haven't insisted on representation."

"If your information's valuable to us, Mr Marlowe, I guarantee you we'll give you a deal, okay? But only if it leads to a satisfactory conclusion of this case, meaning that no one in this room dies, do you understand? If one of your colleagues hurts a member of this team, all deals are nullified. Now, tell us why you murdered Colin Fisher, Brandy Reid, and Kurt Austin? Did you choose to kill all three to throw us off track?"

"I guess that's the best deal I'm going to get out of you, so I'll take it." He moved his hands, rubbing his sore wrists. "You obviously know Colin Fisher was the target, but the colonel thought adding a couple extra bodies would hinder your investigation, which worked to our advantage."

"But when you murdered Henry Curtis, we were onto you," Miller added.

"The colonel knew you'd end up pointing a finger at Melodi Demirci; her prints were everywhere. It was the way he wanted it. But it was my mistake putting the gun to the back of Curtis' head. We actually wanted his to appear as a suicide. The colonel wanted us to get rid of everyone with knowledge of the battery before it became public knowledge."

Travis frowned. "I get Fisher, being Richard's brother, but why Curtis? I mean, he might have been married to the younger brother, but why kill him?"

"Everyone who knew about the battery, detective, and not only did Henry Curtis know about it, he was an investor. He personally gave Richard Fisher a million towards it. That made him a massive target when the big petroleum companies found out about it, I can tell you. When that stupid bitch, Yurika Ishii, went to them about the battery, she started something she couldn't stop."

Hayes folded her arms on the table. "And these petroleum companies, you're sure they're your paymasters? They paid your company to eliminate everyone involved?"

"A hundred per cent. But it's bigger than that. It's not just the big petroleum; it's a couple of the global car manufacturers, CEOs of huge corporations. In fact, it's more like a conglomerate. Think of these companies as the head, and my company as the arm striking Fisher Valves down."

"Yurika Ishii, I assume from what you said just now, she

made a deal?" Miller saw the nod. "So, she's what, out of the country now? Living life in the lap of luxury?"

"At the bottom of the ocean, more like, food for the fish. I didn't do it, but I know for a fact she's been weighed down and thrown off a boat in the middle of the sea, along with her boyfriend. The same goes for Nathan Stewart. A couple of my colleagues took care of him. He won't ever be found either. You see, they want everyone with any knowledge of how to build the battery eliminated." He leaned forward. "They're winning, guys. That's everyone involved dead. Fisher, Parekh, that German bitch, Lang. Nathan Stewart, and Yurika Ishii. The only thing left to do is take the two remaining prototypes. They've even taken care of the guy sorting out the paperwork for Fisher's patent. Hands up, nothing to do with me."

"Hang on! You said two prototypes." Hayes regarded Miller, then went back to Marlowe. "We have one here. Where's the other one?"

"The blue Fiesta," Miller answered before Marlowe could. "It was already fitted with a battery when we were at the workshop. It wasn't there when we went back, though."

Gillan picked up his mobile. "It's been impounded. There are only two places it could be: Perivale or Charlton. I'll get onto this. We need that prototype, guys." He excused himself from the room while he made phone calls.

"Wait! There's more," Marlowe said, desperation in his voice. "I have all the intel you need on the conglomerate safely hidden away. With what I've got on a USB stick, you'll be able to charge all the individuals involved, all the big wigs in these companies. Take me with you when you go to pick up the car from the pound, and we'll take a detour to get the USB stick." He continued, "Come on, detectives, I've got as much to lose as anyone. I'm trying to save my life, sure, but I'll also be helping you win the biggest case of your careers."

Miller was surprised when Hayes said, "He's got a point."

Hayes continued, "I'll tell you what, Marlowe, if Inspector Gillan signs it off, you've got a deal. You give us the intel we need to arrest these big shots, I'm sure we'll be eternally grateful. You've murdered six people that we know of, you can't expect freedom, but witness protection is better than prison."

"Hell, I wouldn't expect freedom," he replied.

Gillan came back carrying his phone. "The blue Fiesta is safe and well at Perivale Car Pound on Walmgate Road, Greenford. I've instructed the sergeant I spoke to there not to let it out of his sight."

"Miller and I will collect it, sir. It's our investigation."

"And Mr Marlowe has requested he join us." Miller stood and stared at their cuffed suspect. "He has a USB stick stashed away somewhere with information we need to prosecute the fat cats in these companies. We'll be going with a fully armed response unit. He won't be any trouble, will you, Marlowe? If he is, he knows we'll have him on his arse so fast his head will spin. Isn't that right?"

"Fine. You'll be travelling with an armed response unit anyway."

65

"You're not going without me," Charlotte insisted. "That's my brother's legacy, his invention. I'm coming with you." She picked up the rucksack and put it on her back, threading her arms in the strap holes. She was met by both detectives shaking their heads.

"What do you think you're doing? You're not bringing the battery with you," Miller barked. "It's too dangerous; we don't know what resistance we're going to be met with, Mrs Edwards. You can come with us, but leave the battery here."

The audacity of the woman. "You're kidding, right? Don't get me wrong, you two seem genuine enough, but if you think I'm leaving this here, think again. My brother's been set up by your lot, and the NCA, and don't say he wasn't. He was no paedophile. They just wanted to smear him, make him fearful of his life in prison as a nonce, so that when they went in and killed him, they could blame it on suicide. This battery is never leaving my sight." She shifted the weight of her bag further up her back. "Shall we?"

Gillan walked towards her, carrying his mobile. Charlotte

was ready to go, but it seemed they were waiting on something, or someone.

Hayes stood from her chair. "What's the plan, sir? Are we taking the battery out of the car, or driving the Fiesta back here? What do you need us to do?"

"I've just spoken to the Superintendent, who's agreed for us to drive the Fiesta from Perivale to Charlton. We have a safe space to store it there until we can set up a press conference. This conglomerate doesn't want to go public, so we'll keep the Fiesta under armed guard until it does. As soon as the journalists get a whiff of this, the conglomerate's failed. There'll be no need for the mercenaries to hang around after that."

"You underestimate the colonel at your own risk, Inspector."

Charlotte hadn't noticed the black sergeant walk over with a handsome man in cuffs. "Who the hell's this?"

"The only way to ensure against reprisals is with my USB stick. I have intel on everyone, including the colonel."

She glared at Hayes. "Who's he?" It didn't take her long to work it out. "Oh my God! This is one of them, isn't it? You said you had two in custody? You're one of the animals who murdered my baby brother, aren't you?" She felt nauseous.

"Hey, I didn't enjoy it, if that makes a difference." Marlowe raised his cuffed hands. "It was just business."

Through an angry red haze, Charlotte launched herself at him, clawing at his eyes. "I'll kill you, I'll kill you, you bastard!"

Detective Miller pulled her off him so easily Charlotte was shocked at the Amazonian's strength. Since their first meeting, Charlotte had been impressed by her. Everything about Miller screamed strong and independent, both of which she aspired to be. "Stay away from me, you hear? Or I will hurt you." The acid in her voice shocked everyone.

"Right, Mrs Edwards will go with Hayes and Miller.

Marlowe, you can sit in the back of one the armed response units." Gillan nodded.

"Be careful, guys," Travis added. "Any sign of trouble, leave the car, get yourselves back here safely."

Charlotte saw the nervous smile on Miller's face.

"Relax, we have backup. Before you know it the blue Fiesta will be safe at Charlton Car Pound."

When Hayes called everyone together, Miller said she would be down in a couple of minutes, so Charlotte went downstairs with Hayes and the bastard who'd killed her brother, who had cuffs around his wrists and ankles. He wasn't going anywhere fast. When they descended in the lift, she daydreamed about kicking him down the stairs, or better yet, dropping him down the empty shaft. "Why is he here with us?"

"I'll explain on the way, okay? For now, though, let's focus on getting to the pound. The only thing that matters is making sure that car's safe."

66

Miller watched Hayes take Mrs Edwards and Marlowe out of the office, then took out her mobile. It was already five o'clock, and she'd not heard any whispers about Luke's unit being suspended yet, which was odd in itself, because cops loved gossip. She couldn't understand it. The IOPC would act on the information Luke gave them immediately; it certainly wasn't a complaint they would sit on. "Damn it, Luke, answer!" she muttered.

His phone went to voicemail after five rings. "Where the bloody hell are you?"

"Miller, are you going, or what?" Gillan gestured the doors.

"On my way, sir," she shouted, putting her mobile in her jacket pocket and heading for the doors. At the lift, she hit the button, then decided to take the stairs instead, which she did, two at a time until she arrived at the fire exit.

Coming from the rear of the building, she surprised Hayes, opened the passenger door and sat down, clipping her belt in place.

"All set?" Hayes switched on the engine of their Peugeot.

She turned and regarded Mrs Edwards, before going back to

her partner. "There's something I need to tell you, but it'll wait until later."

"Don't mind me; I'm not listening." Their passenger put earphones in.

With an armed response vehicle in front of them, and one behind, Hayes took them on the road to Perivale Car Pound. The officers in front didn't turn their lights or sirens on, so her partner didn't either. Hearing Mrs Edwards' music blaring out of her headphones, Miller checked she wasn't listening. She opened her mouth, but no words came out. How could she say it?

"Everything all right?" Hayes studied her. "Charlotte's got her headphones in, if you need to tell me something?"

"I do, but, nah, it can wait," she replied, knowing she couldn't say it out loud. "This is all so mental. To think yesterday we were sure Demirci was the one behind this. What a difference a day makes, huh?"

"Come on! I know you want to tell me something. Just say it," Hayes said, eyes ahead, focusing on the road. "Is it about Luke?"

Hayes could get her back up like that. "Why would it be about Luke? My whole world doesn't revolve around him. I can talk about other things. Why are you like this? One minute we're getting along, and then you go and–"

Her partner put her left hand up in surrender. "Whoa! Where's this coming from? I only asked a question. Wow! Talk about biting my head off. I thought it might be about Zuccari, is all. We haven't really spoken about it."

Miller felt bad for blowing up. Hayes had the best instincts, which Miller admired, more than she would ever let on. "I'm sorry!" she said, reaching out and touching Hayes' shoulder. It felt awkward; she wasn't a tactile person, outside of a relationship, unlike Hayes. "I'm grouchy this morning. Do you forgive me?"

With a tut, her partner forgave her. "I'm just putting this out there, but I'm always here for you if you need a chat. You know that, right? For anything. Work, social, my ears are never far away."

And now she felt guilty. "Thanks. You too if you ever need to talk." Looking out of the side window, she toyed with the idea of telling Hayes everything, but fell short.

It wasn't long before Mrs Edwards' music stopped, and she put her headphones away. "Are you going to tell me why that bastard's coming with us now?"

While her partner drove, Miller filled their civilian in on everything they'd uncovered about the mercenaries after her brother's invention. She also mentioned that Marlowe, the guy behind them in the armed response vehicle, had intel that would help bring the conglomerate behind her brother's murder down.

Before she managed to finish their conversation, Hayes announced that they'd arrived. The car slowed to a stop outside the entrance. Miller had never been to Perivale before. The first thing she noticed was the size of the facility, and its many grey buildings, fences and security gates. "At least we know it's here, although I doubt these mercenaries would have tried to get to the Fiesta, not with this amount of security. They'd have to take out a lot of officers first."

"Marlowe said they don't care how many of us they take out, remember? Their sole objective is to get the batteries and kill the brains behind them. He said he impersonated a detective to get to Curtis and Lang. They could've tried that here, or be planning it."

Miller ended the conversation. "So, let's go and get our baby." She received a smile from her partner, who followed the armed response vehicle inside the pound. She watched a member of staff talking to the driver in front. "Here we go!"

After a short drive through the premises, Hayes pulled up behind the response car. "And there she is. She doesn't look like much, does she? No one would suspect the secret she's carrying beneath her bonnet."

"I think it's time to check her out, don't you?" She opened her door, got out and walked over to the Fiesta. Hayes had a victorious, almost elated, sparkle in her eye. "Amazing, huh? To think she never needs petrol, or recharging. It's madness."

Marlowe appeared, accompanied by two armed officers carrying their carbines. "Don't go getting too attached; she's going to get you killed unless we get out of here. Come on! We haven't got all day. They're watching this place." He turned and scanned the surrounding area.

"He's right; we don't have much time," Hayes reiterated.

"Can we go now, please? Have you finished admiring her?" Marlowe kept turning and scanning the area.

"Right, who's driving what?" Miller hoped, prayed Hayes would let her drive the Fiesta, but when her partner gave her the keys to the Peugeot, she didn't argue. Hayes was the senior officer, it was her call. "Right, if you take Mrs Edwards, I'll take Marlowe. When you get to Charlton safely, I'll take him to pick up the USB stick. How does that sound?"

"Charlotte, I need the key in your bag," Hayes demanded, holding out her hand. "Right, let's go! Oh, and Marlowe, if you try anything, Miller has my permission to put you down, do you understand?"

Miller waited for Hayes to reverse the Fiesta. In front of her, Miller had one of the armed response BMWs, then the Fiesta, and she had a BMW behind her. The four-car convoy made its way to the entrance, where two guards stood. When Marlowe started talking she shut him down. "It's quiet time now, okay? Shh!"

The first BMW turned onto Walmgate Road. The Fiesta

went next. As Miller began to turn left and follow, a dark van appeared out of nowhere. It carried no insignia, but she could tell it was bulletproof, instinctively knowing it was them. She stepped on the accelerator, turned onto the road, and followed Hayes.

Miller grabbed the car radio. "It's them! They're right behind us."

In her mirror, she saw the BMW pull out, turn, and follow her. At first she couldn't see the van. Until it was right on her backup's tail.

The first bullets sounded like distant firecrackers. Miller noticed the BMW swerving, saw one of the officers lean out of his window with his carbine. She saw muzzle flashes in the mirror. Miller called it in to headquarters, requesting backup.

Turning hard to the right, the Peugeot's wheels spinning, she followed Hayes onto Aintree Road by taking another hard left and carried on until she steered hard right onto Bilton Road, all the while keeping an eye on the BMW behind her. So far, they'd staved off the assault by the armoured van.

"We're heading east on Bilton Road, heading towards the A4005. Repeat, heading towards the A4005 at Bilton Road. Need assistance. Under attack. Assailants armed with automatic weapons."

She apologised to Mrs Edwards, whose pallid face told her how petrified she was. "We'll be fine, you'll see. Keep as low as you can, and if I say duck, get your head down, do you understand?" They were approaching Piggery Bridge going over the Grand Union Canal, which meant they weren't far from their turning onto the A4005.

67

Walker sat behind the wheel of the BMW, waiting for Sarge and Vodicka to get back with their evening meal, which would consist of sandwiches from a Tesco Express they'd found. He gave Vodicka his order of a tuna sandwich, and a bottle of Diet Coke. She'd accepted it with her evil eyes glaring at him. He figured then that she would make a terrible poker player, unable to mask her feelings.

He was beginning to regret not complaining about his team to the IOPC. Had he gone through with it, the organisation would have had them off the streets inside an hour. He would be on suspension, but he didn't want that. Hell, with his job, every day carried its fair share of risk of suspension. As soon as they fired their weapons, in fact. Life as a firearms cop wasn't like in the movies: if he shot a person, he would be suspended pending an inquiry. If his act was seen as lawful, he would be reinstated, but only after a battery of psychological testing. "Come on, Sarge."

There was no denying the atmosphere in the car, or the fact that he was the main recipient of their hostility. All day he'd felt Vodicka's stare. At one point, he was ready to turn around and ask if she had a problem. Not that it mattered. He knew what her problem was: him. Walker was the only one who risked exposure.

And there they were, the Sarge and Vodicka, carrying plastic bags filled with goodies. The Sarge sat next to him. Voddy sat behind him. He accepted his sandwich, as the radio crackled to life. "Hey, that's Rachel!"

"Repeat, heading towards the A4005 at Bilton Road. Need assistance. We're under attack. Unknown amount of assailants armed with automatic weapons."

"What're you waiting for, permission?" Sarge took out his sandwich. "Let's go rescue your girlfriend."

68

Hayes held her breath as the BMW in front of her swerved to her right, on the opposite side of the road, then slammed on its brakes, as she surged ahead. In her mirror she saw it move again, only after the armoured van had whooshed past them. "Looks like a van sandwich to me," she muttered to herself.

Charlotte stared at her. "Huh?"

"Nothing, don't worry." It swerved onto their side of the road before a car slammed into them on the other. "That van has an armed car in front and behind it. It's game over for them." When she looked in her mirror again, she swore when a second armoured van exactly the same as the other one appeared. "We're in trouble."

She took an exit right, leading to a big roundabout at Barham Park. Once she was over it, in the distance she saw one of her armed escorts roll, with all three occupants inside. At the roundabout it rolled at least five times, leaving a mess of metal. "We've only one armed escort left, but two vans."

"Do something, then. You're the cop. Get us out of this!"

"Charlotte, yelling at me won't help. In fact, it'll do quite the opposite. Bottom line is, we're in the safest place we could be right now. We're in the one car that doesn't need to refuel. Everyone behind us will, so if we can stay ahead of them, we're safe, okay? And they want this car. They're not going to harm it." She checked the petrol gauge, which said they were almost out of power. "Please work!"

"What? What's wrong?" Charlotte stared at her, waiting to put her mind at ease. "What aren't you telling me?"

"In any other car, Charlotte, I'd be worried at the petrol dash," she said, still praying the empty cell would click over to the full one. "We're running on empty, but you could say this is a field test. Let's hope your brother's battery works."

Behind them, one of the vans tried overtaking the last remaining armed Beamer. They passed Sudbury and were heading for North Wembley. There was a clunk, and the petrol gauge flicked back to full. Hayes whooped, ecstatic that their Fiesta hadn't conked out on them. "It worked! You know what this means? We just need to outrun them."

"I hate to be the bearer of bad news, but we just lost our second escort," Charlotte confessed, pointing out of the rear window. "Look, they're right on us!"

Hayes saw that Miller's Peugeot was outnumbered two to one. The furthest armoured van accelerated, sped past its partner, and pulled up alongside the Peugeot. "No! Miller!" Hayes shouted.

"There's another armed police car!" Charlotte pointed it out.

In her mirror she saw the van next to the Peugeot slam on its brakes, before getting in line. The armoured police car did a skid, a handbrake turn and joined the convoy behind the last armoured van. "Where did *they* come from?"

"What does it matter? So long as they're here to help."

Charlotte was right. Whoever they were, she was grateful for having their assistance. The police BMW kept trying to overtake the vans. Hayes thought she saw one of her colleagues leaning out of their window, carbine in hand. "Take them out, would you!"

One of the vans pulled alongside Miller's car again. Miller steered sharply into it, smashing the side of the van. All Hayes could do was keep driving. She didn't know how this was going to end, and it bothered her. She liked to be in control of her destiny, not have it dictated to by a group of psychotic mercenaries.

With Miller still behind her, Hayes watched in her mirror, as her partner kept the vans back by steering left or right, depending on which way they went. Cars coming the other way blasted their horns at them. All Hayes could do was hold her nerve.

The van managed to nip past Miller. Hayes saw the frontage of the van in her mirror. It was so close to her rear, too close. When she saw a window descend, she shouted to Charlotte, "Get down, now!"

Her passenger did as she was told, crouching as far as she could, when the rear windscreen shattered, the noise making Charlotte scream. Hayes knew Miller was doing everything she could to get rid of them.

69

Miller slammed on the horn, not that she knew why. These guys had already taken out the back window of the little Fiesta. "Shit! We need to get rid of them." She was sick of listening to Marlowe shit himself. "Will you shut up! You're not helping, damn it."

"What do you expect? You're driving like a moron, and I'm cuffed here. Let me drive; I'm an expert." He held his hands out, like she had time to uncuff him. "Come on! Before you get us killed."

"Put your hands down! Christ! I've known you for all of five minutes, and already I want to shoot you." She put her foot down, feeling the adrenaline flow, as she sped alongside the dark van, needing to get in front. "Take this!" Her nose slightly ahead of the van's, she yanked left, her Peugeot colliding with the van.

"Hey! What the fuck are you doing? Are you mental? Are you trying to kill me, or what?" Marlowe moved away from the door, almost on her lap.

"We've got to give them a fighting chance; they're sitting

ducks up front." With her car jamming the van's way, Miller managed to get in front of it, so she was directly behind Hayes' Fiesta. "Come on, Luke, where are you?"

"Who the fuck's Luke?" Marlowe turned in his seat to look out the rear window. "Incoming!" He turned and ducked.

Miller screamed when a bullet tore through the rear window. While driving, all she could hear were gunshots, small pops. "Shit! We need to get off this road."

The second dark van, which she thought was behind the one behind her, shot past, Luke's BMW trailing it. Miller saw Sarge firing at the van, which was clearly armoured. "Hayes!" she shouted, when a Heckler and Koch MP5 appeared out of the passenger window of the van.

If having one van speed past her wasn't bad enough, the second followed suit.

Miller's side window shattered, cutting her face and neck.

She was too busy to bleed.

As though Hayes had heard her, the Fiesta turned left into a small narrow road. While the blue car managed to catch the slip road, the two vans and Luke's BMW didn't; they continued on along the A road. Miller had to slam on the brakes to catch the slip road. "Whoop!" She laughed, watching the vans slam on their brakes too late; they would have to back up and turn. "What's the matter, Marlowe? We've given ourselves a couple of minutes."

Taking her mobile out of her jacket pocket, she handed it to Marlowe. "Get Hayes on here, would you? Do something useful for once." It took a few seconds of following her partner along the thin road with potholes everywhere before she heard Hayes' voice. "Do you even know where this road leads?"

"I wish I could say I did, Miller, but no."

Miller grunted when she saw a sign for a country mansion

and driveway ahead. "Oh shit! It's a dead end!" Up ahead the huge building, the likes of which she'd only seen in magazines and movies loomed large. In the rear view, the vans approached, which meant Luke's BMW wouldn't be far behind. Their immediate problem was figuring out what to do.

"We've got no choice but to stop here, Miller," Hayes said. "We can't turn round and go back through them."

Swallowing hard, Miller agreed. "Get as close to the front door as you can. They're going to take no chances; they'll come out firing."

More pops from behind told her they were firing at them again. As she drove closer to the mansion, she could see a couple of people outside the front. "I think it might be a hotel. Look at those people."

"I think you're right, but there's nothing we can do."

The people out front of the building must have heard the gunshots. Getting closer, they were running away. "That's something, at least. They've seen the vans behind us." Then she saw them running into the house.

The Fiesta was first to pull up outside the front door, followed by Miller's Peugeot. She got out in a hurry, not bothering to wait for Marlowe. At the front door, Hayes banged on it, yelling that she was a police officer.

Behind her, Miller saw the vans getting closer. Bullets hit her Peugeot, as muzzle flashes made her duck. "We need to get inside, now."

Hayes ducked while bashing the door. "Don't you think I know that?"

Marlowe stood, went to launch his foot at the thick wooden door, when it opened a crack, and a woman in a suit appeared through the crack. "Thank God! Let us in, madam, please."

As Marlowe forced his way in, Miller watched the vans.

Luke's BMW made a last-minute dash to beat the vans to the house. "Come on, Luke!" The BMW screeched to a halt behind her Peugeot, the doors flew open, as Luke, Sarge and Vodicka fired at the vans, the bullets barely scratching it.

"Inside, all of you, now!" she ordered, hiding behind the door, holding it for them. "Come on!" She waited until all three were inside, then slammed the door shut, locking it.

Catching her breath, Miller turned to find Hayes trying to urge the hotel staff to leave out the back. "Please listen to her. These are professional mercenaries, hired to kill us. If you're here they won't hesitate in shooting you. Everyone out the back, please."

There were a number of staff, ranging in age from what looked like late teens to their seventies. Miller helped Hayes take them to the rear of the building, where the general manager complained that they were in the middle of an audit, that the hotel was being inspected. He asked if they could come back another time?

Miller scoffed. "Are you kidding? We've got men outside with machine guns about to come in."

"Carry on through the garden. Just keep going, and don't come back until someone with police ID comes to get you, okay?"

By the time they had the hotel to themselves, Miller joined Luke, Sarge and Vodicka in the front bar, looking out of the window. Outside, there were ten mercenaries clad in black, carrying automatic machine guns, waiting. "Why aren't they trying to come in?" she asked everyone.

One of the mercenaries slid beneath the Fiesta and yanked out the remaining battery. He carried it back to the mercenary with the speaker. "You have a choice to make. You can do this the easy way, or the hard way. We have the first battery in the Fiesta;

now we just need the prototype Fisher's sister's carrying. Throw it out to us and we leave quietly, no fuss. No one needs to die here today. But if you push us, we will put a bullet in your foreheads, am I making myself clear? Don't go being heroes, all we want is the battery, nothing more. Don't be stupid here, people."

70

Hayes didn't say a word; she listened to her surroundings. No one in the bar area of the hotel said anything. "Is that a helicopter?" It was faint, but undeniably a chopper. With Charlotte by her side, Miller in front of her, Hayes had the two most important people to her in the same room, where she could keep an eye on them. "Is it one of ours?"

"Not unless we've started using unmarked helicopters, no." Miller pointed at the sky through the net curtains. "Look!"

Her partner gave her space to observe through the window. Coming in towards them slowly was a dark chopper. It didn't say "Police" on its side, which meant it wasn't theirs. Which could mean only one thing. She turned to Marlowe. "One of yours?"

With a nod, he answered her. "In a minute, they'll breach this place, and go room to room executing everyone here, do you understand?"

Sarge turned suddenly. "Wait! What do you mean it's one of yours? Hayes? What the hell are you talking about? Is he a part of this?"

She didn't like the way Sarge was pointing his MP5 at Marlowe. Hayes stood back, getting in between her captive and the carbine. "Listen to me, Sarge, he's in my custody, as you can see. He's cuffed. But in answer to your question, yes, he's one of them."

"And he has information we can use to bring this whole thing down." Miller stepped back, ready to pounce on him if needed.

"You have one minute to bring the battery out, or we breach the building," the tannoy announced. "If you make us go in, none of you are coming out of there alive. Please don't be short-sighted; it's just a stupid battery. We don't want to hurt you."

That was what he was counting on. "We're all agreed this is worth it, right? This car battery will literally change the world as we know it. Companies whose income is based on petrol and oil will collapse, as will oil based economies of countries. What we do here tonight will affect the outcome of our children's futures."

"What's so special about it?" Vodicka asked.

"This battery doesn't need topping up, ever. It doesn't require petrol, or oil. It recharges itself using a dual cell, so while one's in use, the other's charging. Do you understand how big this is?" Hayes checked Vodicka's expression.

"You mean I'd never have to pay for petrol again?" the armed officer asked, her glare replaced with raised eyebrows.

"If you fitted this battery to your car now, it would keep on going, like the Battery Bunny. Just think: no petrol stations or trying to find an electric meter. All of that could be a thing of the past. No more CO_2 emissions; it's zero carbon. No more pollution, no more CFCs. Think of the good this battery will do for the environment."

"It's our job to protect you, but now you've made it a crusade, let's get set up," Sarge said, taking charge of the situation.

"The chopper's right over us," Vodicka said, trying to watch it.

"That means we have three units on us now. There's ten out

there and another God knows how many about to abseil onto the roof. Listen, if you're going to give them the battery, now's the time to do it." Marlowe waited for an answer.

Hayes glared at him. "It's not happening. You'll have to pry it from my cold, dead hands first, Marlowe, you little maggot. You're in as much trouble as we are. If they get their hands on you, they'll put a bullet in your head before they even think about shooting us."

Marlowe put his cuffed hands up, palms splayed. "Hey, just saying. We can all live through this if she gives them her bag, don't you see?"

"How about we send you out there with the bag?" Miller glared at Marlowe. "We can kill two birds with one stone."

Hayes smiled at Miller, who winked back. "How do you want to play this, Sarge? We have an unknown number out there, and only three of us with guns in here." She looked from person to person, from Charlotte, to Miller, Luke, Vodicka, Sarge, and finally Marlowe.

"That's not strictly true." Luke took his Glock out of his holster. "Sarge, we can give our pistols to Hayes and Rachel, can't we? They're trained to use them."

"And we need all the help we can get." Sarge handed his to Hayes, while Luke gave his to Miller. "Here, take the extra magazines."

Taking the Glock and magazines from Sarge, Hayes thanked him. "Right, now we've evened the score a bit, what now? Where do you want us?" She heard the tannoy guy out front say they had ten seconds until all offers were revoked.

"You're kidding, right?" Marlowe moaned. "You're handing out guns, and you're really not going to give one to me? Hey, I have a right to protect myself."

"No! You're a murdering scumbag, you deserve to die." Charlotte narrowed her eyes and glared at Marlowe until he backed down once more. "Can I have a pistol, please, Hayes? I want to shoot this one in his ugly fucking face."

"Will you two behave; neither of you are getting your hands on a gun, is that clear? We've got bigger things to be worrying about." Hayes stepped up to the window again, as the mercenary in charge declared a breach, and his group fanned out. One of them walked past the window. "How about I go upstairs with Miller, Charlotte and Marlowe?"

Sarge nodded. "That's probably the best idea. There's ten down here."

"And the others on the roof," Hayes said to Miller, taking Charlotte's hand. She strode out of the bar, into the hallway. Heading upstairs, Hayes arrived on the landing, looking right and left. "Let's split up?"

"I'll go left with Marlowe," Miller confirmed, giving her a little 'good luck' smile. "Be careful, and remember: take them down – because they won't show you mercy, okay? Head shots." She walked away.

"Come on, Charlotte, let's find a safe hiding place for you," she said, taking hold of her hand again. Hayes heard movement above them and let go of Charlotte. "They're trying to smash their way in through the roof."

She didn't realise how big the hotel was. There were so many bedrooms on the first floor. Passing several, she chose one, turned the handle, expecting it to be locked, but it wasn't. "They must have unlocked all the doors for the inspection. Shit!" she whispered to Charlotte.

Inside the spacious bedroom, Hayes closed the door, looking around for something to use to jam it. *A high-backed chair would be nice about now*. Nope. Nothing. There wasn't time to sort it, so she ordered Charlotte behind the bed. "Stay there, okay?"

With Charlotte hiding, Hayes set about finding something to use to lock the door. The room was devoid of all things useful.

Before she had the chance to wedge it with something, she heard the first gunshot, just a single shot, not an exchange. She gulped, walked backwards towards the bed with her pistol pointed at the door.

Charlotte sat on the floor the other side of the bed. Hayes joined her and knelt with her arms resting on the floral duvet, the Glock in both hands trained at the door. Outside in the hall she heard noises, footsteps.

Breathing shallow, Hayes closed her left eye, looking at the sight when the door handle turned. She held her breath. The door opened slowly.

Seeing the intruder's kneecap in sight, she pulled the trigger, as the noise of the gunshot reverberated around the room, making her ears ring.

The black-clad intruder fell, letting off a couple of shots from his carbine into the ceiling.

Getting up, she pointed the gun at his head. "Move and I'll blow your brains out, understood?" She walked round the bed, saw his MP5, and picked it up, putting the pistol in the back of her suit trousers.

Hayes stepped up to him, took his helmet off while he was screaming in pain, and belted him with the butt of her carbine, knocking him unconscious. "Come on! Give me a hand locking him in the bathroom."

71

Walker squatted behind a chair in the dining room. There were a dozen tables he could have chosen. The table he chose was near the glass patio door, giving him the best view of the incoming mercenaries.

No amount of training could prepare him for this. He'd been involved in several tactical operations, had fired his carbine once, but never had he shot someone before. There was no doubt he would that evening; they were on their way in.

With Sarge in the bar, and Vodicka in the lounge, they had most bases covered, except the hotel was too big for the three of them to handle themselves. His radio hissed, then he heard a female voice ordering all units to converge on the hotel. "Backup's on its way! We just have to survive until they arrive!"

No one replied. He didn't have time to dwell on it. A figure in black holding a machine gun stepped in front of the patio door, glass the only barrier between them.

Raising his carbine to eye level, Walker kept him in his sights, his finger on the trigger, ready for action. He swallowed, hard, making a noise. "Shit!" he muttered. Sweat formed on his lip. He didn't want to kill anyone.

The mercenary tried the door handle.

When it wouldn't open, he stood back, pointed the carbine at the glass and fired.

Without flinching at the noise, Walker stood, kept the mercenary's face in his sights, and squeezed the trigger, letting off one round.

The bullet hit his target in the cheek. He fell to his knees, dropped the MP5, and fell onto his face, dead.

Walker stood, stunned for a moment, while his brain processed the information. He'd just killed a man. By law, it wasn't murder. He had a defence if it came to that in court. The guy would have killed him given the chance. "Sarge! How're you getting on back there?"

Upstairs, he heard gunshots.

Turning his attention back to the broken patio door, another figure in black appeared.

He didn't have time to hide.

Before his enemy had a chance to fire, Walker squeezed the trigger five times, hitting the hired gun in the chest three times, once in the neck and once in the eye. The mercenary fell on his back, his legs twitching from the sudden brain trauma.

Walker made a move for the lounge, where Vodicka had shot one of them. Her victim sat in an armchair, his head tilted to the side. The only way Walker knew he was dead was seeing the bullet wound in his cheek. "We need to help Rachel and Hayes. That woman's got the battery."

"You go! There's more down here," Vodicka replied.

Although what she said didn't sound hostile, her eyes told a different story. Walker agreed, nodded, and walked backwards into the dining room, not wanting to turn in front of her. Once out of the lounge, he ran for the hallway.

"Rachel!" he shouted up the stairs.

More shooting upstairs made him run up one flight to the

first landing. "Rachel!" Nothing, just gunshots. "Talk to me, baby, where are you?"

When he turned left, a door opened. He leapt to safety inside a room before bullets hit the wall. He was in a bedroom, plush, well maintained, with floral bedding and light-coloured walls. Walker opened the door a crack, then shut it quickly, a figure on its way.

Upon seeing the handle turn, he fired three shots into the door, then heard a body slump to the floor. When he opened the door again, his target lay there, a hole in his forehead. He couldn't have shot him any more centrally if he tried.

"Luke, they're everywhere!" Miller shouted from upstairs.

"How many have you taken out?"

"Two. How about you?"

He wished he could see her. "Three, and Voddy wasted one that I saw." When he received no reply, he stepped over the body into the hall.

Bullets came flying at him from nowhere. He ran at speed in the opposite direction to Rachel's voice.

72

Miller wanted to march downstairs, find Luke and kiss him. Instead, she stood beside the bedroom door watching as the handle turned. Sweat formed on her temple. She raised her pistol, kept it pointed skyward, ready to lower to head height at a moment's notice.

Next to her, Marlowe had his hands cuffed in front of him. "If you'd uncuffed me, and given me a gun earlier, we wouldn't be in this shit." His voice was an angry whisper. "Give me that pistol now and I'll take care of this."

"Shh!" She glared at him. Turning her attention to the handle, the door opened slowly, letting the muzzle of the carbine inside. Miller braced herself, held her breath, and barged the thick wooden door, wedging the mercenary between the frame and the wood. The guy's helmet fell off.

With as much power as she could muster, she slammed her full weight behind the door three more times, the guy's head catching the force on two occasions. He slumped to the floor, unconscious. Bending over, she picked up the carbine, putting the pistol in her trousers. "That's three. It's time to finish this."

"Oh what? You think it's going to be that easy?" Marlowe

stayed behind her when she opened the door and stepped over the body, into the hallway. "These guys are trained killers, remember? You think you're getting out of here? None of us are."

"You hear those sirens, don't you? Your mates know that if they take too long at this, they'll be surrounded. It's why they're getting sloppy." As soon as she set foot on the carpet, Miller had to jump back inside, as bullets tore up the door. "Down!" she cried, looking up at the hallway where she'd just been, the MP5 still in her hands. "Quick! Shut the door!"

The unconscious intruder was in the way. She forced Marlowe to drag him further into the bedroom, then slammed the door shut. "Shit! We're trapped!"

What sounded like firecrackers forced Miller onto her side. Bullets blasted their way through a wall. Next door, one of the mercenaries tried their luck. She turned onto her other side, listening. There was movement behind the wall.

"Now!" Marlowe shouted.

Without hesitation, Miller squeezed the trigger eight times at the wall, in the general area of the noise. One bullet hit her guy; she heard him moan, followed by swearing, grumbling. She'd injured one, but he still had his gun. "Damn it!"

She didn't have time to fret, the door burst open and a black-clad mercenary ran in, firing blind. He was firing at chest height, yet Miller lay on the carpet. Waiting until he was all the way inside, committed to his attack, she squeezed the trigger three times, the first bullet hitting him in the neck, the last two missing him.

He fell back, grabbed his throat with one hand and raised the carbine with the other. The mercenary kept using his leg to crawl away from her.

"The next one goes in your forehead," Miller hissed. "Put it down."

Surrendering not his preferred plan, the intruder stopped crawling.

By the time he'd raised his MP5 to fire at her, Miller had already shot him twice, once in the chest and once in the forehead. He lay on his back staring skyward, his dead eyes shocked. "That's what you get for underestimating the Metropolitan Police, you piece of shit." Miller stood, then helped Marlowe to his feet. "See what I mean? Sloppy."

In the distance she heard more gunfire, sporadic, small arms, by the sound of it. Miller could tell Hayes was having trouble. There were two different guns firing. She had enough experience of firearms to tell the difference. "I've got to help Hayes."

"Are you kidding? You're worried about your partner? Worry about us getting out of here in one piece, why don't you!"

"You know, for ex-special forces, you sure are a fucking coward."

"In case you hadn't noticed, *I'm handcuffed, with no gun, you stupid bitch*! I have to rely on you not getting me killed, for fuck's sake."

"I don't give a shit! We're going to find Hayes, stay close." Miller opened the door slowly, knowing there could still be mercenaries out in the hall. She peeked out from behind the door frame. Nothing.

73

"Luke, we need help down here," Sarge shouted.

Walker froze, listening to everything around him. He heard gunshots downstairs. Wanting to ignore Sarge, he took a step away from the stairs, then stopped. Sarge and Vodicka were still part of his team; he couldn't leave them down there with a load of mercenaries. If he lived through this, and they didn't, Walker wouldn't be able to live with himself. There was no knowing how many more there were.

He turned and headed back down the stairs, his carbine in front of him, trained on whatever got in his way. A stair at a time, gunshots going off all around him, above and below, his senses were sharp, his trigger finger ready.

On the ground floor, he turned into the hallway to find it empty.

Walker breathed out, relief flooding him.

The bar was directly in front of him. To his right, flashes made him dive through the doorway, but not before a bullet caught him in his right shoulder. He lay on the floor, the pain so intense he thought he might faint.

Behind him, Sarge was dealing with a mercenary. Walker

used his right leg to try to close the bar door, but before he could, a figure emerged. With his MP5 in hand, he put six bullets in the guy, one bullet catching him in his open mouth.

In the doorway, the mercenary lay in a pool of his own blood.

For a moment or two, his brain forgot about the pain. It came back with friends once the danger was over. Walker groaned, holding his injured arm. "Sarge?"

To his left, Walker saw a mercenary take four bullets from Sarge, and collapse on the floor in a heap. Again, Walker breathed out deeply. "I've taken one in the arm." He tried to stand, until his boss came and helped him up. "It's okay, I can still hold a gun."

"Here, take one of their Glocks," Sarge said, handing it to him. "The MP5's too heavy with one arm. And stay close, I don't know how many are left."

Walker compared notes with Sarge on how many they'd each taken out. He saw three bodies on the floor in the bar alone. "Do you hear that? Backup's on the way. All we have to do is wait it out until these fuckers are surrounded."

"Do me a favour," the Sarge said, nodding at the window. "Go over there and tell me what's going on outside, would you?"

Carrying the Glock in his good hand, he walked over to the window and stared out at the assortment of vehicles out there, from armoured vans, to his police car, the blue Fiesta and Rachel's plain white Peugeot. "Not a lot. Looks like they're all inside."

"Hey, Luke!"

Turning round, Walker froze. Sarge, squatting in front of the mercenary he'd just shot, had the dead man's finger on the trigger of a Glock 17, the pistol pointed at Walker.

"Hey, what the fuck, Sarge? What're you doing?"

"You know this has to happen, right? You should've pulled

the trigger, Luke. Now you're a liability, probably thinking of how you can weasel your way out of this, huh? You see, Luke, you're not one of us now; we can't trust you. And I bet you told that bitch of a girlfriend of yours upstairs, didn't you? Shame, you were one of the best cops I've ever worked with."

Panic set in. Strangely, he wasn't as concerned for himself as he thought he would be. The only person on his mind at that moment was Rachel. By the narrowing of the Sarge's eyes, he intended to go ahead. "Rachel! It's a trap!"

The last thing Luke Walker saw was the muzzle flash of Sarge's pistol.

74

"Rachel! It's a trap!"

Miller stopped. What was Luke talking about? She didn't like the way she heard a gunshot immediately after he'd shouted it. "Luke! Speak to me, Luke!" she yelled down the stairs. His voice came from the ground floor; or at least she thought it had. Nothing. Taking the stairs one at a time, the carbine in her hands, all she wanted was to see his beautiful face.

With Marlowe behind her, she found herself on the ground floor, turned to her right and saw the bar door was open. Figuring it was the best place to search for Luke, she stepped inside. "Luke?"

At the front of the room, in front of the window, she saw Sarge cradling her Luke, who was covered in blood. The net curtains were red. Miller screamed, then rushed over to them. Without waiting for Luke's superior to get out of her way, she took over cradling her dead boyfriend, tears streaming down her cheeks.

In the distance, sirens wailed. Miller didn't care; she'd lost the one good thing in her life. She'd only been going out with him for a short time, but knew she loved him. Luke was perfect for her, and now he was dead.

"Miller! Look out!" Marlowe shouted.

Staring up, she was shocked to find Sarge pointing a pistol at her.

Tears stung her eyes, and a lump strangled her. "You? You shot Luke?"

In hindsight, she should have known, but considering there were mercenaries paid to execute them in the building, she hadn't expected this. Rookie mistake.

At the rear of the bar, Miller noticed Vodicka enter.

"Wait! Let me do it, Sarge," Vodicka said, walking up to him, putting her hand on top of his pistol and pushing his arm down. "I want to take this snooty bitch out."

"Make it quick! Backup's on its way," Sarge replied.

Having no time to think, Miller let go of Luke, ready to lunge when Vodicka was within reach. "I want to see what you've got, Vodicka. Let's see if you're as tough as Luke says. Come on! One on one; how about it?"

Vodicka smiled. "It won't take long."

In the background, Marlowe sidestepped towards Sarge.

Getting to her feet, Miller stepped towards Vodicka, as her opponent slid a knife out of its sheath. "A believer in fair fights, huh? You fucking coward! Let's have it, then."

With no warning, Vodicka took a swing at her with the knife.

Miller ducked, the blade missing her by mere millimetres.

Having a long arm reach, she punched Vodicka on the bridge of her nose.

Angry, Vodicka went for her with the knife. Miller managed to grab her wrist, turn into her and launch Vodicka over her shoulder.

The shorter Vodicka crashed into a table made of wood and glass.

"Luke said you were good. Personally, I think he might have overestimated you."

The knife still in hand, Vodicka stood behind the broken table, her eyes narrow, evil slits of hatred. She flew at Miller.

There was nothing Miller could do against such rage. Vodicka kept swinging and jabbing at her with the knife. Only two made their mark on Miller's wrist and arm, enough to draw blood. Miller didn't have time to bleed; she was countering everything Vodicka threw at her.

Sensing Vodicka growing weaker, Miller lunged at her, grabbed her neck and headbutted her on the bridge of her nose again.

The armed cop staggered backwards, her face a crimson mess.

"You fucking bitch!" Miller lunged at her opponent again, managing to get her on the floor.

Picturing Luke's beautiful face with every punch, she rained down blow after blow on Vodicka's already-damaged face. Her rage took on momentum.

"I don't think so, bitch!" Sarge pushed his Glock in the back of Miller's head.

75

Hayes fired her Glock for the third time, hitting another mercenary in the knee. On the second floor of the hotel, in a bedroom over the bar, she pointed her gun at the intruder, who gripped his leg, blood trickling over his fingers. "Into the bathroom, now," Hayes ordered, gesturing the en suite with her gun. "Consider yourself lucky you came across me first. My colleagues shoot to kill."

She'd ordered Charlotte to stay behind her at all times. "That's it, inside, there's a good boy. I'll have a paramedic here ASAP; I only hope it's in time before you bleed out." The hotel was old fashioned, with bathrooms coming with keys to the door. She locked him in, took the key and pocketed it for later. "I haven't heard many shots recently."

"And your backup's nearly here." Charlotte pulled at the arm straps. "Is it over?"

"I don't know." Hayes pointed her gun at the door and walked towards it. "Only one way to find out. Stay with me, okay?"

The door creaked as she opened it, peeking out, into the

hallway. Clear. She stepped out, beckoning Charlotte to follow her. The mercenary trapped in the bathroom continued screaming in both pain, and frustration. There were two more in other rooms.

Breathing shallow, trying to make as little noise as possible, Hayes descended the stairs one at a time, the Glock out in front of her, ready to fire at a moment's notice.

On the first floor landing she looked in both directions but couldn't see anything. She could spend hours hunting for Miller in a hotel this big. After she decided to start looking left, she heard a man talking, followed by Miller's angry reply.

Hayes knew her partner well enough to know when she was upset; her voice had a harsher tone to it, and the way she spoke to the male, whoever it was, she hated him. Aiming her gun at the bottom of the stairs, Hayes took each step with as much stealth as she could. "Shh!" She held a finger up for Charlotte, whispered, "Not a word!"

The closer Hayes came to the bottom of the stairs, the more she could hear. When she was by the door to the bar, Hayes stood with her back against the wall, listening.

"Why did you have to kill Luke? If he was going to grass on you, the IOPC would have you in cuffs already."

"He told you, that's enough of a reason. Oh, I've heard all about you, Miller. A real stickler for the rules, aren't you? Well, the rules don't apply to people like Demirci, or those vile cousins of hers. No one's going to mourn their deaths. No one's going to come looking for them, either. It's like they never existed."

"Why did you do it? You're a police officer, for Christ's sake," Miller said, her voice bitter, resentful.

"We didn't, as it happens. Voddy here, myself and Luke, we collared the Inan brothers in a kebab shop, bunged them in the back of a van and drove them to a friend's farm. Zuccari and the others brought Demirci along. We were only going to scare them, rough them up, but before we knew what was going on, Zuccari pulled a gun out and shot one of the brothers in the face. Our fates were sealed the moment Zuccari pulled the trigger."

"You could've handed Zuccari in."

"Don't be so naïve, Miller. That's what Luke said, but we were all there, all part of it, all prepared to do our bit for the sake of the unit, except Luke. I didn't want to shoot him; he was the best fucking cop I've ever had the pleasure of working with."

"Sarge, it's time to end this. Enough talking! Let me do it."

Hayes blew out air, held her breath and breached the bar, kicking the door open, finding her targets. "You're under arrest, Sarge. Put the gun down; it's over."

Miller was on her knees in front of Vodicka, who had a knife under her throat. Hayes wanted to open fire on Vodicka first, but the Sarge had his Glock trained on her. Marlowe stood less than a metre away from Sarge.

"You put yours down, or Voddy opens your partner up."

Marlowe winked at her, without Sarge seeing. "I mean it. I heard everything. You're no better than the scumbags we put away, do you know that? In fact, you're worse. At least the dealers and murderers out there know they're the bad guys. You, you're dressing up as cops, but gangsters underneath. You disgust me!"

"Hayes, now!" Marlowe flew at the Sarge.

Hayes turned her gun on Vodicka, who was about to slit Miller's throat. Squeezing the trigger three times, one bullet hit Vodicka in the chest, another in the neck and the third in the cheek.

Miller grabbed the knife from Vodicka, slicing her hand in the process.

Vodicka fell to her knees, staring at Hayes.

Hayes stood with her mouth slightly open as Vodicka drew her last breaths. By the time she noticed Marlowe punching Sarge, Vodicka was on her back, staring up at Miller.

Vodicka died lying next to Walker.

"Give up, Sarge, it's over!" Hayes pointed her gun at him.

Marlowe's fight with Sarge took on momentum.

Before she could intervene, they were wrestling for Sarge's Glock. "I mean it, Sarge. It's over. Give it up before you get yourself killed."

A gunshot reverberated around the large room, making Hayes jump.

Sarge lay on his back with a chest wound. Hayes heard him struggling to breathe. She stepped up to him and watched as his breathing stopped.

Before she could say anything, Marlowe grabbed the Glock and stood up, pointing it at Hayes. "Marlowe, what are you doing? It's over!"

"For you, maybe. But not for me. What've I got to look forward to, huh? What, a lifetime in prison? No fucking way that's happening."

"You bastard!" Charlotte snapped. "Prison's too good for you, you piece of shit!"

Hayes glared at Charlotte. "You're not helping. Shut up!"

"Yeah, listen to Hayes, and shut the fuck up. While you're at it, give me that rucksack, now." He pointed the pistol at Charlotte, then back at Hayes.

"Wait! Marlowe, please don't do this." She pointed her gun at him, glanced at Miller, who stood with her hands up. "That battery's too important. The world needs it."

"Not as much as I do. That little battery's my insurance policy. All the while I have it, and promise not to expose it, the colonel won't come after me. Come on! Bring it over here, now, or I'll shoot you in the face and walk over there and get it myself."

Over a tannoy a police officer ordered everyone inside to exit the building with their hands up.

Hayes couldn't have him take the battery.

When her finger moved, Marlowe lowered his gun and fired at her leg.

The pain was indescribable. Hayes fell to the floor, clutching the wound, which was already bleeding profusely. All thoughts of using her gun fell away at the excruciating pain. "You bastard!" were the only words she managed.

"Hayes!" Miller rushed over to her, placing her hands over the wound.

Marlowe accepted the bag from Charlotte and put it on. "Looks like no one will be coming after me now, huh? If Miller leaves you, you'll die of blood loss. Anyway, I'll be off. See you both around." He smiled, then fled the room.

Hayes was already woozy from blood loss. "Go... after... him."

Miller shook her head. "Are you mad? No way! If I leave, you might die. The battery's not that important. Charlotte, go outside, explain the situation. Tell them we need an ambulance now."

An armed police officer burst into the room with three colleagues. "Identify yourselves!" He stepped up to Miller, his carbine trained on her.

"Detective Sergeant Rachel Miller, my ID's in my pocket," she said, still pressing down on Hayes' leg wound. "We need a paramedic in here, now. And there's a suspect carrying a rucksack out the back. We need the contents of that bag, do you understand?"

"Go after the bag, please," Hayes said, shivering.

Sweat rolled down Hayes' face. She lay back, staring up at the ceiling, which was getting darker by the second. Miller kept telling her to stay awake, but she couldn't keep her eyes open. So tired.

The last thing she heard were gunshots, followed by voices.

DAY 9
WEDNESDAY, JUNE 20TH

76

Miller looked up from the hospital floor to find a doctor in a white coat walking towards them. She stood with Inspector Gillan, and Travis, waiting for the doctor to tell them if Hayes was okay. "And?" Anxious, she studied his reaction.

"It was touch and go there for a while, I'll be honest. The surgeon said she lost a lot of blood. Luckily the bullet missed her femoral artery, but embedded itself so close, it took her a while to free it. Although Hayes' heart stopped twice on the operating table, she was revived on both occasions, and I hope she'll make a full recovery." He smiled at her. "She's one brave lady, I'll give her that. You should all take better care of her."

"Oh we will, and thank you so much. You don't know how relieved I am." Miller went to shake his hand, and a touch emotional, hugged him instead.

"I think I can tell." The doctor's voice was strained. "You're strangling me."

"Oh, I'm so sorry!" Miller relinquished him. "Is she awake? Can I see her?"

"Yes. She's in her room and she asked for you, Detective Miller. I'm sorry! I would allow you all in, except she's still groggy from the anaesthetic. I'll give you ten minutes with her, then she must get some rest."

Miller glanced at the clock on the wall. 04:30. She'd been waiting here for hours, which actually felt like days. The not knowing was over; she could breathe. "Is it down the hall?"

The doctor caught the attention of a nurse, asked her to show Miller to the recovery wing, and Miller followed the portly woman along a corridor. "Thank you!" Miller ran to the end room the nurse pointed to.

Opening the door, Miller saw that Hayes had her eyes closed, and her leg raised, bandaged. Miller thought she looked awful. Her usually lovely brown skin had a pale hue to it. "Are you awake?" Her whisper was met with a smile.

"Sure, come in, Rachel," Hayes replied.

Miller closed the door, then walked to the side of Hayes' bed, picking up a plastic chair as she did so. "How are you feeling? You gave me the biggest scare." Ordinarily, she would hate Hayes calling her Rachel, but it seemed right somehow. All she was trying to do was stop herself from bursting into tears thinking about Luke.

Ignoring her question, Hayes' smile faded. "Marlowe?"

Shaking her head, Miller gave Hayes the bad news. "In hospital. He was shot twice in the legs trying to run away. We have the battery stashed in the station. Since all this went down, every member of Luke's unit is in police custody, including Zuccari. The IOPC are on it now, interviewing them one by one. Inspector Gillan reckons it's only a matter of time until one of them caves under the pressure. All I care about is Zuccari getting his; he started it."

Hayes opened her bloodshot eyes. "And what about us?"

"Suspended, until further notice." Miller said it nonchalantly, so as not to alarm her. "I've made my statement to

Gillan already. I've been told it's a formality, that if my statement's true, the IOPC will clear us."

"But I killed... a cop. I shot Vodicka."

"Yeah, because she was about to slit my throat. Don't ever forget that. You saved my life yesterday. If you hadn't pulled the trigger, it'd be me lying in the morgue, not that bitch. Honestly, you did nothing wrong." Miller wanted so badly for Hayes to believe her words. The doctor wasn't wrong; her partner was the bravest woman she'd ever met.

"I'm so sorry about Luke," Hayes said, tears rolling down her cheek, onto her pillow. "I know how much you liked him."

"Me too." Her chin wobbled. A lump formed in her throat, promising to strangle her. "I really liked him." Hayes' hand reaching out for hers, fingers interlocking, was all it took. Miller put her head on Hayes' sheet and sobbed.

THE END

A NOTE FROM THE PUBLISHER

Thank you for reading this book. If you enjoyed it please do consider leaving a review on Amazon to help others find it too.

We hate typos. All of our books have been rigorously edited and proofread, but sometimes mistakes do slip through. If you have spotted a typo, please do let us know and we can get it amended within hours.

info@bloodhoundbooks.com

www.ingramcontent.com/pod-product-compliance
Lightning Source LLC
LaVergne TN
LVHW040039080526
838202LV00045B/3401